Find Me

ASHTON KHOURY

PREAMBLE

Dear Reader,

If you are reading this, then it was meant for you. Follow the light to find me.

FIND ME

For my daughter, Scarlett, may you always lc
up to the stars and know I am with you.

For my mother, Leigh, who taught me to fir
inspiration in the stars.

For my father, George, and sister, Brittany
whose strength and creativity have inspired r

For Niki, whose positivity has encouraged n
For my friends, who helped me along the w
with unwavering support.

For my readers, who love a thrilling ride—
buckle up.

CHAPTER ONE

ALINA-UNIVERSE A

The city had never felt more suffocating than it did that day.

"Get out of the way!" A man in a navy blue suit barked; his shove jolted me through the throng of rushing bodies. With a hushed urgency, he spoke into his earpiece, "Yes Sir, she's on her way."

I gritted my teeth. *Does he think he's the only person trying to make it to work?* My eardrums ached, assaulted by the noise of school-aged girls making VidReels behind me. To my left, a woman in a red body-con dress boldly talked on her phone that was plastered with gaudy glitter stickers which read: "Boss Bitch" and "Work Hard, Play Hard."

I picked up my pace, eager to escape the smothering grip of the city's chaos. Each step felt like a battle as I barely avoided the array of chewed-up gum buried deep in the pathway. *Just get through this, Alina,* I encouraged myself as I weaved between the crowd.

My mind spiraled into a flurry of thoughts. *I can't be late for work again. Logan will fire me this time. Do I even care?* He was the typical world's worst manager, brown-nosing to the higher-ups. A woman exited Caffeine City, balancing three coffees between her fingers, and I narrowly avoided bumping into her. In her hurried state, a file labelled CONFIDENTIAL fell from her bag. I quickly bent down to retrieve it, but she snatched it away with a huff before walking off. I glanced at my watch and hurried, weaving through the sea of people. My racing thoughts persisted.

Why do I need a job as a receptionist for Ether anyway? Smiling with dead eyes at all the hot-shot physicists every morning while they escort the elites to Building A is not my idea of a good life. It's as if they want to parade their high status to those less fortunate. What do they even do up there? Whatever they do must be important, considering Logan has had me print out countless non-disclosure forms for them.

Logan has always had a distaste for me. I suppose I've given him a few reasons to write me up. Perhaps it's because-

Thwack!

A sudden impact sent a flurry of white papers into the air, and my too-expensive-to-waste praline cappuccino splashed down my button-up top, coating my was-straight chocolate-brown hair in a sickly mixture of syrup, milk, and coffee. A single black pump shot straight up like a missile.

I felt a sharp jolt in my back as I landed on the cement. Lying on the ground, eyes tracing the clouds above, I watched a flock of birds glide effortlessly by, and a yearning surged within me. I wondered if they were fleeing to someplace else or if they were going home. From the corner of my eye, I saw a figure quickly approaching me.

"Are you okay? I saw you run into that pole," a man with olive skin, looking to be in his mid-20s, said. He wore a black sweater that almost perfectly shaped his muscular physique and dark jeans with worn-out dress shoes.

"I'm okay," I said, but didn't mean it.

He brushed his dark, curly brown hair back and held out his hand. "That was a pretty nasty fall." His green eyes momentarily distracted me from embarrassment.

I turned my head to see the brightly lit bank he had come out of. I could see his desk with stacks of paperwork leaning against the window. He had a full view of my fall. My mind shifted to the clownish lighting from the bank. *Why would you light up a bank that way?* I pondered in disgust. But then again, everything seemed garish in the city.

Refusing his hand, I willed myself to stand up and said, "Thank you. I'm okay, really." I lied again.

I hurriedly shoved my paperwork back into my tote and found my missing shoe, leaving the freshly chewed gum stuck to it. I then buttoned up my jacket over my coffee-stained clothes.

Behind me, a bright light pierced through the window, its intensity blinding me momentarily and left a sharp sting in my eyes.

"More clown lights?" I seethed as I quickly spun around to confront the source.

Without warning, a deafening silence haunted the city.

My eyes, still adjusting to the assault, scanned the area. The sky seemed a more vibrant blue. The clouds had dissipated, and I no longer felt the chill of the wind on my face. I shifted focus to my surroundings. To my left, graffiti-strewn walls, tagged with messages of disillusionment, seemed to mock the once pristine façades. Puddles of questionable origin lingered in potholed alleys. Vibrant billboards screamed for attention, each vying to outdo the other in a cacophony of colors that clashed with the city's muted palette.

To my right, the cityscape transformed into a slurry of luxury and neglect. Skyscrapers reached for the heavens, looking down upon the overlooked corners below.

The city appeared unchanged, but a feeling of unease washed over me as I lay my eyes on a green pasture in the distance. A single, white cottage sat perfectly in the middle of the field. It was so out of place and so beautiful. Had I always been too busy before to notice? I stared for a long while. I then turned my attention to the man in front of me, the man from the bank. He was dressed differently, his hair less worn, and his beard neatly trimmed. He appeared deeply concerned; he wore a bulky grey sweater and grey slacks, and his shoes looked less tired. He gazed at me, unmoving like a statue of skin and bones.

"Hello?" I said, waving my arms in front of him. He stood there motionless, his eyes open. Another flash of light came over me. I shut my eyes, which felt like they were burning out of my skull, and then there was darkness. I heard horns honking and a man shouting in the distance. Kids giggled nearby, and I slowly opened my eyes. The man looked at me with concern while adjusting his too-tight black sweater.

I carefully took two steps backward.

"What just happened?" I clenched my phone.

"You hit your head on a pole. My name is Alister, what's yours?" The man, now more animated, gestured to a large pole stationed in the middle of the sidewalk.

I've made this walk a thousand times. I'd have known if a pole was there.

"I, uhm, thank you. I'm Alina." I stumbled over my words, backing away from whatever this was, and hurried off, leaving behind the beautiful, strange man who had helped me.

Behind me, I heard Alister shout, "Hey! You left your…" His voice blended in with the array of noises in the city.

I checked my bag, realizing too late that Alister was telling me I had dropped Teddy's letter. Logan would be furious that I was even later than usual, but I couldn't afford to leave that note behind.

As I turned around to retrieve it, the air went still around me. A woman next to me was frozen mid-stride, and a child was held upside down in a cartwheel as if suspended by invisible ropes. Car engines abruptly silenced as they stalled in the middle of the road, mere inches from collision. I peered down at Alister, who was glitching in and out of view, seemingly advancing toward me with unsettling determination. All the other passersby appeared frozen in place as he drew closer.

The silence was shattered by an unseen voice speaking to me, seemingly emanating from the clouds above.

"Alina, find me," the voice echoed. A loud beep pierced the air. I dropped to the ground, clutching my ears as it blared incessantly—

BEEP. BEEP. BEEP.

BEEP. BEEP.BEEP.

BEEP. BEEP. BEEP.

After what felt like hours, the noise finally ceased. I glanced up, searching for Alister, but he had vanished.

"Are you okay?" the now unfrozen woman asked. I surveyed the surroundings as cars zipped through the streets and people maneuvered around me as if I were now the gum on the ground.

I needed to retrieve my note from Alister; it was the only link to Teddy. But first, I had to face Logan. I willed myself off the ground and continued my race to work.

My mind, an unsolvable puzzle of flurrying images and words, couldn't comprehend what I saw. I ran over the recent events. *I was walking down the street and hit my head. I must have lost consciousness and hallucinated. I clearly can't trust my memory right now. Should I go to the doctor?* I snorted cold air out of my nostrils. *In this economy?* I snorted again.

I had one block left until I reached Building D. *D for Deadweight.* I chuckled to myself. Nobody important ever worked in Building D. Building A is for the physicists and their elite clientele. Building B is for high-performing staff, chasing the carrot of promised promotions to Building A, but rarely making the climb. And Building C is for…well, I didn't know.

I arrived at the grand three steps up to Building D. The once vibrant façade of the office now appeared weather-beaten and worn, its original brown exterior faded under the relentless California sun. The previously pristine lawn was now a patchwork of dried brown grass and stubborn weeds, struggling to survive.

I glanced to my left to see ETHER in wooden letters on a black marble pedestal, a red haze illuminating the words. Each building had its own shrine to the company name, only differing in size and light color. Building C's was cast in bronze with purple lighting. Building B displayed an elegant silver exterior illuminated by a captivating blue glow, while Building A had a glorious white radiance behind its gold lettering. Building A's and B's green grass surrounded the shrines in a colorful prayer.

I looked at myself in the dirty office window one last time before I braved the storm of my boss's wrath. As I took a hair tie out of my pocket and tied my now-sticky hair back, I leaned closer to examine my face—a small cut across my forehead and a large bruise formed.

Taking a deep breath, I inhaled the not-so-fresh air, courtesy of a teenager's marijuana smoke. Taking notice of the camera in the corner of the entrance, I wondered what whoever was watching me would think of my disheveled appearance. I stretched my hand to the door and swung it open. I stepped my scuffed-up pumps inside and was met by Logan's smiling face.

His grin faded as he moved out of view of the physicists.

"You better have a good reason for being late," Logan said through a clenched jaw.

"I do," I said.

"Well, what is it?" he asked.

My mouth opened to speak, but the words were suddenly trapped inside me as I glanced out the window in the far-left corner. A man's silhouette, about six feet tall and slender, ran across the parking lot. Someone with flowing hair, a woman, pulled his arm or held his hand; I couldn't tell.

"Teddy?" I exclaimed.

I darted out of Building D and watched the two figures slide into Building C, shutting the door behind them. I ran to Building C and yanked at the door, but it would not open. After banging my fists against the door and screaming Teddy's name, a passerby whispered and gawked at my outburst. I stopped banging and observed my hands, now red from the impact. Then, I caught a glimpse of myself in the window and jumped back. The girl in the window was me, but she looked...wrong. She was smiling at me, though her eyes were void of emotion. Her complexion looked vibrant but tight, like her skin didn't quite fit her bones.

I watched as tears welled in her eyes and spilled out of existence. Still smiling, she turned around and laid down in what seemed to be a hospital bed. The window flashed a bright light, and I turned away to shield my eyes. I pressed my fingers to my lips; I wasn't smiling. I pinched my cheeks, which felt securely attached to my face and not too tight. I slid my fingers up to my forehead to touch my bruise.

The woman, whom I had narrowly bumped into earlier, walked past me, still balancing the coffees and clutching her file. I quickly reached out and grabbed her arm.

"Did you see a young man go into this building?" I asked.

"Um, no. Please don't touch me," she said, clutching her file.

Glancing down, I realized my hand had clenched into a fist around her jacket, now stained with coffee. Mortified, I instantly released her.

"I'm so sorry. I fell today; I must be losing my mind," I said as I backed away.

The woman side-eyed me, then made a swift escape and scurried into Building A.

I continued to rub the bruise on my forehead as the reality of my outburst came into focus. Taking slow strides back to Building D, I forced a smile and stepped back inside.

CHAPTER TWO

ALINA-UNIVERSE A-PAST

Teddy was my best friend, and up until this morning, he was my roommate. We met in high school during our senior year in health class. He wasn't exactly popular, but he was well-liked. As for myself, I was the quiet kid who drew pictures of sunsets and silhouettes of people I imagined knowing.

One day, I was particularly bored of Ms. Greenwald discussing how babies are born, so I started drifting off to my imagination, drawing a mother holding a baby on a farm.

I shaded in the grass and the sun setting in the distance. Teddy turned around from his seat and nudged me, giggling,

"Why does the mother look so sad?" He asked.

"She was probably being bored to death by Ms. Greenwald," I smiled briefly before my lips turned downwards.

"She's not sad; she's just lost," I said, watching Teddy. He studied my drawing momentarily and then looked back at me.

"Hey, do you want to have lunch with me today? We can talk trash about Ms. Greenwald and eat pizza," he asked.

"Hard yes on the pizza and trash-talking. I'm in," I said.

From that moment, Teddy and I became best friends; we did everything together. We played Monopoly on Saturday evenings after getting ice cream at the now-extinct creamery called *From the Cow*. I was there for him when his ex-girlfriend Dahlia broke his heart, and he stood by me when my mom disappeared and never returned.

We became roommates when we decided to go to the same community college. I dreamed of being a world-renowned physicist, but when my mom vanished, I lost sight of my future, and being with Teddy felt like the right choice. My dad was a fly-in-fly-out worker, but I never seemed to be in the right place at the right time to see him when he'd fly in. Our relationship was strictly phone and bank account communication.

Teddy and I became our own little family. He once admitted he was not close with his family either, though he didn't speak much about them. We spent many nights silently bonding over the invisible glue that held us together.

***

I had awoken from my double-sized mattress as always, my soft, blue flower blankets strewn about and a puddle of drool left on my matching pillow set. The bedding wasn't my typical style, but it was a gift from Teddy for my twenty-second birthday last year.

I sat up, my eyes still groggy from sleep. I yawned, stretching my arms wide as I stepped out of bed and headed to the bathroom to shower. Showering was my favorite time of the day. I cleansed my body and mind from the realities of life and allowed my imagination to drift to a better place. My bare feet padded over the linoleum tile scuffed with marks from over-use. I switched on the pale, dimly lit yellow light and pushed open the shower curtain, which hung limply from a rusting metal rod. My bathroom lacked luxury, but it provided me a sanctuary away from the bustle of daily life. The slightly-too-hot water ran down my body, and I shut my eyes.

I was standing alone in a field of bright green grass. I took a deep breath and was delighted to smell the fresh air. There was no air pollution, just nature. I walked straight ahead to a beautiful cabin, pristine but quaint, its all-white exterior in contrast with the colorful nature surrounding it. I approached the foot of the porch, and suddenly, it faded away into a rushing river of water.

"Back to reality," I sighed.

The water turned cold and forced me to get out. A tan towel, too scratchy for my liking, hung on the wall, waiting for my embrace. I brushed my teeth with my orange toothbrush and threw on my corporate clothing, which never fit or felt right. After checking myself in the frameless mirror, situated over a small but functional off-white basin sink, I stared for a long time, unblinking, as if trying to find the inside of my retinas. I snapped out of it when I heard my phone alarm ping again, a warning blare in case I slept past my first alarm. With my tote looped across my chest, I opened my jaded bedroom door; it squeaked in excitement, announcing my entrance.

The aroma of fresh coffee whirled through my nostrils, and I inhaled deeply. I walked to the tight-spaced kitchen, carefully maneuvering past our thrifted, two-person table, where I saw Teddy. He wore grey sweatpants and a matching hoodie, holding a hot drink. Most mornings, he would wake up early and buy a praline cappuccino for me and a hot chocolate for him.

I selected my coffee from his hand, wondering where his hot chocolate was. "Why aren't you dressed for work? Are you sick?" I asked.

"You know I love you like a sister, right, Alina? You're my best friend." He said, his green eyes refusing to meet my hazel, tired eyes.

Uh oh. What the fuck does that mean? I winced but said nothing.

He continued, "I have some news."

My silence encouraged him to rip the band-aid off.

"Look, I can't stay here any longer. I have to move out. Today." He stared at the floor.

My heart felt like Teddy had yanked it up through my throat. "What? Why?" My face reddened.

"I can't say right now, but I need you to read this when I'm gone." He handed me a letter in a red envelope.

"Teddy, just tell me what's going on. We'll work through this. You can't leave me; you know I can't take another loss after mom disappeared."

"I'm sorry; I love you, Alina!" He pulled me in for a hug. My eyes welled up with tears. That was all it took to lose someone: one fleeting moment of words strung together.

"Please reconsider, Teddy! I need you." Tears spilled down his sweatshirt. I'm not sure if they were mine or his.

He hugged me tightly and whispered a barely audible, "I'm sorry." He broke our embrace first and gestured to the note in my hand. "Read it when you have time. I'll be gone when you get home from work." He wiped away the tears from his eyes.

"Can you at least tell me where you're going? Are you going to come back?" I asked.

"I can't answer your questions, Alina. Please, just go," Teddy replied.

I tucked the note in my tote and gave him one last look goodbye, trying to commit him to memory. I took in his citrusy bergamot scent and studied his pitying face until I couldn't bear it anymore. I walked out the door and crumbled to the floor, sobbing. My heart broke into shards all over the sticky hallway tiles.

I eventually came to, wiping my tears away as I stood up, straightened my clothes, and blinked my tears away. I checked my wristwatch—*8:50 AM.*

Shit. I'm late.

I started running. I only lived a fifteen-minute walk from work, so at least Logan wouldn't notice for a couple of minutes. I ran down the three flights of stairs and pushed the exit door open, allowing my thoughts of Teddy to fade as I joined the rat race of LA's finest.

CHAPTER THREE

UNIVERSE A-ALINA PRESENT

"Ah, yes. Here she is! My star employee," Logan said, forcing a smile as he moved me past the front entrance.

I stared at Logan momentarily and then glanced to my left at the three physicists wearing the typical white lab coats and glasses, making their morning parade through the building.

"Uhm, hi. Yes, that's me. Good morning," I curtsied.

Walking to my desk, I sat down and sifted through random paperwork to appear busy.

"Alina, would you be a dear and wait for me in my office?" Logan said.

His grey hair looked exceptionally grey today, and his brown eyes looked black. The thing is, he wasn't old. He was a twenty-three-year-old man-child dressed in a suit two sizes too big and growing a patchy red beard. I imagined all that anger inside him caused him to age faster.

"Of course," I smiled, clenching my jaw.

With a polite nod to the physicists, I headed to my fate.

Logan's office was littered with alpha male propaganda. *Be The Lion. Less Talk, More Action.* One poster said, *Alpha Vibes Only.* I cringed. There were no family photos on his desk, just a white teddy bear with a blue bow tie perched on the right corner chair. It looked so out of place that I wondered if someone had put it there as a prank.

I should have been rehearsing my apology speech. I heard Logan's fake laugh as he turned the doorknob. He entered his office, still smiling at me. His eyes looked dark and sharp. My nostrils were instantly overwhelmed with the smell of his cheap body spray. His smile disappeared, and his left eye twitched slightly. He opened his mouth to speak, and at that moment, I felt like I was about to be swallowed whole by a predator.

"Do you have any idea what you've done?" he barked.

My face contorted. "No?" I said, and immediately regretted it.

"Not only have you embarrassed me in front of some very important individuals, but you have also disgraced our founder, John Ether, by missing the deadline for project T788C. That was to be submitted promptly at 9:05 AM. I just saved your ass by submitting it for you and explaining that you had computer troubles. However, I can't explain your recent little outburst," he said.

"Don't you mean you saved *your* ass, Logan?" I rolled my eyes and straightened my posture. "This was a task assigned to you; I'm not qualified to submit projects. Don't bother explaining my outburst to them; we're nobody to the Building As," I said.

Logan's face twisted as if he had just eaten sour lemons. He would be handsome if not for the permanent look of bitterness stained on his skin. "That's not true, and you work for me, and if you don't like that, you know where the door is," he said.

"You're right." I slapped my thighs and stood up.

Logan was much less intimidating when I stood three inches taller than him. He sniffed the air near me and recoiled.

"Why do you smell like stale milk and Christmas cookies? My god, Alina, have some respect; it's October," he hissed.

I started giggling, which quickly turned into hysterical laughter. Why was I laughing? He clearly could see I was injured but did not care one bit. He cared that I smelled, which was ironic, coming from someone who dressed and smelled like a fourteen-year-old boy.

My laughter turned into cackling as I hunched over the floor, trying to catch my breath. Debbie, a plump blonde-haired woman with round glasses, sat in her cubicle staring at me. Max, a skinny, middle-aged, soft-spoken man, was in the cubicle next to Debbie, shaking his head in disapproval. I caught a glimpse of my reflection on Logan's glass door, which sobered me up quickly. *I'm a mess.*

My laughter subsided, and I stood up, smoothed out my clothes, cleared my throat, and calmly told Logan, "I quit."

I grabbed my bag, walked straight out the door, and made a detour to Building A. I hurried across the perfectly manicured lawn, ignoring the dampness building up in my heels. I marched up the thirty steps to Building A, panting and sweating. I wiggled my toes to bring some much-needed relief to my blistered feet.

Two cartoonish, plump-looking guards dressed in red formal attire stood at either side of the door. I tried my luck anyway and walked straight ahead with determination. To my surprise, the guards did not stop me.

I entered to see pristine white walls that stretched further than my neck would allow and grand pink and gold flower displays floating from the lobby's walls. A man in a black suit, looking to be in his sixties, greeted me immediately. He was standing in front of two uncomfortable-looking red three-seater couches. My body stiffened; as hard as the couch looked, the founder of Ether, John Ether, stood there waiting for me.

"Alina," he commanded.

My heart felt like it was beating out of my chest. *He knows my name?* I had never met this man before except for seeing his photos on the wall in Building D. In this company, he was a god; someone to look at but never approach. Though, the way he looked at me, it's as if I'd known him for a thousand years.

"You must go back," he told me. "You don't belong here." His voice was gentle but stern. "Now leave and do not come back."

John was not angry. He had sympathy in his eyes, or was it pity?

All I could say was a stuttering, "Sorry," as I ran out of the building.

I took my scuffed black shoes off and ran down the steps and back the way I came.

Approaching me was Betty, the dog walker who always had exactly six dogs and six leashes in her hands. One of her six dogs, a Doberman named Lady, ran full speed towards me. She tackled me to the ground with licks and kisses.

"Oh my God, Alina, I'm so sorry. Are you alright?" Betty grabbed Lady's leash and pulled her off me.

"I'm okay! She was just excited to see me." I pulled myself up from the ground using a bench nearby.

Lady wagged her tail while licking my scratches.

"Where were you running off to, Alina?" She asked.

"Honestly, I don't know. Home, I guess; it's been a rough morning." My mind shifted to Teddy as I searched my bag for his note to confirm it was definitely not there.

Betty had been distracted as she untangled herself from the dogs looping around her.

"Enjoy your walk, Betty! I have to go find something I've lost." I placed my heels back on my feet, and they screamed in protest.

I jumped up and scanned the filthy concrete as I retraced my steps.

I'll need to find Alister if I want my note back; maybe he can explain what happened earlier. I ran as fast as I could manage in my heels.

Nobody seemed to care that I was running in full work gear. No one seemed to notice at all. I didn't stop running until I reached the bank. I stood with my back to the bank, huffing and puffing like I was about to blow a house down.

With my hands on my knees, I stared straight ahead. Where there was a green pasture earlier, there now sat an oversized six-story parking garage—no open land in sight. I blinked my eyes multiple times to make sure. *Nope, a parking garage.*

I placed my hands on my temples and walked over to the curb, littered with wrappers of food long digested, and sat down, defeated. My head throbbed as I tried to calm myself.

Did I just quit my job? What would I have done at Building A had John not stopped me? Blown the place up? I must be losing my mind.

Before I had more time to process, I felt a hand on my shoulder, and I turned to see Alister bending down to sit next to me on that filthy curb.

"Rough day?" He handed me a tissue.

"Not at all," I laughed.

"You left this," he said as he gave me a piece of paper.

It was Teddy's note.

"Thank you." I smiled and held the letter to my chest.

"You ran off so fast before I got to ask if you would like to get coffee with me sometime," he said.

"Wow, you don't miss a beat. That's forward of you," I said.

"That's not a no," he said with a smile.

"It's not a yes either." I stood up while clutching my note.

Alister also stood, retrieved a pen and sticky note from his pocket, and scribbled something.

"Here is my number. If you change your mind about the coffee, or if you find yourself intertwined with a pole again, give me a call," he said.

"Thank you," I replied.

I wanted to say more to Alister, who seemed so kind, yet I had too much on my mind. I glanced at the spot where the white cottage had sat and then back at Alister.

I contemplated asking him about what I saw before I left him earlier, but I couldn't risk sounding crazy. Instead, I simply thanked him for returning my letter.

But before turning to head home, my raging curiosity got the better of me. I asked Alister, "Hey, by the way, have you ever seen a pasture down there?" I pointed straight ahead.

"Umm, how hard did you hit your head?" He chuckled.

"I guess pretty hard," I laughed as I walked away. Maybe I had lost my mind after all.

I reached the front of my apartment complex, where a homeless man named Bob sat outside on a green crate, holding a white cup and singing a made-up song.

"Down the trap, down the trap, close your eyes. Down the trap, down the trap to find your surprise," Bob sang.

"Honestly, A for effort," I said to Bob as I pulled a couple of crumpled fifties from my tote and put them in his cup. "I know it's not much, but I hope this buys you a meal," I offered.

"Thank you, dear. How's it going, Alina Ballerina?" Bob displayed his crooked teeth.

My mom was the only one who used to call me that, and I found it oddly comforting when Bob said it. He had been a resident of the curb since the day I moved into my apartment complex with Teddy. Bob was a kind soul who suffered from paranoia. He told me once that the trees were spying on him and that he would watch over me to make sure the tree men didn't get me. Bob meant well; he did. I appreciated his concern and always gave him what I could in return.

"See you later, Bob. Have a better day than I'm having," I said as went through the main entrance to my building and dragged myself up to my apartment door. I pulled my key out and braced myself, then turned the handle and stepped inside. Only silence permeated through the walls.

The living room, once filled with books of nature and cluttered with shoes, was now bare. I walked to Teddy's bedroom; all that was left was a stripped bed. There were no clothes strewn about the floor, no video game console, just a bare room and the ghost of Teddy. I went to the kitchen to see he left everything there behind, including a mug I had bought him for his birthday. The apartment suddenly felt too big.

I walked to my room, placed my bag on my bed, stripped my dirty clothes off, and put on an oversized t-shirt I had stolen from Teddy long ago. It was red and had holes in three separate places, but I would never get rid of it. I sat on my bed, plucked the note from my bag, held it to my chest, and cried. I cried for my fall, I cried for Teddy, I cried for my job, and I cried for my mom. The world felt too heavy on my chest. I wasn't ready to open his note yet, so I closed my eyes and drifted off to another world.

I descended the spiral staircase to find my mom, dressed in black pants and green blouse work attire, pouring me a bowl of cereal and milk. "Here's your breakfast, sweetie, don't want to be late for school." she smiled warmly.

"Thanks, Mom." I ate my cereal as she kissed my head and said goodbye.

"Be good. Be strong," she said as she grabbed her keys and walked out the door.

I finished my cereal, grabbed my backpack, and headed out the door to catch the school bus. I stepped outside and found myself at Building A of Ether. I stood at the bottom of the steps, looking up to see the back of a slender woman with curly-brown hair ahead of me.

She reached the top, where John greeted her with a tight embrace. They entered the building as the ground shook beneath their feet. Pieces of the building broke off, slowly at first and then all at once. The building shattered into a million pieces, and in the background, I heard the homeless man's song, "Down the trap, down the trap, close your eyes. Down the trap, down the trap to find your surprise."

I jolted awake, drenched in a cold sweat, clutching Teddy's letter. I inhaled and, with shaky hands, unfolded the paper. It read: Dear Alina,

I'm sure you feel very confused and hurt right now. Please know you did nothing to make me leave. But, it's because of you that I had to go. I arranged a new roommate who will move in tomorrow at 10 AM. I can't tell you where I'm going, but the truth will find you soon. I had to leave so you can find me. You don't belong here.

P.S. Don't trust anyone. They are watching you.

All my love,

Teddy.

CHAPTER FOUR

UNIVERSE A-ALINA PRESENT

I stared at that letter for a long time, grasping it with trembling hands.

"You don't belong here." First, John Ether, now Teddy. What could they possibly mean by that? I don't want another roommate. What is Teddy thinking doing this to me?

My stomach growled, and I realized I hadn't eaten anything that day. I checked the time on my phone, and it read *8:07 PM*.

Did I nap that long?

I jumped out of bed and walked to the kitchen, avoiding looking at Teddy's mug on the counter. I rummaged through the fridge for last night's Thai and ate it cold. The Pad Thai looked like hard worms, but at that moment, chilly leftovers felt like all I deserved.

When I finished, I entered the bathroom and saw myself in the mirror.

"How did my life turn out this way?" I said to my reflection.

The bruise on my forehead had turned a deep purple now, and my skin looked dry. I made a mental note to drink more water. My eyes looked sunken in, and I looked too skinny.

"Why is this happening?" I asked myself, half expecting my reflection to give me the answer.

After finishing my nightly routine, I slowly returned to bed, pulled the blue comforter over me, and closed my eyes.

My alarm went off promptly at 7 AM. I forgot to turn it off the night before since I quit my job the day prior; I no longer needed it.

I groaned in defiance at this noise assaulting my ears and threw my phone across the room. I opened my eyes to find it was pitch black.

Confused, I searched for my phone, thinking it must still be the middle of the night. I dropped to the floor and felt around for my phone until the unmistakable plastic phone case grazed my hand. I tapped the front, and the time popped up: *7:03 AM, October 24th, 2030.* I furrowed my eyebrows.

The sunrise should have happened a while ago. I stood up and felt around my room until I reached the window and pulled the blinds up. There were no streetlights on. There were no lights in any of the neighboring houses. No cars drove by. No sight of the moon or the stars either. I started slowly backing away from the window when, in the corner of my eye, I caught a glimpse of light. It had been far off into the distance, but its shimmering strobe-like effect drew me in to investigate.

I tried deciphering where it was coming from, but the surrounding darkness made it impossible. I changed into a blue hoodie, black jeans, and running shoes and grabbed my phone to use as a flashlight so I could investigate further.

I turned the doorknob to my bedroom door, and, to my surprise, the living room was bright. The sun was spilling across my coffee table, illuminating every scuff and coffee stain.

The sudden light made my already injured head pound to a sickening beat. I placed my fingers on my temples and slowly massaged to ease the pain.

My head drooped as the thumping continued. An invisible force squeezed my head like a watermelon, ready to burst. With my eyes still closed and my hands grasping my head, an image of myself appeared. She was the same girl I saw at the Ether window. She was me, but she was someone else. A hand clasped hers as she lay in bed, her eyes closed. A man I recognized leaned in close to her and kissed her cheeks, which were covered in scratches and bruises. She smiled at him, or was it directly at me? It was hard to tell.

"Alister, you're here," she said softly.

Alister rubbed his thumb over her hand and wiped a tear from her cheek.

"I'm never going to leave you," he told her.

I released my hands from my head as the images turned back to a blend of swirled colors behind my eyes. The thumping abruptly stopped, and I mustered the courage to open my eyes again, allowing the light to return to me. My headache was completely gone. Can a simple bruise on your head make you hallucinate? I wondered. I looked up and welcomed the sun shining through my window, now that it didn't feel like it was trying to kill me.

I flipped a light switch to check if the power was back on. It worked, and I quickly flicked it off to save myself from a second headache that was increasing by the second. Perplexed, I walked back into my room, which appeared bright and cheerful, too.

"Huh. I guess someone fixed the power." I shrugged.

Thump. Thump. Thump.

Someone was banging on my door.

I grabbed my head and yelled, "Ugh! Who is it?"

Thump. Thump. Thump.

My door rattled.

Thump. Thump. Thump.

Are they serious? I stomped over to my front door and swung it open. A blonde woman, looking to be about my age, dressed in all-pink athletic wear and stowing seven bags behind her, stood before me. She was grinning from ear to ear with her pink, freshly glossed lips. It was the kind of grin that showed no expression in the eyes. This is who produced those strong knocks? My brows raised.

"The You Can Do It yoga studio is three blocks over." I rolled my eyes and pushed the door to shut.

The woman wedged her expensive purse, which I'm too broke to know by name, between the door.

"I'm Cecelia! Your new roomie!" she said as she spun for me, knocking her bags over in the process.

She didn't acknowledge the fallen luggage. Her eyes were only focused on me.

You've got to be kidding me.

"Oh. Yes. Teddy's friend. Hi, I'm Alina. Come in. Sorry, I didn't dress for the occasion." I motioned down my body.

"That's okay, babe; we all have our ugly days," she said.

I bit my tongue.

"Yeah, so do you need help with your bags?" I clenched my fists together, trying to overlook her ignorance.

"Yes, that would be perfect!" she said as she handed me the two smaller bags gripped in her hands.

After assisting Cecelia with all her belongings and searching around to ensure there wasn't a tiny puppy hiding in a handbag, I showed her around the place, which took a whole three minutes.

"…And, finally, this is your room," I said. A lump formed in my throat as I stared into Teddy's room.

She hugged me and said, "Thank you, Alina! Teddy said this would be the perfect place for me to stay."

I swallowed hard.

"So…" I walked over to the couch and sat down. "How do you know Teddy?"

"Oh, you know, I've seen him here and there. I've helped him several times, and he helps me out," she replied.

"Okay…What does that mean?" I said, not hiding my annoyance.

"He's very special to me, and I'm here to help," she said.

"Did you and Teddy work together at the restaurant *Fun For Fettucine*?" I asked.

"No," Cecelia stared at her phone as she scrolled.

"Where do you work?" I probed further. I guessed that it was probably at a fashion magazine based on her attire and designer bags.

"Ahh, I could tell you, but…" she trailed off.

"Then you'd have to kill me?" I snorted.

Cecelia did not laugh.

"What do you do for work, Alina?" She perked up, finally putting her phone away, and sat beside me, resting her fist on her chin.

"I work for Ether, very important stuff. You wouldn't get it," I lied. She didn't need to know yet that I quit and couldn't pay the bills.

"Oh, I think I would." She laughed gracefully, yet somehow like a hyena.

Was she challenging me?

"Anyhow! It's so lovely to meet you. I'll start unpacking my things now, and maybe we can have some more girl chit-chat later!" She wiggled into Teddy's, excuse me, her room. She fiddled with zippers as she hummed an unfamiliar tune.

I forced a smile until I was out of view and allowed my lips to return to their natural frown.

Girl chit-chat. What are we, sixteen? I'd rather just have her kill me. I thought.

I walked to my room, thinking about Cecelia dodging my questions. She didn't seem like the type of friend Teddy would have. Maybe I didn't know Teddy as well as I thought. I stripped off my clothes and left them to their fate on the floor. I switched on the light, which barely illuminated anything, a stark contrast to the natural light pouring from the windows in the rest of the apartment. I pulled the mildew-stained curtain to the side, stepped into the shower, and let my mind drift away. The pitter-patter of the water consumed me, and my vision turned inward.

I saw my mom sitting in her car in our driveway, talking to my dad on the phone. He was always a businessman first and a father second. He was away a lot on trips, so I never saw him much. Mom looked angry, yelling and slamming her hands against the steering wheel. I saw her hang up the phone while streams of tears rolled down her face. She stayed there, motionless for a moment, and then wiped her tears away. I ran outside to see Mom after her long day of work. "Mama!" I yelled out. She stepped out of the car and smiled a big, warm smile. She opened her arms for a hug, and I ran faster towards her. "Hi, baby. I missed you." She stroked my hair as we embraced.

I turned the tap off and braced myself for the scratchy tan towel awaiting me as it hung from a tilted metal rod on the wall.

I dressed in my office attire: a white blouse, navy-blue pantsuit, and my only non-scuffed pumps. I had to play the part of a still-working and put-together girl to Cecelia. I retrieved my bag from my bed, checking the contents to ensure Teddy's letter was still there.

Pushing open my squeaky door, I entered the living room, where Cecelia was still unpacking her things. I saw her bringing fresh daisies in a glass vase into her bedroom. *Maybe another girl in the apartment would do this place some good,* I thought. I peeked inside and noticed the luxurious white bed set she had put onto her double mattress. It was beautiful and looked like it would feel like sleeping on a cloud.

But, truthfully, it was as if she was erasing Teddy's memory. My stomach filled with knots as she sprayed a sweet perfume across the room and on practically every inch of the carpet.

I cleared my throat to make my presence known.

"I'm off to work. Please make yourself at home, and I'll be back later in the evening," I said.

She didn't appear to hear me as she furiously scrubbed the windows with what looked like a very expensive blouse. I assumed that was her equivalent of an old dishrag.

"Hopefully, the power doesn't go out again. If it does, there's some food in the pantry that doesn't need cooking. Help yourself," I offered.

Cecelia perked her head up and looked at me.

"The power went out?" Cecelia looked surprised.

"Uhm…yeah, you were in the building when it happened," I said.

"No, the power was on the whole time," she insisted.

"No…the power went out and turned back on right before you knocked on the door. You would have been in the building during that time. The sun didn't rise until much later, too. Are you sure you didn't notice?" I squinted my eyes.

Cecelia paused and looked at me with sorry eyes. "Listen, I didn't want to bring this up so soon…but Teddy told me you've been having a hard time lately. It's not surprising you're misremembering things after your fall," she said.

How did she know about my fall?

"I want us to be friends." She smiled sweetly, but it left a bitter taste in my mouth.

"I want you to know you can come to me with whatever you need." She rested her manicured hand on my shoulder.

Her blue eyes gazed into mine for just a beat too long for comfort. She reeked of strawberry and vanilla.

Who does this girl think she is? She doesn't know me, and she barely knows Teddy. How has Teddy never mentioned her if they're so close?

"Thanks." I stepped backward while pushing my hair behind my ears.

I opened the front door, noticing the floors now looked pristine.

"Make yourself at home, but please don't go into my room," I said as I glanced back at her.

I didn't wait for a response. Maintenance must have finally come by to clean the building floor. My shoes didn't stick with every step, and I had to hold onto the wall to not slip from the freshly mopped tiles. I walked through the hallway, down the three flights of stairs, and pushed open the main entrance door. I reached into my bag, ready to give Bob a couple of dollars again, when I spotted two cops approaching him. I nudged his arm.

"Bob, wake up," I said.

Bob startled awake.

"Wha- what's happening? He's here. He's come to take me away." Bob frantically jumped up from his crate.

"Bob, stay calm; the cops are here, so just follow my lead," I said as I laughed dramatically. "Uncle Bob! You're so funny. Let's get some breakfast at the Egg House Buffet."

Bob followed me down the sidewalk as the cops looked him up and down but continued past us.

"Thanks, Alina. You're a good girl," he said.

"Anytime, Bob. Maybe you can go to the park near the old ice cream shop on Hillside Road and lay low for a bit," I suggested.

"Yes, I think I'll do that, Alina Ballerina." Bob crossed the road, singing his song.

"Down the trap, down the trap, close your eyes. Down the trap, down the trap to find your surprise."

Bob's song was so bizarre, yet I found it oddly comforting. His terrible lyrics were endearing.

Caffeine City was only a short block away. This was the first time I would have to step inside now that Teddy wasn't around. I stood before the brightly lit neon sign and wondered if he was in there. Perhaps he wanted me to find him and have a lovely best-friend coffee date, and all this sadness would mix with my caffeine hit, and my worries would fade away. No, this wasn't a fairytale; there wouldn't be a happy ending on the other side of that door.

CHAPTER FIVE

UNIVERSE A-ALINA PRESENT

The atmosphere inside was worse than the café's cheesy name. I was visually harassed by bright orange chairs and contrasting blue tables. The walls were a vibrant green with no artwork, just a complex rainbow of paint fighting for attention. It would be overstimulating to anyone, but for me, this was especially unbearable. Teddy's kind soul used to spare me from this coffee circus and let me drink my cup in peace. I miss him so much.

I stood in the middle of the room as people maneuvered around me. I knew I should step aside to let them by, but I felt frozen in thought.

How could he just leave me like that? How does he expect me to find him? What does that even mean? I searched the room for him. Maybe he would be seated at a table ready to yell SURPRISE, claiming the title of worst prankster ever.

Perhaps he got a job as a barista and wanted me to find

out this way. But that wouldn't explain why he got me a new and very much less improved roommate. I scanned every inch of the room and came to the gut-wrenching conclusion: Teddy wasn't there. He was gone with no substantial explanation, leaving me alone. I felt tears welling up from behind my eyes and diverted my attention quickly before I lost it and caused a scene. I sniffled up the congestion forming on the inner edge of my nose and stepped into the line.

A woman behind me muttered, "Finally," to herself as I moved out of her way.

A line of seven people waited to order. A mother sighed as she juggled holding her baby and stopping her toddler from grabbing the chips from a brown, woven container. Behind her, two businessmen discussed the stock market, gracefully ignoring the toddler weaving between them. A teenage girl with blue hair texted on her phone, eying the children and the mother, and a man in a suit at the front of the line was ordering his drink.

He seemed frustrated and stiff as he repeated his order to a barista wearing an in-training name badge. The man turned around, and I saw those familiar, striking green eyes: Alister.

He saw me and a big smile stretched across his face.

"Alina! So great to see you," he said as he walked over to me and placed a hand on my shoulder.

"Alister, hey! Do you often frequent Caffeine City?" I asked.

"Every morning, sweetheart. However, I've never seen you around here. It's a pleasant surprise," he said, and I blushed.

"Yeah, it's a new routine I'm trying: buy the coffee and don't spill it on myself. I'll let you know how that works out," I said.

"Hey, I've got time before my shift starts. Would you like to sit down with me? Let me buy you your coffee," he offered.

"Yeah, I've got time," I said without checking the clock.

All I had was time. I may as well have spent it with him.

Alister walked to the front of the queue, whispered something to the barista while slipping them a fifty-dollar bill, and grabbed my hand.

"Bold move." I raised my eyebrows.

"In this world? You can't afford not to be." Alister led me to a small table in the corner of the coffee shop.

I sat against the wall, facing the window and the coffee shop's front door. Alister sat down next to me, not across. *Bold*, I thought to myself.

We exchanged pleasantries, and a barista with pink braids and braces brought my coffee to the table. Alister had ordered me a regular cappuccino with one sugar. Thankfully, he didn't get me the praline flavor like Teddy always did, so I was spared the mortification of losing it in public yet again.

I swirled my coffee, mixing the heart-shaped foam from the top.

"So, Mr. Bold, tell me about yourself. So far, I know that you work at a bank and often save women in embarrassing situations," I asked.

"Not often. Only for the cute ones," he sipped his coffee before continuing. "I grew up in multiple foster care homes, but I had great mentors who helped me become the man I am today. I went to Salent High School and graduated in 2025. I initially wanted to be a physicist but dropped out of college when I realized I wanted a regular job and an exceptional family. I'm still working on the latter. Oh, and my favorite color is red." His eyes stared into mine and waited for a response.

"Wait, you went to Salent High? I went there, too, and graduated the same year. How have I never seen you before?" I asked, bewildered.

"It was a big school. But I have a confession to make." Alister leaned in close.

"Oh yeah?" I leaned in, too.

"If I had known you back then, I'd have made my move much sooner," he whispered. I smiled.

"Well, what was your move in the first place?" I challenged.

"Saving you from that evil pole. That's a move, right?" He laughed.

"That's definitely a move." My shoulder brushed into his, sending a jolt of excitement through me.

I had never met anyone quite like Alister before. He was so easy to talk to, confident and sure of himself. His every word was gentle yet with forceful energy. I think, had I known him back in high school, I would have welcomed his first move. But unlike Alister, I wasn't ready for a confession like that.

We gazed at each other as we sipped in silence for a moment. *Another tick off the list of why he's perfect. Silence isn't awkward with him. Cecelia could take notes.*

Alister broke the trance first. "So, Alina, what do you do for work?" He was still laser-focused on me while he sipped his coffee.

"Well…" I paused and sipped my coffee, too. *Should I admit I quit? I suppose there is no harm in telling him.*

"I just quit, but I was working as a receptionist for Ether in their lower-tiered building." I held my breath for his judgment on quitting.

Alister's bushy eyebrows lifted in surprise. "You worked for Ether? As in for John Ether?"

"Uhm yeah, I did, why?" I shifted in my seat.

"A buddy of mine is an investigative reporter and…" Alister leaned in closer to me, "he found out that John Ether did some messed up experiments on his family. Supposedly, his wife found out and tried to shut down the company, but rumor is that he killed her. He stabbed her right in the stomach as she bled out in front of him." He leaned back into his chair and studied my face. I was shocked that I'd never heard that story before. We weren't told much about John Ether, except that he's phenomenal at his research projects, but a story like this wouldn't usually go amiss.

"Wow, I had no idea," I exclaimed.

"Yeah, luckily, you don't work there now, or who knows what experiments he'd do to you. Maybe give you a monkey's brain and a rat's tail," he poked fun at me.

"Who says I don't have a rat's tail?" My lips curled upwards, forming a smirk.

"Oh, I hope you do," Alister's eyes squinted.

"So, what about you? What got you into banking?" I asked.

"To be perfectly honest, I'm only in it for the money. As I said before, I want a family one day, and I want to provide for them."

My ovaries ached. "I love that!" I beamed.

I changed subjects abruptly as I remembered the strange occurrences this morning and suddenly felt uncomfortable in my skin.

"Hey, did you have a power outage this morning?" I asked.

"Hmm, nope, can't say that I did. Why?" He questioned.

"Ah, mine went out briefly, but don't worry about it. I think the building is just faulty. Weird about the sun rising late, though."

Alister sipped his coffee with a confused look. "Did it?" he asked.

The conversation lulled as we sat together in a moment of silence. I stared out the window, observing the pitter-patter of rain falling from the ever-darkening clouds above, until Alister glanced at his gold watch, rimmed with tiny diamonds. I found myself studying it as well—not because it gleamed so brightly that it demanded attention, but because it reminded me of my father's watch. Or, at least, I thought it did. But since my fall, my mind felt too fuzzy to be certain.

"I've got to make my way to work now, but I'd love to take you out on a real date sometime. How's this Friday at 7?" he asked, although it felt more like a statement.

I pretended to check my schedule for an opening when I knew damn well I had no plans. Alister would be a good distraction from the misery that surrounded me. He awaited my response while gathering his bag.

"This Friday is perfect!" I smiled.

"It's been a pleasure talking with you, Alina," he said.

"The pleasure is all mine." *The pleasure is all mine?* I cringed internally. I tried to play it off. "Text me, and we'll figure out where to go," I said nonchalantly as we walked out the door onto the busy sidewalk.

"I'll call you with a plan. Bye, Alina," he said as we embraced awkwardly.

I watched him walk away, and I couldn't deny that I was smitten. "Bye, Alister."

It occurred to me that I had nowhere to go and no plan in place. I couldn't return to work because I didn't have a job. I couldn't go home because Cecelia thought I was at work. To avoid making things uncomfortable, I walked in the opposite direction of Alister until I finally found an empty bench. It was covered in bird poop; I could see why no one wanted to sit there.

I took a napkin I had stuffed in my bag from the coffee shop, wiped it off, and sat down. The rain had subsided, and the sky was back to showing off its bright blue hues. The air felt warm, and my face flushed, still reeling from my unexpected coffee date with Alister. He had a way of showing up at the right time. *I guess this is what fate looks like.*

The passersby dwindled as they entered their places of work for the day, the sidewalk now reserved for the unemployed and those who enjoy working from home. A girl in a revealing top with too much makeup danced through the street with no music while a man following her with his phone encouraged her.

Betty, the dog walker, was approaching my direction. She only had four dogs in tow.

"Hey Betty, only four dogs today? What happened to Lady and Luna?" I said.

Betty was on the phone.

"Hang on, Milly. Some girl is talking to me." She pulled out her EarPods and looked at me, annoyed. "Sorry? Who are Lady and Luna?" she said. I stared up at her, confused.

"The dogs you usually walk every day…you always have six. Lady, the Doberman, where is she?" I asked.

Betty looked at me, puzzled. "No honey, it's always been just these four dogs," she replied.

"I've passed you on my way to work for the last three years; it's been six dogs. We even joke about them as we pass by, and I give Lady pets," I said.

I felt desperate for her validation.

"Sorry, hon. I think you have me mixed up with someone else. I have never met you before." she placed her EarPods back in and continued her conversation as she trailed off.

I sat there, perplexed. *Am I going crazy? Why is she acting like she doesn't know me? There were always six dogs. Or maybe there were only four dogs. I rubbed the bruise on my head.*

My train of thought was interrupted.

In the distance, across the road, I saw it: a flickering, vibrating white light. This light was not like any other in the city. It pulsed like a heartbeat. Its rays shot out in every direction as it bobbled up and down in rhythm.

I could see the light behind a small building that used to be an ice cream shop named *From the Cow* but had since been vacant for the better part of two years. I scanned the area, and nothing else seemed out of place. I checked the time on my watch, which read *10:35 AM*. I took a closer look at the year, 2030. Had it really been five years since my mom had disappeared? As I realized how fleeting time could be, I knew I shouldn't waste any more. I stood up, stretched my legs and arms, and announced to no one, "Let's go be BOLD."

I searched for the nearest crosswalk, waited for the go-ahead to cross, and made my way to find that light.

CHAPTER SIX

UNIVERSE A-ALINA PRESENT

The light shimmered and pulsed just ahead of me, illuminating an otherwise dark part of the city. That side of town always gave me the creeps. It was a failed strip that didn't get much traffic. The rain picked up again, and droplets trailed my face. The hustle and bustle of the city turned to a faint blur of noises in the background. I checked my surroundings to find no one else was on this street with me. I didn't know if that made me feel better or worse. I took giant strides closer and closer to the light. *Just a bit further*, its vibrations taunted me. My blisters rubbed against my heels, and I'm pretty sure the soles were filled with blood.

The ice cream shop was approaching; I took more strides to reach the light. *Is it getting further away?* I walked faster, but the distance to the light stayed the same. The pulsing sped up, seemingly telling me to hurry, yet it appeared even further away now. I took my heels off and ran, leaving small spotted blood trails behind me. I was ten feet away from the light before it poofed out of eyesight.

I came to a halt as I reached the ice cream shop.

"No, no, no! Where did you go?" I frantically searched high and low for the light, but it was gone.

I pressed my face to the glass of the empty ice cream shop. Nostalgia mixed with a tinge of sadness thickened the air. Teddy and I came here often before it closed down. We single-handedly kept them open for a year before they finally shut shop. I peered inside through the dusty window. The once-bright walls, painted in cheerful pastels and adorned with whimsical murals of dancing cows holding ice cream cones and children frolicking in the sun with ice cream sundaes, now appeared dull and lifeless, the colors muted by years of neglect.

I sat down against the window, picturing our memories in the shop. Teddy always got a scoop of peppermint ice cream and a scoop of cherries jubilee. He would mix the two. I'd make a face of playful disgust while I ate my chocolate chip cookie dough, and he'd offer me a sample of his mixture. I never accepted the offer, and he always responded the same way, "More for me, Jubilee," and took a comically large bite. I wish I had tried it just once.

I searched around for the light one more time. Why was it bringing me to memories of Teddy? Was the light capable of being cruel? As I gathered my shoes and bag to stand up, I noticed a white envelope on the ground to my right. I pulled it closer with the heel of my shoe and read the name on the front.

Cecelia Abernathy

I peered over my left shoulder and then to my right. *Was Cecelia here?* There was no sign of her unless she was lurking inside the abandoned ice cream shop, ready to pop out like a Barbie Boogeyman. I turned my attention back to the envelope between my fingers. Curious, I read on.

The envelope said:

OFFICIAL DOCUMENT. DO NOT OPEN.

So, naturally, I opened it.

My face paled as I pulled the content from the envelope.

There was one single piece of paper inside, and it read:

Cecelia: Employee 85-75:

You are assigned to ProjectAlina. The QR code on your smart tablet has your instructions. Do not lose this copy, as it is the only one.

Do not speak to anyone about this, and do not let me down.

Yours truly,

Ether

My mind raced as more questions flooded my brain than I could manage.

Cecelia works for Ether? Is she the one messing with me? Is she the reason Teddy left?

My head was a balloon drifting in a hazy sky. I needed to stand up, but my body forced me to lie down. I laid my head on the pavement, and my vision blurred into darkness and then light.

I stood in the green pasture enclosed with trees from every direction. I saw a clear blue sky and birds flying above my head. The air felt crisp, and I smelled baked cinnamon apples wafting in the wind. Horses and cows sang as they made their presence known beyond the trees. I spotted a white cottage with two square windows on either side.

The front door was ajar, inviting me in. I walked slowly to the porch, finding a white swing in motion with no occupant. I entered the cottage to see my mom. She wore a light blue apron over a white dress. She turned around, holding a freshly baked apple pie.

"Honey, I made dessert," she smiled sweetly as she placed the pie on the wooden countertop. Her arms stretched out wide, waiting for an embrace.

"Mom!" I called as I moved towards her.

I heard footsteps behind me and then the voice of a small boy.

"Mama!" he exclaimed.

The boy poofed out of existence before I could catch a glimpse of him, and the house faded into static.

"Mom!" I called again, but she was gone.

Darkness engulfed the space around me. Voices called from somewhere far away. I focused hard to hear what the voice was saying. "I me," I heard, but that wasn't right.

"Hello? What are you trying to tell me?" I shouted.

"Find me." I finally made out the words.

"Who are you?" I shouted back.

The air sent chills down my spine. The voice did not talk to me again. A hand grabbed my shoulder and shook me.

I opened my eyes to see Bob hovering over me as I lay on the sidewalk.

"Hey, wake up, Alina," Bob said.

I felt groggy as I sat up, holding my pounding head.

"Cops'll be on you any minute, girl. You can't sleep here." He helped me stand up.

"Sorry, I'm…I'm not well." I blinked my eyes forcefully.

"Yeah, Ether will do that to you," he said.

I shot my eyes up at him. "What do you know about Ether?"

"You're asking the wrong question, sweetheart," he smiled.

"What does that mean?" I asked.

"What does what mean?" He grabbed his bags, not looking at me.

"Tell me what you know about Ether, Bob," I demanded.

"Ether? Alina, if I knew anything interesting about Ether, do you think I'd be homeless?" He chuckled.

"But you just said I'm asking the wrong question." I folded my arms, not in the mood to play games.

"I said you're asking the wrong man. I can see you're not well; let me help you back to your apartment," he said.

I stumbled my way back down the pathway with Bob holding me upright. I tucked Cecelia's envelope under my jacket.

"No cops in sight; I'll be here if you need me. Go get some rest; you look like you need it." Bob opened the door of my complex for me, and I walked inside. Bob mumbled his song as the door closed behind me. *Down the trap, down the trap…*

The images of my dream were still freshly torturing my mind. *I saw my mom. She was so happy. And that boy, was that her son? Did my mom leave me and start another family? How could she do that to me?* I was furious, or maybe sad; the two emotions had intertwined like a bitter cocktail. Was she dead, and I entered another realm to see her? Wherever she was, I hoped to see her again one day.

I arrived at the front of my door, remembering I was not supposed to be there yet. Cecelia would wonder why I was home early and looked like I just returned from war. I pulled out my phone and scrolled through my contact list until I reached Alister's name.

Should I call him? I could really use a smile right about now.

No, don't call him. It's too soon.

I scrolled through my contact list again and stopped at the name, Dad.

I stared at it for a moment, contemplating calling. He was usually too busy to answer my calls, but maybe this time, it would be different. I hit dial, and, to my surprise, he picked up on the first ring.

"Hi Alina! It's so good to hear from you," Dad said.

"Dad! I didn't think you'd pick up," I said.

"Are you alright?" he asked.

"No, not really." I tried to think of a way to explain what was happening, but before I could, he responded.

"Listen, Alina, there's something…"

"Dad, hello? Can you hear me?" I asked.

I realized the call had disconnected and sighed.

Thoughts of Alister popped into my mind again; the image of his perfectly straight teeth and deep pink lips stretching out to form a smile was soothing. I decided to call him. The phone rang once, and he picked up.

"Alina, hello!" he said cheerfully.

"Hey Alister, I know I just saw you a couple of hours ago, but I was wondering if you wanted to meet for lunch?" I held my breath for his response.

"I'd love to, but it's two o'clock, and my lunch break was two hours ago," he said. I checked the time on my phone: 2:03 PM.

"Oh my gosh, I'm so embarrassed. Sorry, time must have gotten away from me; I was enthralled in an excellent...book," I said.

"Oh yeah? What book were you reading?" he quizzed.

I smacked my head. *Oh no, he caught me in my lie.*

"Oh, uhm, the phone is breaking up. Can I call you back?" I hung up quickly and pinched the bridge of my nose.

Okay, calling him was a bad idea. I sniffed the air around my body, my own aroma nauseating me. I needed to sneak into my room and freshen up. I pressed my ear to the door to see if I could locate Cecelia's high-pitched voice on the other side.

"What are we listening to?" a voice whispered behind my ear.

I jumped to the side and grabbed my chest as it nearly pounded through my shirt. "Oh my god, Cecelia, you scared me!"

I could feel her letter scratching my skin beneath my clothes and held it tightly in place.

"Geez, I'm not that scary looking, am I?" she asked.

"I forgot my key; I was listening to see if you were home," I lied.

"Why didn't you just knock?" She eyed my bare and bloody feet and continued. "And what happened to you?"

"It's a long story; I need you to unlock the door. Where were you, anyway?" I asked.

She retrieved a bottle of wine from her bag, "I got us wine!" She wiggled it in front of my face. "I thought we would celebrate new beginnings tonight," she said cheerfully.

Absolutely no way was I spending my night with her.

"Oh, yeah, okay, let's do that," I said, eyeing the still-locked door.

Cecelia took notice of my impatience, pulled her blue key from her pocket, and unlocked the door. Teddy must have given her his key because I remember painting his blue with my nail polish when we moved in together.

I swiftly moved to my room, yelled, "Thanks," and closed the door behind me.

I changed out of my clothes and into fresh black jeans and a long-sleeved black top. I carefully cleaned my bloodied toes and placed bandages from my medicine cabinet onto the tender wounds. After slipping into black tennis shoes and tucking Cecelia's letter next to Teddy's in my bag, I retrieved my phone and scrolled, stopping at the DriveMe app. There was no way I was going to walk to my next destination.

Cracking my door, I saw the coast was clear, and Teddy's old room was shut. The floorboards creaked with every step I took to the front door and crept out of my apartment. I was relieved to walk on the sticky tiles, away from Cecelia. Bob was napping on the ground, using his worn-out coat as a pillow. I welcomed the chill in the air while waiting for my ride to arrive.

Moments later, a black Hyundai pulled up to the side street, rolled its window down, and a woman in her mid-forties leaned in.

"Alina?" the woman said.

"Yes, thank you." I opened the car door and hopped in.

The driver made small talk with me, and I appeased her, although I'm not one to enjoy small talk. I smiled and gave short answers, hoping she would get the hint. I learned about her two dogs, Honey and Homer, and her boyfriend troubles. He wouldn't commit to marrying her after nine years together. She told me this was her side gig, and selling weed was her main job.

I asked, "Shouldn't it be the other way around?"

"Oh no, honey. Have you seen how people tip these days?" She glanced at me through the rearview mirror.

I laughed and made a mental note to tip her well.

I rested my head on the window and admired the view of the hills and nature. It was a breath of fresh air to avoid the hustle and bustle of the central part of town.

The woman pulled up to a grey and white two-story house at the end of a court.

"Is this home?" she asked.

"It was," I said as I unbuckled my seatbelt and opened the car door.

"Thank you." I shut the door, and the woman drove off.

I gazed upon the familiar sight of my old home. I glanced at the driveway to the left, once filled with chalk stick figures, now bare asphalt. My mom and I used to ride our bikes together around the block until the sun dipped below the horizon.

My eyes trailed the freshly cut grass to the right and moved up the apple tree to find many red apples waiting to be picked. Every weekend during apple season, we would fill baskets with apples, and Mom would make apple pie for us and the neighbors. I walked to the apple tree and plucked the closest red one and took a bite. Its crisp flavor hugged my taste buds as I walked to the back of the tree next to the fence.

I saw a large trampoline on the other side of the fence that was not there when Dad sold the house.

The new family that lived here had two kids—ages nine and fourteen. I met them when my dad was selling the house. He had just broken the news to me over the phone that he was permanently stationed outside of California for work and that I would need to find an apartment to live in. I lived alone in that two-story house for two years after my mom disappeared. My dad had paid for all my expenses until then but cut me off when I moved in with Teddy. He was angry that Teddy and I were so close, although he never could give me a valid reason.

After meeting with the family that would live in my home, I remember feeling a sense of dread wash over me. This was our family home, and part of me believed my mom would return someday. I spent many nights overthinking. What if she came back and saw a new family there? What if she couldn't find me? I cried for weeks when I moved out, but Teddy was always there to cheer me up. One morning, I was crying in my room, and Teddy knocked on the door, holding my favorite coffee drink: a praline cappuccino. That's when the morning tradition started.

I stared at a home that was not mine and a life I barely remembered. I traced my hand along the spot on the fence where I carved my name when I was seven. My mom wasn't mad when she found out. Instead, she traced her name, too. I ran my fingers across her name and smiled. I stopped at the next set of carvings below her name. I didn't remember ever seeing it before. Maybe it happened when I moved out? But if it did, then that meant she came back and didn't want to look for me.

I read it repeatedly. Four words were carved into the fence. Four simple words that were now etched into my memory deeper than the wood they were cut into. The words read: **Alina, Mom is here.**

"Alina?" a man behind me called.

Startled, I spun around. "Oh, hi, Mr. Jacob."

My old neighbor, who lived across from us, stood before me.

"Alina, it's so good to see you! What are you doing in this neck of the woods?" he asked.

Mr. Jacob was a kind man who used to let me have sleepovers at his house with his daughter, Riah, and he would bring out all the best toys. One time, he let us have a water balloon fight inside the house. Mrs. Jacob wasn't too happy about that.

"Just stopping by. I wanted to reminisce," I said.

He looked in all directions, leaned close to me, and whispered, "You know…she hasn't come by. I always hope she will one day. But I haven't seen her since…" he suddenly looked uncomfortable as he glanced at the window to his house.

I felt a lump building up in my throat and couldn't manage to say anything back.

"Take care of yourself, Alina; you don't belong here," Mr. Jacob said.

I froze. Those words. *You don't belong here.*

"What did you say?" My breathing quickened.

"I said take care of yourself, Alina; you are always welcome here," he smiled.

"What. Th-thanks. I, uh, I have to go now."

I panicked. I ran. I ran out of the court and around the corner to the playground.

I know what I heard. Is this some sick joke that Cecelia is playing? How could she have known I was going to my old house, though? I sat

64

down on a swing and loaded up the DriveMe app again. It said Amy, the driver who dropped me off, would be here in two minutes.

Amy pulled up to the curb, rolled down her window, leaned forward, and said, "Are you Alina?"

I waved, responding, "Yes. It's good to see you again."

Amy looked perplexed. "Honey, I haven't seen you before."

"Yes, you have; you dropped me off less than twenty minutes ago." My smile faded.

"Hmm, nope. I just dropped off a teenager at the movies. I think you have the wrong gal, but come on in!" Amy said as she gestured to the door.

What is happening? I bolted in the opposite direction. *How can she not remember me? What is happening to me?* I ran until my chest felt like it was going to burst. I walked up to a sandwich shop, exhausted, thirsty, and starving. I ordered a large chicken sandwich, a bag of barbeque chips, and ample water. I sat down at the booth and pulled out my phone again. *7:04 PM. How is it already so late?* I ate my sandwich while I dialed Alister's number.

"Alister? Hi, I need a favor," I said.

***

Alister parked in the lot where I was standing. He drove a silver Range Rover. A little bobble Hawaiian girl danced through the speed bumps on his dashboard.

I opened his car door and slumped into the passenger seat. The seat warmers were on, and I was grateful for the heat.

"Thank you so much for picking me up," I said.

"Of course. Are you alright?" He rubbed my shoulder.

I couldn't hold back anymore, and I burst into tears.

"No…something weird is happening to me, Alister. Something is not right," I said, through heaving breaths.

He moved his hand to my back.

"It's going to be okay. Tell me all about it." His warm smile put me at ease, and I took a deep, shaky breath and started from the beginning.

CHAPTER SEVEN

UNIVERSE A-ALINA-PRESENT

"Wow. That is a lot to take in." Alister was silent for a moment.

Relief flowed through my veins as the weight lifted off my shoulders.

"Okay, the way I see it, one of three things are happening here," he paused. "Option one: you hit your head and have a concussion, and it's more serious than we thought. In which case, I should take you to the hospital right now. Option two: someone is messing with you and is either trying to scare you or wants to hurt you, but why would they want to do that? Or option three, that letter is real, and Ether is involved in this and targeting you."

"Yeah, I agree. We can skip the hospital run, though. They'll tell me to rest and send me home with a bill the size of an elephant," I said.

"An elephant?" Alister raised a brow.

"Yeah, you know, because they're big," I stated.

"Yeah, no, I got that. It was just an odd comparison," Alister held in a laugh.

"Okay, Mr. Poet, what would you compare it to?" I crossed my arms and smiled.

"I'd say it would be as large as your heart." He winked.

"Keep your day job. Besides, you can't say that to me yet. You barely know me." I rolled my eyes playfully.

"Well, I'd like to know you," he paused and then continued. "There's a twenty-four-hour diner around the corner. Would you like to go?" He asked.

I thought about the sandwich I had demolished. "I could go for some dessert," I said.

Alister started the car, and we drove in calming silence to the restaurant. We pulled up to the empty diner, usually reserved for college students after their escapades at the bars, but it was too early in the night for their arrival.

He opened the door and gestured for me to get out. "M'lady," he said.

I envisioned a red carpet leading me to the front door. My daydream turned back to reality as I approached the dimly lit diner. *Maude's* banner dangled loosely from the front building.

Alister opened the door for me, and stale coffee and bacon overwhelmed my senses. A woman with dark circles under her eyes and a tight brown bun walked with a limp to escort us to our pick of the booths. We were the only customers there. She handed us the menus, unceremoniously placed water in blue plastic cups, and walked away. I took my napkin to clean the droplets from the table and put on my best smile to hide the uncomfortable stiffness in the atmosphere.

"I'll take you somewhere nicer next time," Alister said as he rubbed my shoulder. *I guess my smile isn't fooling him.*

"No, it's okay. I'm with you, and that's enough." That was true. Something about Alister's presence was calming like I had known him all my life.

"So, Alister, what do you like to do when you're not working?" I looked up from my menu after deciding to get the unidentified flavor of surprise pie that was rated #1 on the menu.

"Well, I love physics and teach a class to underprivileged teens free of charge." His phone pinged, but he kept his gaze on me.

"Oh wow, that is such a lovely thing to do," I said as I glanced down at his phone going off again.

"Yeah, they remind me so much of myself at that age, and my mentor helped me become the man I am today, so I owe it to them to give back," he said. His phone dinged again, yet he didn't look away from my eyes.

"Do you need to get that?" I gestured to his phone.

"Don't worry about it, sweetheart; my time here with you is exactly what I need to do." He winked.

The increasingly grumpy waitress brought our food out to the table. She placed a chocolate cake in front of me and a pumpkin pie in front of Alister.

"Oh, we haven't ordered this," I said shyly to the woman while waving it away.

"He did," she pointed to Alister and walked off.

"When did you order this? We were talking the whole time," I asked, perplexed.

"Okay, I have a confession; I called ahead before I picked you up and ordered already." He dug into his pumpkin pie.

I stared down at my cake, thinking about my mother; it was her favorite. Every year my father would make her a chocolate cake for her birthday. He was terrible at baking, but he tried his best, and she ate it and never said anything other than a gracious thank you.

My childhood memories come and go. Sometimes, I had distinct memories of my past, and sometimes, they blurred so much that I questioned if I ever had a childhood at all. My mom had been missing for so long that I had to look at pictures to remind me of her appearance. And my dad had morphed into the image of his name on my cell phone. Alister couldn't have known this dessert was special to me. He couldn't have known I had never touched a chocolate cake since my mom's last birthday before she disappeared.

"Do you not like chocolate cake? I'm sorry. I just figured it was a safe choice to order for you." Alister looked disappointed with himself.

"No, no, it's great; thank you. I'm just not very hungry," I said.

"Oh, that's okay, we'll pack a to-go box," he gestured to the waitress, who glared at Alister.

We packed up our desserts, and Alister paid for the uneaten treats. He led me back to his car with his hand on the small of my back and opened the door for me again.

The car stopped at a red light, and he looked at me.

"We'll figure out what is happening to you, Alina. I'll help you. If you see the light again, or if Cecelia does anything, and I mean anything to you, let me know, and I'll be there." He placed his hand on top of mine.

It was warm; I hadn't felt warmth radiate through me in so long. "Thank you, Alister; I'm so glad I met you. I think it was fate that I fell that day in front of your office," I said.

"Fate is just energy showing you the path you were meant to be on," he said as he pulled up to the curb, where Bob was sitting, hunched over with an oversized jacket, drinking from a steaming cup.

"It's going to be okay, Alina. I'll call you tomorrow, and we can figure this out together," he reassured me.

I hugged him and took in his cologne. Hints of black leather mixed with cinnamon lingered on his neck. I pulled from his embrace. It felt like too much too soon, but something about him seemed to draw me in like a magnet. I leaned back towards him, just far enough to reach his lips. This strange magnetic pull seemed to draw us together as he placed his lips on mine. His hands ran through my hair while mine grazed down his back. Time seemed to stand still. For a moment, it's as if we existed in a universe of our own creation.

A slew of pings radiating from Alister's pocket stole the moment from us. I pulled away as reality shifted back to me. I suppose it was too soon. I grabbed my bag and my untouched cake and opened the door.

"Thank you for being here for me." I smiled.

"Of course. I'm here whenever you need me. See you soon, beautiful," Alister said while smoothing his hair and picking up his phone.

I stepped out of his car, carefully closed the door, walked to the front of my apartment building, and pushed open the main entrance door. Alister sped off, and Bob called to me from his crate.

"You be careful, Alina; men that smooth are standing on jagged rocks," he said as he sipped from his Styrofoam cup.

"Bob! Were you watching me?" I laughed.

"Trust me, girl, no one wants to see that." He offered a smile.

"Here, this is for you. It's sweeter than the man who dropped me off." I handed him the bag with my untouched cake.

Across the road, a red light, the size of a pea, flashed in and out of the trees.

"Hey, Bob, do you see that?" I pointed behind him.

He turned around and observed the light. "Yeah, that's the tree people. They're always watching," Bob said as if it was common knowledge.

"The tree people? Have you ever seen them?" I asked.

"The tree people are everywhere and nowhere. You can't see them, but they can see you. Stay safe out there, Alina." Bob dug into his cake.

"You too, Bob," I said as I eyed the red blinking light. Chills ran down my arms as I walked up the stairs across the sticky floor to my unit. I turned the keys in the knob and entered.

Cecelia was on the couch watching a reality show on TV, The Single Charade. She was giggling at a fight between three ladies hoping to win a man's heart.

"Hi, Alina. You're home late!" she chirped. I glanced at my phone. It was 9:10 PM.

"Hi, uh yeah, I had dinner with a friend," I said, avoiding eye contact.

"Come watch this show with me; I opened that wine for us!" She waved her wine glass around.

"Erm, oh gee, I wish I could, but I'm just so tired from work." I glanced around the room and found she had made a few changes. The round table beside the kitchen had daisies in a glass vase. An air freshener plugged into the wall next to the table was making the room smile like strawberries. Light blue and pink throw pillows were piled along the couch. A soft blue blanket was draped over her legs.

"Oh, just sit down, roomie." She patted the couch beside her.

"Yeah, okay, sure." I grabbed a glass from the table that she poured for me, stiffly walked to the other side of the couch, and sat down. My fists were red from clenching my bag so she wouldn't see her letter from Ether I found earlier today.

"So, you like this show, huh? I do, too, but I haven't kept up this season," I offered small talk to make it less awkward.

"This is the first time I've seen it! It's so hilariously bad!" She giggled.

I must admit that her cheerfulness was contagious. Maybe in another life, we would have been friends.

"You haven't seen it before? Your job must keep you busy." I glanced at her from the corner of my eye with my head still facing the TV.

"They don't have this where I used to live," Cecelia said.

"Where did you live, Amish country?" I looked at her fully now. She looked uncomfortable like she regretted asking me to sit with her.

"Hmm?" She brushed off my question and did not look back at me.

I quickly downed my drink and stood up.

"I've got to get to bed now. Goodnight," I said.

Cecelia's eyes were glazed over from too much wine. "Goodnight," she mumbled.

I rushed to my room, closed the door, and locked it. I took out the envelope, pulled the paper, and re-read it.

Rage encompassed me; my cheeks felt hot and flushed. It could have been from the wine, or maybe it was that my new roommate was fake as hell and planned to destroy my life.

I can't believe I thought for a second that we would be friends.

Maybe she's a mad scientist and is doing secret brain surgery on me? No, that wouldn't work. I'd know if my brain was cut open.

I paced my room as my mind swirled with rows upon rows of angry conclusions. *I knew she was creepy. No one is that perfect and put-together. Nobody is that cheerful. It's like Bob said: She's too smooth; she's got to be a secret jagged rock. She probably shut the power off to my room, too, just to mess with my head! Whatever she's doing, I will get to the bottom of this. Maybe she's John's mistress, and that's why he killed his wife.*

I took off my clothes and showered before bed. Thoughts of the past twenty-four hours consumed me. *What did Cecelia do with Teddy? He asked me to find him. Maybe she's holding him hostage somewhere. Is she the person I saw dragging Teddy to Building C? Should I go to the police? If she's involved with Ether, then there would be no point. Ether basically owns the police with how rich he is. It would be too dangerous. I'm going to follow Cecelia to her work tomorrow. I need to see what she's up to.*

I turned off the shower, more stressed than before I got in, and reached for my scratchy tan towel. But when I looked down, I saw a beige towel that was soft as feathers. That was the last straw. I screamed and ran out of the shower, quickly wrapping myself in the luxurious material, and stormed out of my room to see Cecelia looking at me.

"What's wrong, Alina?" She jumped up from her alcohol-induced trance.

"Did. You. Change. My. Towel.?" I seethed.

"Why would I do that?" Cecelia laughed.

"Answer the question," I demanded.

"No, Alina, I did not change your towel. That's not even one of my towels. Mine are pink." She rolled her eyes.

"You were here all day. It had to be you."

"Was I?" she challenged.

"Don't touch my stuff!" I stomped back to my room and threw on some fresh PJs.

Who did she think she was, touching my stuff like that, going through MY room?

I walked into the bathroom again, pulled out my blue toothbrush, and examined my bruise. It was fading to a nice yellow. It was healing. I wondered if my heart could fade to yellow, too.

As I placed my toothbrush back in the holder, I spotted a tiny, red flashing light through the mirror. It was in the top right corner of the shower behind me. I spun around and stepped onto the edge of the shower. I extended my fingertips to the very top of the wall while holding on to the shower rod above me. I felt the light's rough, jewel-like surface, but my fingers slipped off the surface with each effort. I clawed into the wall with my nails like a feral cat until the tiny light loosened and bounced to the floor behind me. I jumped down to my knees and scanned the floor with my hands.

My eyes darted to every corner and crevice of the small bathroom, but it was gone. Defeated, I remained on the floor, crouched in a child›s pose, and sobbed. I held my face as I rocked back and forth, trying to make sense of a world that seemed to be collapsing around me.

Bob said they were watching us. *Who? Who is watching me? Cecelia has to be the one trying to harm me, but I won't let her. If she's going to watch me, then I will watch her back.* With newfound strength, I willed myself off the floor and gripped my hands against the counter as I stared and examined my reflection.

My face and eyes seemed narrower. My usual chapped and thin lips, now perfectly plump, contorted into a smirk. I blinked my eyes furiously, and my image returned to normal. *Cecelia messed with my brain. I know she did.* I walked to my door and opened it with the lightness of a feather. Cecelia's hair was no longer spilling over the edge of the couch. She must have gone to bed.

I exited my room, carefully stepped across the creaky floorboards, and walked towards her bedroom. I twisted the knob to Teddy's old room and pushed the door open to find an empty, un-slept-in bed. I quickly spun around to find Cecelia emerging from the kitchen with a spoonful of peanut butter in her hand.

"Whatcha doing?" she asked through licks of peanut butter.

"I, uh, wanted to apologize for my outburst before," I said.

"Oh, okay. Go ahead." She sipped milk from a glass on the counter.

"I'm sorry," I said as I glanced at my knife set in the kitchen.

"Apology accepted," she chirped and sauntered to her room. I stood still as my poorly thought-out plan went to shit.

"Well, goodnight!" Cecelia said as she closed the door.

Just before it closed, I caught a glimpse of the ceiling in her room. In the corner of the left wall, there was a small, flashing red light.

I stumbled back to my room and locked my door.

My mom used to say that no puzzles can be resolved with tired eyes. Granted, she was talking about actual puzzles at the time, but I'd like to believe she would give me the same advice now. I had to find out what Cecelia was up to and how Ether was involved in all of this, but I'd start fresh with my plan tomorrow. That night, my mind belonged to a better world. I tucked myself under the duvet that Teddy had gotten for me long ago and closed my eyes, allowing my world to go dark.

Beep. Beep. Beep. Beep. Beep. Beep.

The sun intruded through my window from the morning glow, straight into my eyes.

"Ugh," I groaned as I rolled over in my bed. I checked the time—7 AM.

I was about to fall back to sleep when I remembered my plan: find out what creepy Cecelia is up to.

I jumped out of bed and threw on a new set of business attire: a grey long-sleeve blouse and matching pants. I opted for flats today; I learned my lesson not to wear heels out again. I shoved my phone, keys, Teddy's note, and Cecelia's envelope into my black tote and quietly opened the door. Cecelia was in the kitchen making coffee, dressed in casual clothes. Her hair was perfectly curled, and her makeup was done, complete with red lipstick. *That's what she wears to work? Maybe she does a side gig at Lady Baze, the expensive makeup store next to Caffeine City.* It was the only nice store on the block, probably because Ether owned the company. I walked straight to the door and opened it cautiously, checking behind me to ensure she was not standing there holding a knife. She was still in the kitchen, humming a catchy song I had never heard.

I stepped into the hallway and slowly closed the door, swiftly moving out of the building. I gave Bob a nod but continued to turn the corner,

I passed a run-down convenience store and then ducked into an alleyway beside it. I texted Alister to let him know my plan to follow Cecelia, and I switched on my location so he knew where I was. I had seen enough horror movies to learn not to be completely alone. My phone pinged, and I kicked myself for not turning it on silent.

"Good luck! I'm a text away if you need me," Alister's text read.

I put my phone back in my bag and waited.

I expected to wait a while, but I could already hear the click-clack of Cecelia's shoes approaching. She was talking on the phone.

"I know, I know. She's making this hard, but it's a little amusing," she giggled.

She was just a few feet from the alleyway where I leaned against a wall. I held my breath as she passed me and continued ahead. *Phew*, I breathed a sigh of relief but waited a few more beats before I ducked out of the alleyway and followed her. I kept my distance, making sure I stayed back but not far enough away to lose her in the crowd.

Betty, the dog walker, was approaching me.

"Hey, Alina! How are you?" Betty smiled.

She remembers me now?

I looked down at her dogs: six dogs and six leashes in her hands. Lady ran up, jumped on my leg, and gave me a doggy hello.

"I'm uh, I'm good, thanks." I pet Lady as Luna emerged from behind.

I will deal with Crazy Betty later.

"Listen, I'm late for something. I'm sorry, I have to go," I said, focusing my attention on the growing crowd ahead of me while searching for Cecelia. Betty frowned when I brushed past her. My eyes darted through the people in front of me as each person blended into the next. I couldn't find Cecelia.

Shit. She couldn't have gone that far. I sped up, nearly knocking over a little girl in a blue dress.

"Sorry," I muttered.

I locked eyes on Cecelia's curly blonde hair, bouncing with her steps.

"Got you." I grinned.

She passed Oh My Pizza, and I followed shortly after, careful not to be seen.

Is she going to Ether? She crossed the pathway onto the unmanicured grass of Ether's property. She was in front of Building D, making a left turn. I crossed the path and followed her footsteps. She stopped at Building C, and I observed her as she lifted a small placard that read *Building C* and revealed a keypad with a fingerprint scanner and numbers. She looked to her left and then to her right. I ducked behind Building D and prayed to the Ether Gods that she wouldn't see me. I peeked back over the wall and watched as she entered the building, closing the door behind her.

"Alina?" a voice behind me shouted.

I froze.

"Alina, what in God's green earth are you doing?" I turned around to see Logan standing before me with his arms crossed.

"I, uh, no, you must be mistaken," I stuttered.

"You're standing right in front of me." His nose wrinkled, and his lips curled downwards in a grimace.

"No, no, I'm not. You don't see me." I placed my bag in front of my face and walked through the grass back to where I had come from.

"I do see you, and you're lucky I don't call security!" he yelled as I moved further away.

I ran.

I can't believe I got caught. Logan won't do anything, though. He's all bark and no bite. At least, I hope so.

I stopped running when I reached the bank that Alister worked at. I took a piece of paper and pen out of my bag and wrote, *we need to talk*. I held it up against the window and quickly tapped, allowing my breathing to return to normal. Alister was sitting at his desk, working on his computer. He looked up and chuckled. He stood up from his desk and walked over to the door.

He opened it an inch and whispered, "You know you could have just come in, right?"

I straightened my clothing. "Yes, but I'm in stealth mode. Now, do you want to know what I found out?" I didn't wait for his response before I blurted, "Cecelia works in Building C. She's the reason all these terrible things are happening to me."

"Oh my god. Okay, did you find out anything else?" he asked.

"I was going to follow her in, but I got caught by my ex-boss." I rolled my eyes.

"I'm off work tomorrow; we can follow her back to Building C. I'll show you how to actually be stealthy." He smirked.

I turned in the direction of home and started walking back. "Game on," I yelled over my shoulder.

CHAPTER EIGHT

UNIVERSE A- ALINA-PRESENT

I sat on my couch for an hour, picking at the strings that had worn thin long ago. The silence in the room was comforting. I used to play a game with Teddy where we would sit silently, staring at each other, and the first person to break the silence had to buy dinner. I imagined Teddy was next to me, and we played a game. I pulled out my phone and dialed his number. A loud automated message blared through the speaker. *We're sorry. This number is no longer in service. Please hang up and try a different number.*

I sunk lower into the couch and closed my eyes.

I walked down the stairs with my backpack in tow, ready to say bye to Mom and catch the bus to school. I saw her sitting on a stool, wiping away tears from her eyes as she noticed me.

"Hey baby, I'm going to take you to school today before I start work," she said. I grinned from ear to ear.

"Yay! What's the occasion?" I asked.

"Can't a mom get a little quality time with her girl?" She smiled.

I skipped to the garage, threw my bag in the back, and sat in the front seat. Mom got in the car and started the ignition. The garage door whirled with force, and the car revved in excitement.

"Alina Ballerina, do you remember when you were five, I taught you how to ride a bike, and at first, you were scared and said you couldn't do it?" Mom glanced at me as she pulled up to a red light.

"Yeah, I remember," I said.

"Do you remember what I told you when you were scared?" she asked.

"You said, be brave, be strong, and do not let go." I smiled and looked at my mom.

"And then you rode your bike so far in the distance that I had to chase you down the road to catch up." We laughed together.

She pulled up to the school drop-off and gave me a tight hug. When I broke away, I noticed her smile had faded.

"I love you, my Alina Ballerina. Be strong. Be brave. And do not let go."

"I love you too, Mom. See you when you get home from work." I grabbed my backpack from the backseat and walked the pathway to the

steps of my school building. I turned around to see Mom's car still sitting there. I waved, and she waved back. I returned to the steps and heard the car engine start as I reached the top.

The school faded away; the red brick turned white, and the trees and grass on either side of me lost their color and shape. I was transported to an empty void of nothingness.

I stood in an all-white room. There were no walls or furniture, and time and space seemed not to exist. A mirror, standing six feet high, was in front of me. I saw my eyes gazing back at me. I took a step forward. I took three more, until I was almost touching my reflection. My reflection looked brighter and more vibrant. She seemed happy, yet cold. She smiled, but I was not. She gestured with one finger for me to come closer. I leaned in…closer…closer.

My reflection's eyes narrowed into slits and darkened. She inhaled and screeched, "STAY AWAY!"

The mirror shattered; shards of flying glass surrounded me like a gust of wind blowing leaves into the open air.

I woke up soaked in sweat, breathing heavily, and Cecelia stood over me.

"Alina, are you okay? Here, I'll get you some water." Cecelia hurried to the kitchen, retrieved a glass from the cabinet, and filled it with tap water. She rushed it over to me, and I took it out of politeness. I would never drink the dirty tap water in this city, though, unless it was a dire situation.

I assessed my sweat-soaked clothes and concluded that it was dire enough.

I gulped down the water and made a face at the earthy, metallic taste. Cecelia hovered over me as my vision blurred.

"Wha-what did you do to me?" I slurred my words. Cecelia's eyes darkened, and her lips curled upward.

"Bye-bye, bitch." She waved to me in slow motion. I released the empty cup from my hand, and the glass fell to the floor, which shattered, as I succumbed to the heavy pressure on my eyes.

I was back in the all-white room, stretching endlessly in every direction. I heard chattering coming from an unknown location.

"Hello?" I said.

"Hello," a voice responded. I spun around to find myself standing before me.

"Am I dead?" I said to the other me.

"No. Come with me." She held my hand as she led me to a group of women circled around a table.

As they turned their heads toward me in unison, I realized who they were. They were all me.

"What is this? Where am I?" I said as my eyes desperately searched for an answer.

One of the women stood up; she looked like me, but a prettier version, one untouched by pain and suffering.

"You need to stop searching. You don't know what is at stake here," she said.

Before I could respond, another version of me with kinder eyes jumped out of her seat and pulled me away from the other.

"No. It's time for you to remember everything, Alina," she said.

"What do I need to remember? I don't understand." My eyes pleaded with them to help me understand, but they continued to provide me with riddles of conflicting advice.

One version whispered in my ear, "You can only trust Alister."

Another version whispered back, "You don't know him." They continued whispering until it became undeterminable chatter.

They circled me, chanting my name now. "Alina. Alina!" I cupped my ears to drown the noise and closed my eyes.

One in the sea of voices shouting was not like the other. I tried to decipher who it was as they continued. I listened over and over again. Who was this other voice? I opened my eyes and could only see rows and rows of myself chanting my name. But I heard her; I listened to that familiar voice that had called my name so long ago. It was my mom's voice.

"Mom?" I shouted.

"Alina! I'm here!" my mom shouted back.

I spotted a gap between the deranged women's legs and dropped to the all-white floorless ground below me. I crawled between them and emerged unscathed on the other side.

The room around me changed again, like a puzzle that had been forced together, and I was transported into a small library. My mom was hunched over on a couch.

"Mom, are you okay?" I approached her slowly.

"No, baby, and you aren't okay either." Her head stayed down, focused on the floor.

I took steps closer to her and saw her holding a knife. Teardrops mixed with blood as they dripped down her shirt. It was then that I noticed my body lying on the floor, blood spilling out of my stomach. This version of me whispered as she took labored breaths. I crouched beside her and placed my hand on her wound to stop the bleeding, but there was too much blood pouring between my fingers to stop it.

She whispered again, and I brought my head to hers to hear the barely audible sounds.

"Cecelia," she whispered.

"Did Cecelia do this to you?" I asked her. She did not answer me. Instead, she coughed up blood. I pressed my hands tighter on her wound. She looked up into my eyes.

"You have to kill her; it's the only way out," she said.

"Kill who? Cecelia?" I asked.

"You know the answer to that already." She coughed up more blood. Her body stiffened as she closed her eyes.

"No! No, you can't die. Please wake up!" I shouted.

I turned to my mom, who had stopped sobbing.

"Mom! Help her! Help me!" I begged.

She sat straight and pointed to the window as the sun set behind a green field.

"Follow the light," she said.

My eyesight blurred as the shouting of my name returned. The voices sounded like an angry mob in some far-off realm.

"Alina!" they shouted in unison.

"Alina! Alina!" the voices continued.

My mom faded out of existence, and I shut my eyes, trying to drown out the noise. The mob of angry Alinas turned to one single voice— Cecelia's.

"Alina!" a hand grabbed my shoulder and shook me.

My eyes burst open to Cecelia standing over me. I squinted my eyes together a couple of times as I scanned my surroundings. I was back on my couch. I felt my frayed blanket still draped around my body. I kicked it off to reveal my clothes, which were soaked in sweat. I felt my stomach to check for any bleeding. There was no wound, but my heart was working overtime. I looked back at Cecelia, who was holding a glass of dirty water in her hand.

"You were screaming in your sleep. You look unwell. I brought you a glass of water," she said.

My mind's brain fog faded, and my thinking became clear. I jumped up from the couch, keeping my distance from her.

"Stay away from me, Cecelia," I snapped.

"What are you talking about?" she asked with her doe-eyed gaze.

"Just stay away." I ran towards my room.

"I was just trying to help. I'll be gone tonight; you can have the place to calm down," she snapped back.

I slammed the door shut and pulled out my phone.

I texted Alister: *Change of plans. Meet me in front of my apartment building in one hour.*

My phone dinged back almost instantly.

Alister: *See you soon!*

I showered and changed into fresh clothes. black pants, a black hoodie, and running shoes. On top of my dresser sat a silver watch Teddy had given me. It wasn't a gift for a special occasion. He just bought a new watch and gave me his old one. It's funny how something seemingly so mundane and non-memorable can become special once someone is gone. I reached for the watch and clasped it around my wrist.

My breathing finally returned to normal, and a sense of calm and focus flowed through me. I knew what I needed to do. I pulled a flashlight from my nightstand and put it in a backpack along with my wallet and keys. I pressed my ear against my bedroom door to hear Cecelia's heels clicking and clacking and the front door shutting.

I watched the clock on my phone as I gave her a two-minute head start and then bolted out the door.

Alister pulled up right as I stepped outside, and I got in his car.

"It's lovely to see you again, Alina." His smile pierced through my soul as he grabbed my hand.

My worries seemed to fade away as soon as we made contact. I no longer felt the urgency to discover the horrible truths of what Cecelia had been planning for me. The normalcy of being in his car, smelling his cologne, and feeling the warmth of his skin distracted my mind from any burden in my life. I contemplated telling him to come upstairs to have a movie night together. Just one night of feeling normal, and we could stalk the crazy girl the next day. However, memories of my haunting dream quickly drove away the peaceful idea. *No.*

Snap out of it, Alina. We have a task to complete. I needed to find out what Psycho Cecelia was up to and make her fix my brain.

"It's great to see you too," I said as he pulled onto the road.

"Cecelia just left. She drives a red Buick; we need to catch up and see where she's going," I said.

"Roger that!" Alister was getting really into the spy role. *God, he's perfect. Stay focused, Alina.*

"This is going to sound crazy, but I had a dream that made me realize just how dangerous Cecelia is. So, I'm going to follow her and find out what she's up to. You don't have to come in with me if you don't want to. I'll understand," I offered him an out.

Alister turned his head towards me with soft eyes.

"You are not crazy. Cecelia is clearly dangerous. I am coming with you. Wherever you go, I go." He placed his hand on mine, warming up my cold fingers.

"There she is." Alister pointed to her car at a red light.

I ducked down in my seat while he narrated for me.

"Okay, she's turning left. I'm turning left now. She's turning into a parking lot. Should I turn in, too? It's empty, so that might be too obvious," he said.

"She's too daft to notice," I snorted.

"Roger that!" he said again.

"Okay, buddy, you only get to say that twice. Now it's just excessive." I laughed.

Alister laughed, too, and mimicked the sound of a radio.

"Don't do it!" I warned him.

"Shhrkkrkkkrrr. Roger. Shkkrrrr. That."

I was in hysterics. How did he manage to put me at ease when I was in such a terrible situation?

"Okay, I'm pulling in. Cecelia just entered Building C," he said.

The energy was instantly more serious.

My laugh subsided, and I suddenly felt like vomiting.

We unbuckled our seatbelts, and Alister stepped out of the car. I hesitated for a moment.

"Are you coming?" he asked.

I thought about what my mom told me the last day I saw her. I repeated her words in my head. *Be strong. Be brave. And do not let go.*

CHAPTER NINE

UNIVERSE A-ALINA-PRESENT

Alister and I made our way through the empty parking lot, carefully checking our surroundings. Building C was straight ahead of us, and Buildings B and A were to our left.

"What do you think the password is on that code box?" Alister asked.

"It's probably my name because she's such a stalker," I joked.

I stopped dead in my tracks, and Alister followed suit. In the far-left window of Building A, at the very top, I saw the glowing, pulsing light.

"Do you see that?" I asked.

"Yeah. What is it?" he asked.

"I don't know, but I think it wants us to find it," I said while watching it pulsate.

We made a swift left turn down the pathway, passing Building B, and approached the thirty steps. I held Alister's hand, and we walked up them together. This time, there were no guards waiting at the top. I hoped John wasn't going to appear out of nowhere like the ghost of Ether waiting to scold me again, or worse.

A fingerprint scanner was situated on the side wall of the front doors, and I nudged Alister to try it.

"You know, just in case it's boobie trapped," I teased.

He didn't hesitate and pressed his finger against the pad. To both of our surprise, we heard the whirring click of the doors unlocking. Silence fell between us as our eyes widened in unison, brows shooting upward.

"How did that actually work?" I asked.

"I have no idea, but let's get inside before someone sees us." He opened the door for me, and we walked inside.

The lights must have been on an automated trigger because it lit up as soon as we stepped inside, casting a spotlight on our intrusion.

The colors of the grand building looked duller than when I was last in there. The red couch was now a dark burgundy. The pink and white flowers had wilted. The floors looked like they hadn't been cleaned in a week. I looked back at the middle of the room where John Ether had spoken to me last. What had he meant when he told me I didn't belong here? I needed to find out.

We walked to the elevator and pressed the button with an arrow pointing up. It dinged and opened, inviting us in. I pressed the 20th floor button, the top level. Alister held me in a gentle embrace as it transported us. His scruffy beard tickled my cheek. This was by far the creepiest thing I had done in my life, yet I felt at peace as he held me. The world was ours for that brief moment. The doors opened to a bright, blinding light.

"Agh!" I shouted and shielded my eyes.

Alister grabbed my hand and pulled us forward. We made a right turn, and the light faded away.

"I think the light is helping us," I said to Alister as my eyes adjusted to the now-dim lighting of the top floor.

"Yeah, it's helping us go blind," Alister said.

There were six offices in the hallway, each with its own plaque on the door.

The first door was labeled *John Ether*. We opened that one first. We entered the room and found a pristine, sterile room. I spotted a chrome-colored filing cabinet and rummaged through the labels, stopping at a file entitled *Project Universe*.

I pulled it out and laid the contents on the desk: only three pieces of paper. I picked up the first and scanned its contents.

"It's a machine," I said to Alister, who was searching through the cabinet.

There was a drawing of a prototype machine connected to a massive computer with code scribbled on the screen. Behind it, a large mirror with a thick coil connecting the two together.

"Alister, look at this." I showed him the drawing. I turned my attention to another piece of paper containing John Ether's notes and read them aloud.

The first human trial using my family has been a success. They will be the first people in history to successfully transfer to an alternative universe of my choosing. Other variations of my family, and every human, exist in bubble universes on different dimensions. These bubble universes are similar to the one we are from, a place I call UNIVERSE A. Each version of ourselves lives their own life and has their own free will and experiences. I have created a way to duplicate worlds and the people in them. This innovative technology I have created will shift how we live our lives—the elite can now control and bend their worlds to how we see fit.

I look forward to building the Ether empire in all worlds and will ensure my family's name lives on.

"Oh my god!" Alister exclaimed.

"They're creating other worlds here?" I asked.

"Not just that, Alina. They're altering them," he said.

Alister handed me the last paper featuring a black web of interconnected bubble universes. Each bubble contained a letter. My eyes shifted to the two colored spheres in the middle: a green bubble with the letter A connected to a red bubble with the letter B. In the far-right corner, the last bubble on the page was a bubble with a green X in it.

I hurriedly put all the paperwork back, placed it in the cabinet, and shut the drawer.

"We need to investigate the rest of the rooms," Alister said.

"I can't imagine we'll find anything more horrible than this," I said.

Alister headed out first, and I followed. "Alina…" he stopped at the next office. "Come look at this."

I stood next to him and read the plaque on the door. It read—*Alina Nobleman.*

"Why is your name on this plaque? And why does it have my last name on it?" he asked.

I stood there like a deer in headlights, searching for an answer—any answer—but came up short.

"I don't know." I said, unable to make sense of it.

"What is your last name?" he asked.

"I … have no idea," I said. I searched my brain as hard as I could, but for some reason, my last name felt fuzzy to me.

"You don't know who you are?" Alister raised his eyebrows.

"I do. I mean, I think I do. This is just too much to take in. I don't understand. We have the same last name?" I asked.

"It appears that way on this door, at least," Alister said.

I turned my attention to the next office door, hoping to find an answer there.

It read: *Alister Nobleman.*

"Why is *your* name on there?" My cheeks reddened as panic slowly crept into my mind. There was no answer, only more questions.

"We need to go. We don't belong here." I swallowed hard as I grabbed Alister's hand and pressed the button to go down.

The doors opened, and we rushed inside. I pressed the bottom floor button, and the doors closed. The ride down felt painfully slow. We stood in silence. The doors opened, and to my surprise, we were not on the main floor.

"I think we went to the storage unit," I said as I stepped out of the elevator. I turned to Alister, who had yet to exit.

"Alina, I have a bad feeling about this. Let's go back up to the main floor," he urged.

I walked to him and grabbed his hand as I gently pulled him toward the room. "We got this far. Come on. What happened to being bold?" I said, even though I was seconds away from a panic attack. Something about that room was telling me to explore it.

Alister took a deep breath in and chose to walk with me. "Okay, but everyone knows nothing good comes out of dark, quiet, empty basements," he muttered.

"I have you to protect me." I smiled up at his barely visible face. I was relieved I couldn't see his expression because I didn't think I could have looked him in the eyes after what we found upstairs.

He kissed my forehead; I guess he wasn't as bothered.

As I looked around, I discovered rows and rows of shelves and tables.

"Let's check the shelves out," I said.

I dug through the far-left shelf filled with boxes while Alister explored the middle shelf beside me. Each box I opened contained various office supplies. One box was all plastic cutlery, and another was toilet paper rolls.

"I've got nothing. Did you find anything?" I asked.

"Just printer paper and pens," he replied.

I focused my attention on the walls. At first, I thought it was a small room with four basic walls, but from the right corner of the room, I noticed it stopped short, leading to an open section that looped around.

"Alister, let's check behind there, and then we can go," I said, taking note of how stiff he looked. Alister appeared weary of the room; perhaps he felt claustrophobic. Or perhaps he was wondering why his new love interest was stealing his last name. I wouldn't have blamed him; I was wondering the same thing.

"Okay, I'm right behind you," he said.

I walked around the looped wall, which led to a stretched-out hallway. At the end, there was a small room, dimly lit by flashing red lights I could see through the narrowly open door.

"Alister, come see this," I whispered as I moved forward further.

Alister did not respond. I pushed the door open to find a wall of flat-screen computers stacked atop one another. There had to be at least fifty laid out in there. The only other things in the room were a single desk and chair pointed at the devices. Each screen displayed a different image, but a tiny red light flashed in the corner of all of them.

Upon closer inspection, the screens on the left side played images of the outside of the town. Two cars waited at a red light that soon turned green. Another screen showed a man and a woman entering a bar further down the road. I brought my attention to the middle monitors after catching a glimpse of something familiar—my apartment. One screen showed my bedroom. Another next to it was blacked out with no video feed to show. The other screen was Teddy's room, which now belonged to a crazy person.

A hand touched my shoulder, and I gasped as I spun around.

"Oh my god, Alister, you scared me!" I held my chest as it thumped.

"Sorry! I found something," he said as he handed me a notebook.

Alister observed the room, taking in all the images on the screens.

"It looks like Cecelia and John have been surveilling the entire city," he said.

"Yes, and that's not all. They put cameras in my room. I found one of them in my bathroom and tore it out. You can see the empty screen right here." I pointed.

"That is sick. Why would they do that?" Alister scrunched his nose and clenched his fists.

"I don't know, but we need to find Cecelia and stop this." I stared at the notebook that Alister had handed me. "What did you find?"

"It's a written journal from Cecelia, marking your every move. I thought that was bad enough, but this..." He gestured to the screens. "This is too much. We need to get out of here." He placed his hand on the small of my back and guided me through the hallway. An exit sign over a door on the other side of the room illuminated our path.

As the shock from our recent discoveries wore off, panic set in full force. I felt dirty, like mud and bugs were crawling all over my body, violating my right to just—*be*.

"Let's get to your car," I whispered, and my voice cracked.

Alister stopped in the middle of the parking lot and held both of my hands as he gazed into my eyes.

"Alina, I know you're scared. I am, too. You were right before; we've come this far. I don't know what's happening or what Cecelia and John Ether are up to, but I think we need to see it through. Let's go to Building C and find Cecelia before she has a chance to find us," he suggested.

"Are you crazy? She's probably waiting there, ready to kill us!" I pulled my hands from his.

He placed his hand on my head and stroked my hair, tucking a loose strand behind my ear.

"If you return to your apartment, she'll be watching you. She may even be watching us if I take you to my house, too. It's not safe to go back. Besides, if we die, we'll die together." He smiled.

"Very comforting." I rolled my eyes.

"Sorry, that was a bad joke. Listen, I'm not going to let Cecelia get away with this. As long as I'm here, I'll protect you."

I took a deep breath in and looked at him. "Alister, if we go in there, we might not return." I swallowed hard as a lump formed in my throat.

"If we don't go in there, you'll never get the answers you're searching for. Come on. I'll be with you the whole time, I promise." Alister extended his hand to me.

"Okay. Fine. Let's go be bold," I said, although I was feeling far from it. I grabbed his hand, and he nudged me forward.

"Atta girl." He kissed my cheek.

Alister had a way of putting me at ease, even in the most dire of situations. There was just something about his demeanor that made me feel like he had everything under control.

We looped around the corner to the front of Building A and walked down the pathway until we were standing in front of Building C. The wind blew my hair back while my breath floated in the chilly air, but I had so much adrenaline running through me that I was not cold. I looked up at the night sky; the stars were barely visible from the light pollution. My eyes fluttered back and forth, searching for the three stars in a row. They eventually rested on Orion's Belt.

As a child, I discovered I could open my window and crawl out to the roof. It was a primarily flat ledge. Our neighborhood didn't have many lights illuminating the roads at night, so the sky could show off its impressive design.

I had snuck out every night since discovering my new spot. I'd gaze up at the moon and wonder what it might be like to be so far away yet still visible. I wondered if it ever got lonely up there being watched by us below. Did it want to be seen? Would I want to be the moon, trapped in a fishbowl of the universe, for everyone to gawk at?

I shifted my eyes to the neighbor's cat, Billy, who roamed the fences, searching for something or someone. I heard a tap on the window. It was my mom. Startled, I grabbed onto the roof tiles and opened it for her.

"Honey, what are you doing out here?" she asked.

"Sorry, Mom, it's just peaceful out here," I said.

She turned around without saying another word, and I moved to go inside. To my surprise, she grabbed the blue throw blanket off my bed and walked back toward me.

"Make some room; I'm coming out here with you," she said.

A wide grin stretched across my face, reaching all the way up to my eyes, which sparkled with delight. She sat beside me and draped the blanket over us.

"Do you see those stars, just there?" She pointed to three stars positioned diagonally next to each other. I looked up and followed the direction of her fingers.

"Yeah, right there." I pointed upward.

"That's Orion's Belt. Ancient Egyptians believed it represented the resting place of the soul of Osiris, the god of the deceased," she said.

"Mom, that's morbid." I laughed.

"I think it's beautiful. I see it as he watches over you, protecting you. And when you most need that protection, you can look to the sky and know you're safe." Mom held my hands, which were shaking from the frigid temperatures; well, frigid for California, anyway.

"Alina, your hands are ice-cold. Come on, let's get inside. I'll make us some hot chocolate, and we can put on a movie," she said.

I looked up at Orion's Belt and wondered if my mom was up there, protecting me. Alister's voice came back into focus.

"What? Sorry, I spaced out." I blinked my focus back to him.

"I said, do you want to do the honors?" Alister gestured to the keypad.

"Why, of course." I pressed my thumb to the keypad, and the door clicked. I pulled open the door and walked inside, with Alister following right behind me.

We were in a dimly lit, long and narrow hallway. The place looked abandoned. What was once fresh white paint on the wall had a yellow tint. The floor was filthy. Rat droppings and old food wrappers scattered the tile floor. The lights above flickered. We walked forward to what looked like a break room. There was a worn-out couch against the side wall. I turned the faucet on—no running water. Beside the sink, there was a coffee cup with a coffee company's name that I didn't recognize.

"Caffeine Couture? Never seen that place around here," I said as I turned to Alister, who was opening cupboards and coughing with a face full of dust.

"This is where Cecelia works?" I asked Alister.

"Maybe there's another room that has power. Let's check the back rooms." He led us out of the break room, and we saw the unmistakable pulsing light at the end of the hall. It faded darker with every step until we were face to face with it, and it blinked out of existence.

The final door was unmarked, but I could see a light on the other side. I glanced at Alister, and he rubbed my back.

"Ready?" He held his breath.

"No, but let's do this." I exhaled for him.

I opened the door; we walked in, and Alister closed the door behind us. There was no sign of Cecelia. In front of us was a machine, John Ether's prototype. The spherical shape had wires and buttons protruding from hundreds of tiny holes. Above it was a large computer screen with constantly cycling green code. In between the codes, there were small words. It was moving at a rapid pace, so I tried to read fast.

I managed to catch three separate lines.

One line said, *Find Teddy*.

Another line said, *Green pasture*, followed by *I'm here*.

The last line I was able to read before it blinked out of existence was *Child*.

"What does that mean? Is Teddy sending me a message? How would Teddy know I'm here?" I said to Alister, who was standing in front of the mirror, seemingly too busy checking himself out to respond.

"Alister, you look great. Now come over here and look at this computer and see if you can find something in this database," I said.

"Do I look different to you? This mirror makes me look jacked." He flexed his arms.

"You are jacked. It's not the mirror." I rolled my eyes.

"No, really, you have to see this." Alister continued flexing. "You are already the most gorgeous girl in the universe. I bet you'd look so beautiful in this mirror that you'd break it." He finally stopped flexing and winked at me.

"You think so?" I blushed.

I cleared my throat as I remembered the task at hand. There was no time to flirt with Alister.

"Just come over here." My voice was stern.

"Yes, ma'am." He complied.

Alister walked toward me, leaned behind me, and pressed the touchscreen. His breath smelled faintly of mint and berries and warmed my skin as it hit the nape of my neck. I watched as he searched through endless files. Each one had a different letter named after it. Alister clicked on the file labeled *Universe B.*

Just as the green code popped up on the screen again, the mirror illuminated and began humming. Alister and I looked up in awe. Its silver plating faded out of focus as purple and blue colors danced to the rhythm.

The swirls soared to the top of the mirror, which nearly reached the ceiling. It was easily three times my height, and I was taller than average. I walked to the mirror as its hums seemed to whisper to me. If I just walked closer, maybe I could hear what it was saying. I stood in front of the lights, now swirling in reverse. The whispers intensified, but the words were unclear.

I turned back to Alister, who was laser-focused on the computer, typing something. When I looked back in the mirror, the lights had disappeared. I only saw myself staring back at me. Only, I looked different. My hair was perfectly curled rather than fried at the ends of my usual straight hairstyle. My skin looked softer, the dark circles under my eyes from the most recent events were gone, and my face looked fuller. I looked healthy but not happy. My eyes seemed to be glaring at me. I lifted my hand to the mirror, and my reflection lifted hers.

The other me began swaying as the whispers turned to humming. The noise grew louder, and someone shouted my name from behind me. Was it Alister? I couldn't tell. The humming intensified as I inched closer, my hand stopping just before the glass. My reflection was smiling as she swayed. Was I smiling? I couldn't feel my face; I couldn't look away from the more put-together version of myself. My hand touched my reflection as if it had a mind, and the glass shattered around me. I felt a suction of air pull me in, and the humming was deafening. I screamed in agony but couldn't hear myself as the force of the wind pulled me in every direction.

"Alister!" I tried to call but couldn't hear an answer.

I was caught in a tornado of something resembling air but felt like fire and smelled like the ocean. I free fell, or was I being pushed upwards? I couldn't tell up from down or right from left. Tiny translucent specs filled the vortex around me, and I focused on the three that seemed to form a perfect, vertical line resembling Orion's Belt. Was my mom there with me, protecting me? A rush of energy flowed from my toes to the strands of my hair. It didn't hurt; it felt like the first hug you get after not seeing someone for a long time. Suddenly, the wind stopped. The noise settled as I felt my back hit a hard surface. The rush of nothingness turned to a still, yet seemingly tangible, darkness.

CHAPTER TEN

UNIVERSE B- ALINA-PRESENT

My eyes were open, but I couldn't see a thing. I stretched my hands and felt the cold tile floors beneath me. I smelled smoke, but the air was not thick. My body ached with each breath. Every inch of my skin felt like it had been torn apart and clumsily put back together. My head throbbed, and my ears were ringing in a high shrieking pitch. My mind was foggy as I tried to piece together the unfolding events. *There must have been an explosion. I must still be alive if I'm in this much pain.* I thought of Alister. *Is he alive?*

"Alister?" I cried out in a barely audible whisper.

I pushed myself to stand. My hands desperately searched for something to grab onto. I felt a round metal surface and used it to brace myself as I inched to where I thought the wall with a light switch was.

"Alister!" I called out, stronger that time—still no answer.

I felt around in front of me, waving my hand, searching for the next object. I took a careful step forward. Then another, and another. I heard the crunching of glass beneath my shoes with every step.

"Alister, please answer me," I whispered, now by choice, as the air around me sent chills down my spine. I reached a roughly textured wall and placed both hands against its surface as I moved along it. *I think the door is to the left.* I took slow steps towards it. My fingers grazed four light switches. *What if I flip the wrong switch?* I hesitated, then called Alister one more time, but there was no answer. With shaky hands, I flipped up all four switches.

Lights illuminated the room from every direction, making my head spin. I yelled out in agony, closed my eyes, and grabbed my head. I needed to be brave for Alister. I was the reason he was in this mess, and I needed to help him. I counted down from three…two... one.

My eyes opened to a perfectly untouched room. The glass from the mirror was not shattered. The machine was clicking, and the green code on the screen atop the circular metal machine was changing with every passing second. I darted my eyes around the room, searching for Alister. He had been standing by the machine before I touched the mirror. I made a loop around it, but he wasn't there. I opened a closet door next to the mirror to find only bare and dust-covered shelves. My shoulders sank as I came to the realization: Alister was no longer in the room.

My stomach felt like it was plunging over a thousand waves. I ran to a small trash can situated by the entrance door and lost what little food was left in my stomach. I sat down, feeling sorry for myself. *Alister must have run out of the room before the explosion. Someone must have heard it, and security will surely be here to arrest me for breaking in. Cecelia will get a good laugh at my expense. And I'll probably be sent to a psych ward if I try to explain to anyone what I've been seeing.*

I turned to the trash can and vomited again. After grabbing the door handle and pulling myself up with all the strength I had left, I spotted a red emergency exit sign lit up at the other end of the room. I took short, slow strides to the door, pushed the handle with my whole body, and stumbled outside into a parking lot. I was in the back lot of Building C. It was daylight out, although I was unsure what time it was. I felt my pockets for my phone, but it had gone missing. I checked the watch on my wrist; it was cracked in three places, and the time was stuck at 11 PM.

I wondered if Alister's car was still parked up front. My body recovered quickly; maybe the adrenaline rushing through it sped the process up. I looped around to Building C's front and searched the parking lot. Alister's car was still there. *Maybe he's waiting for me!* My pace picked up as I approached his black Mercedes. I pressed my face to the window and peered inside. He was not in there. There was a heart-shaped pendulum hanging on the rearview mirror that was engraved, "A & A." I must have been too busy worrying about Cecelia before to notice that. He'd parked in front of a sign that read: *Reserved.* I turned around to head back to Building C. *I have to find him. He didn't leave me, so I can't leave him.*

My strides were longer now; my strength was coming back. I inhaled a deep breath, and the air felt clean. The sun shone down on my face, providing a burst of comfort. I walked up to Building C, raised my right thumb to the fingerprint keypad, and was interrupted by a familiar voice.

"Alina! Good morning." I spun around to see a cheerful Logan grinning from ear to ear. His smile flowed up to his beady little eyes.

"Oh god, Logan, come on. Are you the one stalking me?" I said with the rage of a thousand yapping dogs bubbling up inside me.

I didn't have time for Logan's nosiness.

"Ahh, Alina, your sense of humor always gets me!" He nudged my shoulder playfully.

I furrowed my brows and tilted my head, studying him. His hair was styled, and he no longer reeked of cologne. He was wearing an expensive-looking suit that fit him, one that you could only get at Forever Men's Apparel in the city. Now that I think about it, his eyes didn't look beady at all. His smile was warm, and the way the sun shone on his face, he almost looked handsome.

He extended his arm and handed me a coffee.

"Here you go, miss. Your favorite praline latte. We must get you caffeinated for today's big day!" he chirped.

I examined the coffee cup; the label on the side said: *Caffeine Couture. Drink Elegantly.* I raised an eyebrow and took a sip. This sure tastes like a Caffeine City coffee.

"When did they revamp Caffeine City?" I asked, switching my gaze back and forth from examining the cup to examining Logan.

"Caffeine City?" Logan asked. "That sounds gaudy and disgusting."

Gaudy? Yes. Disgusting? No. It's the best coffee in town. I wanted to correct him, but I caught a glimpse of his brown eyes and slicked-back hair.

"Did you change your hair or something? You look good, Logan." I couldn't stop taking him in. I never thought those words would flow from my mouth. "Well, I have been working out more; that means a lot coming from you, Alina," Logan blushed.

Was he flirting with me? Do I like it? Suddenly, I remembered Alister. *I need to find him.*

"Well, thanks for the coffee. Bye!" I turned around and started to walk away briskly. Logan caught up with me.

"Oh, actually, Alina, I'm coming with you to prep you for today's big launch!" He grabbed my shoulders and guided me toward Building D.

"How are you feeling after your fall?" he asked.

"My fall?" I rubbed the tender spot on my forehead.

"Jeez, that pole must have done a number on your head. And that dog, my god, I can't believe it just attacked you like that out of nowhere. But we're all so glad to have you back, especially John. We weren't expecting you to be out of the hospital this soon. You can barely see the cuts, just those dark circles under your eyes." He beamed with excitement.

There's the Logan I remember, the not-so-charming Logan.

He opened the door to Building D and waited for me to enter before following me inside. I stopped dead in my tracks to see *her. No, this can't be. Cecelia?* Suddenly, I felt the need to vomit again, but I held it down as Cecelia stood up from *my* desk and walked herself over in her baby pink heels and pink and white suit jacket. *Does she think she's in the movie Totally Blonde?* My nose flared as I observed her prancing around, practically taunting me.

"Good morning, Mrs. Alina. Here's the project you requested." She handed me a file labeled **Project Undesirable** and click-clacked back to her desk. *My desk.* My mouth was stretched so far open it could have probably mopped the floor. *What did she do to me last night? What has she done to me* *now? What has she done to Alister?* I marched straight up to her pink computer and matching pink keyboard and poured my cappuccino all over it. It splashed on her perfectly curled hair.

"What did you do with Alister, you evil bi-?" Logan stopped me from continuing as he grabbed me by both shoulders and pulled me towards the door. "So sorry, Miss Abernathy. She's still recovering from her fall." Logan gestured to my head and produced an embarrassed smile. Cecelia cried while she cleaned up my mess with tissues.

Logan yanked me outside and looked me dead in the eyes.

"Pull yourself together, Alina, for god's sake." He grabbed my arm and dragged me past Building C. I wondered if Alister was still in there somewhere.

"Let go of me; I'm fine, Logan!" I whipped my hand away from his grasp.

"I can't go into Building A dressed like this." I gestured to my clothes.

"Dressed like what? You look fine." He continued walking.

I peered down at my clothes. I was no longer wearing my jeans and hoodie from last night. I had been too focused on Alister to notice my blazer atop a navy blue button-up and suit pants. *When did I change my clothes?* My feet suddenly felt sore. I looked down to see shiny black pumps, which were definitely a size too small for me. They were much shinier than any shoe I had ever owned.

Cecelia has done a number on my mind. I swallowed to push down my rising panic. I needed to confide in someone, but who could I trust?

I caught up to Logan as he gestured toward Building A. "He's waiting for you," Logan sighed. Please try to keep it together for your father. He's very excited about the launch."

My…father? No. No, my father works for an oil rig company and lives in Texas. I haven't seen him in years. Why would he be at Ether? I wiped the sweat off my brow. I didn't know if I was relieved or nervous to see my dad again. It had been so long since he was anything other than just a name on my phone.

I peered up at Building A; its grand stature taunted me. I noticed the Ether logo sat on a gold pedestal, but it no longer said Ether. It just had a figure-eight symbol turned on its side, with two hands cupped together, holding it up.

Logan led me up the steps, and we were greeted by plump guards with smiling faces. They eagerly opened the doors from both sides. I entered first, and Logan followed.

I took a deep breath and exhaled as I stepped inside. Logan led me to the elevator, and we rode it to the top. It dinged at each level, slowly rising, unlike my blood pressure, which was undoubtedly climbing at lightning speed.

The doors opened, and I took a step forward.

"Why am I here?" I turned to ask Logan. But he was gone.

I heard the ding and the rumbling of the elevator going down.

"Coward," I whispered in the elevator's direction.

I approached the door marked *John Ether*, and I knocked.

"Come in," a voice called through the door.

I twisted the knob to see John Ether sitting at his desk, his eyes focused on his computer, where he was typing furiously.

He raised a finger, and I stood there awkwardly adjusting my clothes until he finished.

A photo frame situated on his desk caught my attention. I saw myself as a kid, sitting on his shoulders at Little Land. I remembered that trip; we rode all the rides I wanted twice. Mom was there, taking as many pictures on her camera as possible. It was annoying then, but now I was glad she did. I remembered my dad being there, but I couldn't recall what he looked like until just then.

"Dad?" I said with a quivering breath.

"Yes, honey?" He looked up at me from his computer, and we were both stunned into silence. He stared at me, his mouth forming silent words as if he was deciding what to say. He eventually cleared his throat and broke the silence. "Are you okay? It's good to see you." He jumped up from his chair and moved toward me with open arms.

"I…I have to go," I said as I ran out the door and clicked the down button on the elevator repeatedly. After an agonizing ten seconds, the door opened. I didn't check to see if he was watching me. My breathing was out of control; the doors shut, and I took quick and forced breaths in.

The elevator dinged again, whirred open, and I ran. I ran so fast that the surroundings of Building A were a blur.

"Alina!' I heard Logan calling my name, but I didn't stop. I took my shoes off and rushed down the steps. I ran to Alister's car, where I came to a complete halt. There, leaning against his vehicle, was Alister.

"Alister! Oh my god, I'm so glad you're okay." I wrapped my arms around him and hugged him tight.

"It's great to see you too, sweetheart. Why wouldn't I be, okay? I was just grabbing my wallet from the car." He tucked his wallet in his back pocket and wrapped his arms around me.

"When I couldn't find you in Building C, I thought something bad had happened to you," I said.

"Baby, why would I be in Building C? We work in Building A. Are you feeling okay? Is it too soon to be out here? I can drive you home, and you can rest before the launch party if you would like." He brushed a stray hair behind my ear.

My face paled, and my eyes widened. I slowly let go of Alister and observed him. He was dressed differently. He wore a suit that accentuated his form. His hair was combed back, with the curls trapped between a glob of gel. His scruffy beard was gone, showing off his angular jawline. His posture was better; he stood tall with his chest naturally pushed out. I glanced at the wedding ring on his finger. I then examined my hands to see a diamond ring that cast a kaleidoscope of shimmering reflections. Much like Alister's stare, it commanded attention with its brilliance and allure. My nails were perfectly manicured, a soft shade of rose, and my skin was lusciously moisturized.

My eyes widened further than I thought possible, and my muscles tensed. I took two steps backward.

This is not Alister, not the Alister with me last night in Building C, at least. And somehow, I'm not the Alina they think I am. I took in my surroundings. Everything looked off. The town appeared cleaner, there were no clownish lights, and every building, as far as I could see, seemed as perfect as the Ether buildings. I glanced at Building D to find that it was the only building that resembled what I remembered. I thought about the coffee I dumped in Cecelia's hair. It had an unusual name, one I'd never heard of before.

My vision blurred as my mind was overwhelmed. *Where am I? This is not my life. These are not my clothes. That is not my Alister. I don't belong here.*

CHAPTER ELEVEN

UNIVERSE B-ALINA-PRESENT

"Alina?" Alister's voice slowly came into focus. My vision returned as Alister frowned in front of me. "Alina, are you okay? Let me drive you home," he said.

"I'm fine," I lied. "I think I just need to lie down for a bit. I can drive myself. I grabbed the keys that dangled from his front pocket. Alister leaned in for a kiss goodbye, and I quickly moved to my left to dodge his lips.

"Bye, Alister." I opened his car door, started the ignition, and shut the door as I raced out of the parking lot. Alister jumped backward to avoid being hit. I watched the rearview mirror as he mouthed something, but I couldn't make out the words.

All the cars on the road were monochromatic. Each car was filled with ghost drivers. Businessmen and women in tailored suits tapped on their invisible screens in the air as they sat in the passenger seat. I looked down at my wheel and realized I was not driving either. The screen in front of me said, *Auto-Drive Activated.* I let go of the wheel and the gas pedal, and it continued down the road.

The sky above was so blue it looked fake. Maybe it was. I spotted Betty walking four dogs past what was now named Gourmet Buns. The old hot dog stand had been replaced with a bougie and, likely overpriced, hot dog cafe. Ether's horizontal figure-eight logo was attached to the sign of every business I passed.

"Oh my god, Ether owns the whole town?" I gasped.

The car pulled over to the side of the road, seemingly reading my thoughts, next to a beauty spa for pets. The *Zoomy Groomers* that used to be situated on the corner was now a *Beauty Paws and Spa* boutique. Unbelievable.

I felt my jacket pockets for my phone and pulled it out. I thought I had lost it in Building C. This one had a silver case, not the clear cover I had on mine. After tapping the front of the phone, a screen popped up out of thin air on my dashboard. The background was a picture of Alister and I on our wedding day. My dress had a beautiful sweetheart neckline and was dazzled with too many jewels to count. Alister had dressed in a black tuxedo with a violet handkerchief poking from his suit pocket.

"We look happy," I said aloud.

I swiped up, and it unlocked using facial recognition. I went to the maps application and searched for recent addresses. I tapped on *home*, and the automated voice flowed through the car to guide me.

"Wait. Stop the car," I told the voice. It pulled to a safe spot on the road and turned off the ignition.

Glancing out of the rearview mirror, I watched Betty, who was a few steps behind my car. I rolled down my window. "Betty," I said, and she peered into the car.

"Yes?" she said.

"Cute dogs. Where are the other two?" I asked.

"What other two?" She raised her eyebrows.

"You don't know me, do you, Betty?" I said dryly.

Betty paused for a moment. "Oh." Her eyes widened.

"Alina, I'm so sorry I didn't recognize you. I thought you were still in the hospital after…" She suddenly stepped back and appeared uncomfortable.

"After what?" I said just as a Rottweiler jumped up on my car door and wagged its tail.

"I…I'm sorry, I have to go. I won't bother you again. Just please don't tell your father you saw me," she begged.

"Betty, tell me what's going on. How do you know my father?" I yelled to her as she hurried away with the dogs.

"Car, take me home," I sighed.

I rolled up my window as the car turned into the driving lane and drove off.

That's not my Betty. And neither was the Betty from a few days ago. I'm not crazy; I know Betty. She walks six dogs every single workday. She's friendly, and she has four kids and an ex-husband who left her high and dry when they divorced. That's why she walks dogs for extra money. This is not my Betty. This is not my life. But if I'm still Alina, then whose life is this?

"Turn left on Drummer Street," the map voice said. Oddly, it told me the directions when it was leading the way. Maybe it was designed to make the driver feel more human or to feel anything at all. This town didn't exactly scream warm and emotional.

The heat shining down from the sun's rays wasn't enough to offset the cold pallet of muted tones chosen for this city.

"You have arrived at your destination. 7585 Drummer Court," the car announced.

It turned into a driveway with a large steel gate, which automatically opened. My mouth opened as I stared at a three-story black and grey mansion. It stood like a majestic fortress against the backdrop of the rolling hills, its grandeur almost overwhelming. It seemed to stretch endlessly. Windows lined the façade as if inviting passersby to look in. I stepped out of the car and walked through a lush garden filled with vibrant flowers that surrounded the estate.

I approached the front door; it was metal and so thick that nothing or no one could get in uninvited. There was a loud beep, and a green light cascaded down the door. It opened painfully slow, as if reluctant to reveal its secrets. It finally opened fully and beeped again.

I guess this means I've been invited in.

I stepped onto the marble floors, which gleamed under the soft glow of crystal chandeliers. A grand spiral staircase swept upward, its marble steps less than inviting. I stood at the bottom of the stairs, and the darkness at the top was even less welcoming. As I forced myself up the steps, I couldn't help but feel I was trespassing.

At the top of the second floor, I was surprised to see it was just one large room. A giant bed, too high for me to get into without steps, sat in the middle. A grand painting stretched across the wall. It was of Alister and I in an embrace. Our eyes sparkled, and I looked happy. To my right was a large desk with a single chrome button in the middle. I pulled out the chair, which had no cushioning, and sat down.

I pressed the button and brought up an impressive array of images that sprawled across the length of the desk.

"It's a computer! Now, where did that mirror transport me to?" I said. I tapped on what looked to be a search engine named *EtherQ* and searched my name using a virtual keyboard. I selected a search result and read it aloud. *"John Ether welcomes his daughter, Alina Nobleman, to join the Ether corporation alongside her husband, Alister Nobleman, who was named John's business partner in July 2025. Alina expressed in an exclusive interview that she was 'looking forward to expanding my father's empire and improving the life of her fellow Americans and allies in other countries.'"*

"No, no, this can't be. My father founded the Ether corporation? Alister and I are a part of it? Is that why our names were on the office doors?" My stomach twisted in knots.

I willed my hands to type *Sandra Ether* in the search bar floating in the air. No articles or images of my mother appeared. There were no articles about her disappearance, no photos of her, and no social media links. It was as if she didn't exist.

I typed Teddy's name into the search database. No mention of the Teddy I knew popped up either. It was mostly just advertisements to buy Ether-branded chrome and gold teddy bears.

"Where are you, Mom and Teddy?" I bit my lip and pressed my fist to my mouth. "Wherever you are, I'm going to find you," I said as I pressed the button on the desk, and the images warped out of existence.

I hurried back down the staircase. To my right was an ample, open space filled with dark-toned, luxurious furniture. The fabrics were rich but suffocating. A library stretched along the entire wall behind the couch. Books upon books filled the monochromatic shelves.

Photos of Alister lined every shelf. One picture stood out to me; it was the same photo on my phone that I saw in the car earlier. The gold-plated frame was engraved with a date. It read: Married in June 2025. I graduated high school in June of 2025. *I didn't know Alister back then, did I? If that's true, we've been married for five years, right out of high school.* I didn't see any mention of children; there were no photos on the wall of anyone but Alister and me.

I heard a loud engine roaring and the creak of the gates opening.

Shit, someone is here.

I squatted down to the ground and crawled to a window next to the front door. Alister stepped off a chromatic motorcycle and walked quickly towards the front door. He paused briefly when he caught my eye, catching me crouched on the other side. He opened the door, and I felt like I was about to be scolded like a schoolgirl who didn't do her homework.

"Alina, sweetheart, what are you doing?" Alister asked.

Sweetheart. I felt relieved. *Okay, he must not be mad.* "I, uh, was just excited to see you, so I waited by the window when I heard you pull in," I said as I jumped up.

"I'm excited to see you too, but I'm worried about you. I told Dr. Liv you were too weak to attend today's launch and not to release you until you were fully healed. Next thing I know, I see you in the parking lot of Ether headquarters. Looks like I'll be having a chat with him soon," he said, then pressed his lips together tightly.

He must be referencing when I hit my head on the pole. I must have fallen harder than I thought and hallucinated everything that's happened since then.

"So, I hit my head and was in the hospital this whole time?" I asked.

"Yes, darling, but it wasn't the pole that hurt you; it was that damn dog. Your father is in the process of pressing charges on that irresponsible woman."

Betty. So that's why she was so uncomfortable talking to me.

"Why don't you lay down for a bit, and I'll have Logan bring you your favorite dessert, the chocolate cake from that cafe you love so much."

"No, no, that's okay. I'm feeling too nauseous to eat." I waved his suggestion away as he guided me around the corner to another couch that looked just as uninviting as the last. Alister sat beside me and turned the channel to the news. At least, I think he did. He blinked with aggression at the TV, and it changed channels.

A man dressed in a suit was pointing, discussing the weather. *"In today's weather report, we expect no rain and a bright cloudless day. Here in Ether Angeles, the weather will never hold you back from living out your dreams."*

"Did he say Ether Angeles?" I asked Alister.

"Yes, sweetheart, this is where you live. You grew up here. Your memory is fuzzy right now; try not to strain yourself too much until it comes back." He stroked my hair.

I had a sudden urge to watch trash TV. Maybe Cecelia was rubbing off on me.

"Can you put on The Single Charade? I need a comfort show right now," I said as I rubbed my eyes.

"I've never heard of that show," he said, but he entered the name in the search bar for me.

The search results displayed an empty page.

My eyes felt heavy, and I allowed myself to drift off to sleep.

Alister waited beside me as I slept. I could feel his presence before I opened my eyes. He held a chocolate cake in his hand, and Logan stood at the doorway, shifting his weight back and forth. I felt lighter and comforted knowing Alister cared enough to stay with me. This was my life; I had hallucinated everything in the hospital, and all my worries faded away. Struck with a newfound energy and hunger, I grabbed the chocolate cake and inhaled it. The memory of this being my mom's favorite suddenly seemed made up.

This is my favorite dessert, and I am being comforted by my favorite person, the man of my dreams, and the real Alister.

"It's good to have you back, Alina. That sleep must have been exactly what you needed. Why don't you go get changed, and I'll drive you to Ether headquarters if you're feeling up to it. Your father would love to have you read the speech you prepared for the launch." Alister smiled.

I gulped the glass of milk next to me on the side table, ignoring my back, which ached from the stiff couch I'd been sprawled on. "Sounds great, thank you," I said as I stood up.

"I can drive her, Sir." Logan's voice cracked as he uttered the words.

Alister shot back a daggered glance. "No, that won't be necessary. Go gather her speech prompts, and we'll meet you at the launch in an hour," Alister said.

"Yes, Sir." Logan hurried out of the house and closed the door behind him.

I stepped into the most luxurious shower I could remember ever experiencing. Grey matte tiles formed a fishbowl-like serenity around me connected to the glass exterior. Instead of my view being tarnished by mildew-coated shower curtains, I enjoyed the peaceful fireplace that burned fake embers above a bathtub that hung from the ceiling.

My shower had four heads that rained like soft clouds onto every part of my body. Steam filled the glass as I washed away the dirt and grime from my aching body. I thought of Teddy.

Had I made him up? My life here is perfect; why would I dream of such pain when surrounded by people who love me here?

I turned off the water with the push of a button. A large white robe hung from the wall beside the shower entrance. Its warmth embraced me as I draped it over my clean skin. On the bed lay a beautiful red shimmering dress and a pair of black heels. The lights above created a spotlight on the gown, illuminating hundreds of jewels along the bodice.

"It's beautiful, isn't it?" Alister leaned against the doorway, grinning.

"Yes, it is," I said as his smile pierced my soul.

"When you're ready, meet me downstairs, and I'll take you to the event," he said and vanished from the doorway.

I cascaded down the staircase, holding onto the railing, careful not to trip in the high heels. Alister stood at the bottom, wearing yet another perfectly fitting black suit. He gleamed with pride as I strutted down the staircase. I felt like a princess as he extended his hand, and I placed mine in his. He guided me to the car, and I stepped inside. Alister followed me in and sat beside me as the automated vehicle drove us away.

He retrieved a stack of silver-plated flashcards and a small case the size of a quarter.

"Open your eyes as wide as you can," he said while opening the case. He produced two contact lenses and placed both in my eyes.

"Ouch! What are these for?" I fluttered my eyes repeatedly until the uncomfortable feeling dissipated.

Alister waved the flashcards in front of my face. "Keep these flashcards in your purse, make a flicking up motion with your pointer finger when you're ready to give your speech, and the lenses will show you the words," he said.

"Wow, that's a cool invention," I said and then placed the silver cards into my purse.

"Well, I should hope you find it cool; you invented it." He winked at me as he took a bottle of champagne and two thin flutes from a secret compartment in the door's side panel.

The car pulled up to the back entrance of Building A, where I saw Logan standing at attention. He opened the door on my side and extended his hand.

"Just in time. Your father is inside waiting for you," Logan said.

I placed my hand in his; it felt warm and a little clammy. My eyes met his, and he quickly looked away.

Alister exited the car behind me. "Mr. Nobleman." Logan nodded towards him, but Alister did not respond.

Alister placed his hand on the small of my back and guided me toward the open door to the back entrance.

"What's your issue with Logan? I mean, I know he's a kiss-ass, but you could be a little nicer," I said.

"You don't need to concern yourself with Logan, darling," Alister quipped.

Before I could ask more questions, I saw my father standing on a circular concrete slab, dressed in a tuxedo, and smiling from ear to ear.

"Alina, I'm so glad to have you here today to present the launch with me." He opened his arms for an embrace.

I obliged. I had imagined this moment for a long time. I had pictured how warm and fuzzy I'd feel when my dad finally came home from his work travels. He'd hug me and tell me how much he missed me. But I guessed I had imagined that life, too; he had never been away from work. He had always been right there, ready to embrace me. Still, I missed it just the same. I wrapped my arms around him and lay my head on his chest. It wasn't as warm as I had expected it to feel, but still, it felt like my dad's hug I remembered from a long time ago.

I let go of the embrace first, and he held my hands. He studied my features briefly before parting his lips to speak. Alister cleared his throat behind us, and my dad stiffened, seemingly losing whatever thought was forming.

"Are you ready?" my dad asked.

"Ready for what?" I questioned, looking around the room.

Alister flicked a switch beside the wall.

"Good luck, Alina; I'll be watching in the audience," Alister said.

The circular platform shot up into the air, not a slow-moving ascent like I've seen in movies. It made an angry growl as it sealed us onto another floor. Burgandy curtains stretched across a stage. People in headsets were walking frantically from one end to another as I heard the chatter from the other side of the curtain die down.

"You'll do great, Alina; you were made for this. Just read from the prompts in your headset, and I'll take over from there." He straightened out his suit while a woman I'd never met before fixed my hair and touched up my makeup.

He must have noticed that his little pep talk was not enough to calm my nerves because he frowned as he held my hand again. "Alina Ballerina…" He paused, seemingly lost in thought. He opened his mouth to continue, but just as he was about to say his next thought, the auditorium fell silent.

A man in the far-right corner of the stage counted down with his fingers from five, and the curtains opened, flickering out of existence just as they reached the end of the stage. I wondered if I also invented those.

My father gestured and moved us toward a spotlight, illuminating an otherwise dark space. As my eyes adjusted, I noticed Alister sitting in the front row; he winked at me and motioned to his eyes. I flicked my finger up as he instructed me to do in the car, and the flash card prompts lit up in front of me. I waved my hand in front of my face and felt the empty air.

My father nudged me and cleared his throat. "Welcome to the 2030 launch of Ether's latest and most profound project to date. You have all been carefully chosen and invited here, to this world, for one specific purpose: to invest in your future, in your past, and in your now. Invest in you. Invest in MultiU."

My father gestured to the invisible prompts, and I read them as they flowed through the air.

"As you know, my father and I have had many scientific breakthroughs. Many of which you all enjoy today, but we strove for more. We strove for perfection. What would a world look like where you could be the perfect version of yourself? Imagine you could bend reality to your own desires. What if you could live in a perfect town, a perfect city, unbothered by

141

the hardships of life and unburdened by people who are less than you? You have all accomplished profound things in your life, and that is why my father and I have brought you here. We invite you, the elite, to invest in yourselves by paying a fee of one billion dollars, to live in this universe, or one of your choosing, and live the life you deserve." The prompt ended, and my father ripped the sheet beside him to show the familiar machine and mirror.

The machine that brought me to this world. The machine that I didn't dream up. This is real; I've been sent to this world, this evil, wrong world, and I helped my father make this happen. Where is my mother? What did he do to my mother? Where is Teddy? What did I do to them?

Sweat soaked my jeweled dress, and I felt lightheaded. I eyed the machine, calculating my risks, and no doubt, it was calculating me back.

I have to act quickly and get out of here. This may be my only chance. Taking two steps backward, I charged at MultiU, ready to leave that universe for good. Bracing for impact, I closed my eyes. To my surprise and horror, I found myself stumbling forward towards the exit wing and crashing onto my knees. The gasps and chatter from the audience were blurred in the back of my mind while I assessed what I had done.

I'm still in this universe, on this stage. It's not real. I went through a hologram of the machine.

I steadied my breath as I peered up at Logan, who was hovering over me. He held his hand out to assist me off the floor, and I took his offering.

"Alina, get back out there, please," Logan said as he gently nudged me. There was desperation in his eyes, and I guess I felt bad for him for how Alister treated him, so I chose not to push past. The audience fell silent, the only noise were the footsteps of Alister rushing to the center of the stage to join my father.

"I can't do this, Logan; I'm going to pass out," I said as I tried to focus on his face.

"Alina, you can do this. I'm right here, okay? Take a deep breath and go back out there before your father's face turns into a tomato, and before Alister…just go." He handed me a bottle of water with Ether's logo.

I drank the whole thing and stumbled back to the stage, joining my father and Alister. I looked to Alister for reassurance, but he faced forward, clenching his jaw into a tight smile. My father glanced at me, before clearing his throat and speaking to the audience.

"Please excuse Alina; she has recently suffered a terrible accident. As you can see, this is indeed not the real MultiU. Our creation is in a protected environment, specifically designed to contain its powerful energy source." He looked embarrassed as he spoke to the crowd. But as he turned his head towards me, his eyes drooped, appearing sad or disappointed; I couldn't tell.

My father then nodded at Alister, urging him to continue. Alister flicked up his invisible prompts and proceeded with John's speech.

"I present to you MultiU, the AI machine that will transform not just the world but every world. This system is more than AI; it can create, in real-time, anything your mind can think of. It is the connection to every universe that exists. There are infinite universes that lie on top of each other, each with a different version of you and your life. Every decision you make creates new universes where the different possible outcomes occur. We're offering you the opportunity to alter those lives as you see fit.

I have selected this universe, which I call Universe B, to hold only the best outcomes. But alas, there must be balance. Energy is neither created nor destroyed. So, if the best outcome for you is here, the worst outcome for another version of you is in another universe.

You, the people in this room, will never have to know that pain. This machine allows this version of you to never experience those outcomes. It is designed to create the perfect you." He stood upright and appeared proud as he inhaled a deep breath.

Chatter ensued across the auditorium.

"We don't believe you!" a man I could not see shouted from the crowd. I shifted my weight, wiping the sweat from my brows and neck.

My father smiled and began speaking. "Ah, you want proof that it works? My daughter, Alina, and I are the first people in history to transcend the old universe and enter a new one. You see, there are infinite versions of you existing in infinite realities. You are only capable of perceiving one version of yourself and living in one reality. And that is where MultiU comes into play. MultiU allows you to choose your reality. When you enter through the mirror, the transformation happens instantaneously. MultiU has three functions: you can enter a new reality where your old self and the people around you would never know unless you told them; you can erase your previous existence altogether in your original universe; or let MultiU decide for you. It is the smartest AI known to man; its capabilities know no bounds." John glanced at the still-displeased faces of the audience.

"If you still don't believe me, ask yourself how you got here. Do you recognize the person to your left? To your right? Do you remember entering this building? You were all given an invitation in your original universe to view the prototype. You signed a waiver in your universe, consenting to the use of our mind control device to wipe your memory for the purpose of this showing. If you flick your EyeBrowse, you will see the waiver consenting to use MultiU to transcend to Universe B. You were brought here by your free will to leave the old you behind. Your old selves are back in your original universe, believing to have never crossed the mirror. But your new selves are here, in this universe, in this auditorium right now. You all chose option one for the showing, but if you sign with us today, you will have the freedom to choose not just your own destiny, but to choose infinite destinies for yourself and loved ones. What we are offering you here today is to invest your money in yourself. Be a better you and cross the threshold of time and space as we know it. Be a MultiU!" John waved his arms proudly.

The audience erupted in cheer.

My stomach felt like it was going to erupt in vomit.

I noticed one man who was not cheering. He was not standing with the crowd. He was in the back of the room, arms folded, and face contorted. I recognized his round face and plump belly. Bob was here.

"Who is that?" I yelled to my dad over the roar of the auditorium.

"It's no one. He was not invited." He frowned, glancing to Alister, then pressed his radio button, and whispered something into it.

Two guards rushed in from the doors beside Bob and escorted him out. He yelled loudly as they dragged him away. The audience didn't seem to notice as they were too busy clapping and cheering, but I noticed. Bob looked terrified as he fought against the guards.

"Alina! She's out there. Find her!" he screamed.

My head was spinning. *Was he talking about my mom? I needed to get out of that room, away from those people. They are not my family. How could I have helped create this machine? This evil machine. I wasn't hallucinating anything. I need to get out now and get to the real MultiU.* I ran down the steps from the stage that led to the audience's floor. I sprinted to the exit where I had watched the guards take Bob, and I stumbled out onto the cold pavement.

Bob was being dragged to Building C.

"Bob! I'm going to help you!" I yelled out to him.

"Alina! No, it's too late for me. They erased our memory, but I got it back. Your mom is—" A guard punched him in the face, and he fell silent. The plumper of the two guards opened the door and dragged him inside. I started toward him, but two hands pulled me back by my arm.

It was Logan. "Alina, please, for your sake and mine, stop."

There was fear in his eyes.

"Logan, tell me this isn't true. Tell me that my father isn't behind this. Tell me that he didn't ruin my life so he could have a perfect version of me in this world?" I said.

"I wish I could, Alina. But what do you mean, ruin your life? Your life is perfect. What do you have to complain about? This is what you wanted."

Logan still thinks I'm the other Alina. The Alina who belongs here must still be in the hospital in this universe. She must be the Alina I saw in my visions. No one knows who I am here except, seemingly, Bob, and he's been taken. No one is coming to help.

"Logan, I need to get out of here. I think I can do this if you help me," I said as he sat me down on the sidewalk. Logan looked around nervously.

"Just stop talking. Alister will be out here shortly," he said.

"Why does Alister treat you like he hates you? Why are you scared of him?" I asked.

Logan looked away, staring into the distance. I studied his face. He was handsome. The kind of handsome that is unassuming and strikes you at unexpected moments.

"You know, I used to think you were a suck-up to the bosses. But I see now why you were always so hard on me as my boss. It starts from the top down," I said.

Logan raised an eyebrow. "Alina, I have never been your boss. Not in this universe, anyway. Maybe it was too soon for you to come out of the hospital."

My shoulders sank. I had hoped I'd found an ally, someone who understood and could help me escape, but Logan was trapped here, too; he just didn't know it.

Rage bubbled up in my blood. How could my father do this to me and innocent people? How could I have done this to them? Well, another version of me. How could any version of me agree to let other versions of myself suffer?

Logan looked at me, or rather, through me.

"Did you know this area used to be a children's park? Kids would play on swing sets, couples would walk hand-in-hand down a long pebble pathway, and families would have picnics. Now look at it; they pave paradise…" he trailed off.

"To put up a parking lot." I finished his sentence.

"What?" he asked.

"You know…like the song?" I asked, raising my brows.

"No, never heard any song like that," he said.

We sat in silence, watching our breath leave our mouths. His hand bumped against mine, and I found myself slowly inching my hand onto his until they were interlocked. I don't know why I was drawn to him in that moment. It was as if an energy pulled my body to his. I thought of Alister; *I thought I loved him. I do love him. I never got the chance to tell him that before he got left behind in my original universe. But the Alister here isn't my Alister. I may never see my Alister again.* Logan's hand felt soft; it sent shivers through my body. I can't believe I'm saying this, but Logan felt like home. Even if he wasn't the Logan I remember, he wasn't trying to take over the entirety of life. He was the only one there with me on that curb. No one else came out to check on me.

I gazed into his brown eyes; I didn't remember them being as beautiful in my universe. He stroked my hair and pulled me in. I didn't know why I was allowing it, but it felt like I had done this before. Our lips nearly touched, but the spell was broken by the sound of a gunshot ricocheting from the walls of Building C. *Was that gunshot aimed at Bob?* I pulled away from Logan's embrace and grabbed my chest while I mourned for my dear friend, Bob. I should have been there helping him. *Maybe there's still time.*

"I'm sorry; I have to go help him," I said as I stood up and moved toward Building C.

"They'll punish you if you try to leave. Please be safe. I'll do my best to cover you," Logan said as he walked back into Building A.

Logan was scared, but he wasn't a coward. I admired his bravery then; even if he didn't understand why I was running, he allowed me to.

I scanned my finger at the entrance, and the doors opened. Before I had a chance to walk down the hallway, a hand wrapped around my mouth, and another hand yanked me inside the abandoned break room to my left.

"Do not make a sound. Follow me, and you won't get hurt," Cecelia whispered as she released her hand from my mouth. My eyes widened.

Is she kidnapping me or saving me? I don't know, but I have no choice right now but to listen to her.

She led me to the unmarked room, where MultiU awaited us. The lights stayed off to help us go unnoticed.

She switched the power on the spherical metal machine and walked up to the mirror, her silhouette barely visible. Seconds later, lights shot out from every orifice of the sphere. Now that I could see more clearly, I noticed her clothes; she was no longer wearing one of her pink over-the-top outfits. She sported black jeans and a loose T-shirt with a big yellow taxi on the front. She wore black eyeliner but less heavy makeup on her skin. Her hair was still perfectly curled.

She raised her finger to her lips and said, "Shhh."

Her smile was unnerving. Chills flowed through my body, and I had the urge to run, but my feet stayed put.

She extended her hand. *Does the Grunge Barbie Exorcist expect me to follow her?* I weighed my options. *She may be my only chance out of here. Even if I did run, who would help me? Where would I go? Ether controls this world and has technology that can track me down instantly. If I have any chance of making it out of here and finding Teddy, I have to try trusting her.*

I inched towards Cecelia, took a deep breath in, and grabbed her hand. Cecelia's smile widened.

She leaned her lips into my ear and whispered, "Run."

Cecelia tapped her hand to the mirror, and an explosion of glass fell behind us, while darkness flooded ahead.

CHAPTER TWELVE

UNIVERSE X- ALINA-PRESENT

I found myself amidst a lush green field enveloped by towering trees adorned with ripe red apples dropping to the earth. I looked up and allowed the sun to warm my face. A light breeze brushed my skin as birds sang from their nest beside me. I looked straight ahead to see a glowing-white cottage situated over the surrounding greenery; a white swing hung from the porch. I recognized this place. *This is the place I saw in the city after I fell. This is the place I've been dreaming about.* I was about to walk towards the cottage when a shadowy figure appeared in the doorway.

A thin woman looking to be in her fifties with curly, honey-brown hair ran down the porch steps and through the grass.

"Alina Ballerina!" She wrapped her arms around me tightly.

"Mom?" I wrapped my arms around her as my eyes welled up with tears.

"Oh baby, I've missed you so much. I'm so sorry I left you alone." She hugged me tighter.

My mind flooded with five years' worth of questions.

"Where did you go? Where are we?" I asked.

She pulled away from the embrace and then grabbed my hands. "Come inside with me; let me make you some coffee, and I'll explain everything."

Mom held my hand as if letting go might mean she'd lose me again.

She guided me into the house, where I found Cecelia sitting cross-legged on the couch.

"It's so good to have you back, Alina," Cecelia said as she stood up to approach me. I stuck my hands out in front of my chest.

"Stay back, you bimbo devil," I yelled.

I turned to my mom and blocked her from Cecelia's view. "Mom, don't trust her; she's why this is all happening! She's working with Ether!" I pleaded.

Sandra took a sidestep to view Cecelia. They shared a glance and burst out laughing. I felt rage boiling inside me, bubbling up to my throat.

"What's so funny?" I snapped.

"Sorry, Alina, it's not funny; it's just that, honey…I am the Ether you're referring to. Cecelia is your best friend, and she's the one who helped bring you back to me." She handed me a cup of coffee in a blue mug and gestured for me to sit down.

I felt like I should cry, or laugh, or ask more questions. But my mind wouldn't allow me to feel anything right then.

I took a sip of the coffee and silently gagged. Caffeine City coffee would be a treat compared to this dirt-like substance.

"Mom, did you know that Dad is in another universe? He's created a device that can control everyone and everything. And I'm apparently helping him. Well, not me, but another me is," I said to Mom as she sat beside me.

"Yes, I know, honey," Mom said.

I looked to Cecelia, who was nodding in agreement.

"And Alister, oh my god, I left him behind in our universe. Another version of him is on Dad's side, and then there's Teddy. You never got to meet Teddy, but he's missing, and then there's a note—" Mom cut me off.

"Breathe, honey. Just take a deep breath. I know what's been going on, and so does Cecelia. I know about MultiU because I created it. It was my biggest mistake in this world and in every world. I know where Alister and Teddy are."

"Wait, what do you mean you created it? Where is Teddy? Where is Alister? Tell me what's going on right now!" I demanded. My emotions finally returned. My coffee spilled onto my pants as my hands shook.

She brushed a stray hair from my face and placed her hand on my shoulder.

Cecelia cleared her throat. "Sandra, it's too much for her; let me just try to explain it."

Cecelia stood up from her seat. "You are the original Alina, but every action has a consequence, and the universe requires balance. You are here and also there. A different you, with different outcomes in life, but it is still you. It is still your soul. This happens for everything and every person. John— your father, stole the blueprint your mother created many years ago. She never wanted it to come to fruition. Your father is using MultiU as a means of control and to rig the outcome of life in specific universes, while discarding the other versions of each person, leaving them to live the worst outcomes. At the same time, John's family, you and Alister, joined the elite in a single perfect world where everything is controlled by them. They call that world Universe B."

Cecelia placed her hands on her hips, appearing proud of herself for explaining it as if that was meant to make me feel better. As if any of it made sense.

I rolled my eyes at Cecelia. "Mom, if that's true, then why are you here? Why did Dad not create a perfect version of you?

Why was there not even a version of you anywhere when I looked for you? And where is Teddy? I searched for him in the other universe, and he didn't exist. I need to get back to Alister in my universe. He's probably worried sick, or worse, maybe my father got to him."

Cecelia jumped in. "Alina...Teddy and Alister are here and—"

"They're here?" I jumped up from my seat.

"Cecelia, it's too soon." Mom shot her a look of warning.

The bedroom door opened.

"Alister!" I said and jumped up to greet him, but a little boy, whose voice I recognized, ran to me yelling, "Mama's here!" The boy from one of my dreams, the boy I thought was running to my mom, jumped into my arms. I turned to my mom for clarity.

"I don't understand what's happening," I said.

"Darling, I'm so happy to have you back. You've been through a lot, and I've missed you more than you could imagine. I know this is a lot for you to take in, and none of it makes sense yet, so let me start from the beginning," Mom took a deep breath in, and then exhaled.

CHAPTER THIRTEEN

UNIVERSE A-SANDRA-PAST

Sandra opened the door to Alina's room, walked in, and kissed her forehead.

"Mom, ugh, ten more minutes," Alina grumbled.

"Okay, honey, I'll be downstairs making breakfast." Sandra walked down the staircase, opened a bag of cereal, and poured it into Alina's favorite bowl. She set the milk to the side as John entered the kitchen.

"Good morning, dear," John said but didn't look up from his phone.

"Good morning. Don't forget we have the meetings with the physicists today at 3." Sandra kissed John.

"Yes, of course. Are you ready to show off your coding skills?" John said—Sandra's brows furrowed.

"John, we didn't create Ether together to show off my coding skills. We created it to provide groundbreaking research in alternate realities. We can change the world for the better," she said.

Sandra was a passionate woman. John liked to get a reaction out of her.

"Yes, dear, I know, I'm teasing you." John adjusted his glasses and grabbed his keys. "I'll see you in an hour in our office," he yelled to the kitchen as he closed the door behind him.

Sandra spotted his work bag left on the counter.

"Ah, John, lucky I'm here, or you'd lose your head," Sandra said to an empty kitchen.

She had planned to take it to John after she saw Alina off to school, but she spotted pieces of paper sticking out of the bag she recognized; heat rose to her cheeks. Her heart thumped as her eyes scanned the blueprints for the invention Sandra had been working on for the last ten years. MultiU. It was Sandra's most significant work yet. An AI machine that could transport you to other existing dimensions. Her coding skills hacked the computer system of life. It would change society as we know it. But when Sandra discovered that her creation was far more capable than she had ever imagined, she hid her work away somewhere no one would think to look.

The meeting with the physicists was for another project Sandra and John had created. They were using AI to alter reality in real time. They had discovered how to recreate particles and make anything out of thin air using the energy surrounding us. Augmented reality becomes, simply, reality.

Sandra envisioned this discovery to help people in need of transplants or to help starving people have food to feed their families. This discovery would revolutionize the world, making it a better place for her daughter, which was what Sandra spent her life doing; everything was for Alina.

Sandra spotted another paper tucked under her blueprint that she didn't recognize. John's notes. They read:

The creation of MultiU has proven a success. Trials on my family are set to begin shortly. If proven to work consistently, I plan to contact a list of the top 5000 elite to join me in our new world. Sandra believes this to be her biggest failure. I believe this to be true, too. I will take over what my wife was too cowardly to see to completion. The world will not only know my name, but they will breathe my name, eat my name, sleep my name, and be my name. The world will be ETHER.

Alina appeared at the top of the stairs. Her hair was in a messy bun, and whisps surrounded her face. She zipped up her grey jacket as she descended the stairs. Sandra took quick photos of the papers and shoved them back in John's bag. She clenched the kitchen island to hide her shaking.

"Good morning, honey; I've got your cereal ready for you. I'll be back this evening. Be good. I love you." Sandra hugged Alina, grabbed her car keys, along with John's work bag, and walked towards the front door.

"Thanks, Mom, I love you too," Alina smiled through a mouthful of cornflakes.

Sandra slammed the car door and threw John's bag in the passenger seat. She sped out of the driveway, knocking over Mr. and Mrs. Jacob's trash can.

She muttered, "That good for nothing, lying sack." She slammed her fist on the wheel.

When she arrived at the newly constructed Building A, she parked at the curb next to a no-parking zone sign and stormed up to the top floor, where she found John sitting in his office.

He was speaking to the intern, "…and have those files ready by noon."

The intern nodded and slipped past Sandra.

Sandra was sweating from head to toe and breathing like a snarling beast. "How dare you!" She slammed the bag on his desk. John sat still and did not flinch.

"You know." He let out a sigh.

"Yes, I know. I know you stole my work. I know you are planning something heinous for our family," Sandra seethed.

"Not just for our family; for the world. The world will be better this way. My way," he said.

"And our daughter? How could you do this to her? She deserves a good life in every universe," Sandra said.

"This universe will not matter soon enough." John looked bored as he examined his fingernails.

"John, this isn't you. You're a sweet man. You'd never betray your family like this. What's going on?" Sandra said.

"You don't know what I'm capable of, Sandra. Do you have any idea what it's like to be married to a genius? You take all the credit, and I'm here on the sidelines. Well, no more. I'm here to finish what you started. I will not be humiliated any further!" John slammed his fists down on the table like a child throwing a tantrum.

Sandra's face stiffened, and she straightened her posture. "Where is it? Where's the machine?" she asked.

"Building C. But you can't get in there. I've locked you out of the system."

"When did you have time to do that? I've only been here for two minutes," Sandra asked.

"MultiU is the smartest technology in the world, Sandra. Or rather, in the universes. Think about it." He smirked.

Sandra's face paled. "You've been tracking me. You already knew that I knew." She sat on the black leather couch at the other end of the office.

"Oh, Sandra, I wanted you to know. I left the bag there on purpose. I'm sick and tired of you getting all the credit. We started Ether together, yet here you are, the big shot of the company. Well, not anymore. I built this. I will build the new world, with or without you." John's eyes looked hungry.

"I won't let you do this to Alina. I won't let you do this to the world." Sandra stood up from the couch and rushed to her office. She could fix this. She could delete the code blocking her from Building C, and she would destroy that machine.

She typed her password into the system and searched for the file *Ether Building C controls*. A red pop-up blared on the screen.

ACCESS DENIED.

"No!" Sandra pounded the keyboard.

John appeared in the doorway, his arms folded into each other as he smugly leaned against the doorframe. "Obviously, I blocked your access at Ether."

"I will burn this place to the ground, John. Let me into the system," she demanded.

John sauntered to Sandra's desk. He leaned in behind her, squeezing her shoulders.

"Let me make things very clear, Sandra. You will be the smiling face of Ether, but I will be making all the decisions from now on. And if you try to stop me, you will regret it," he said.

Sandra swatted his hands away and stood up from her desk. She stood so close to him she could smell the coffee on his breath. "I will stop at nothing to protect Alina."

She exited the office, called the elevator, and waited for it to open.

"You've been warned," John called out.

Sandra arrived back home and picked up her cell phone. She scrolled to the name *Bob* and pressed dial.

"Bob? Something's happened. I need you to get over here quickly."

Bob lived in the neighborhood over; he arrived within minutes.

"Bob, thank god you're here!" She hugged him.

"Of course, Sandra, what are brothers for?" He hugged her back. "Now tell me what's wrong?"

Sandra showed screenshots of the notes and blueprints from John's bag and said, "We must get Alina and get out of here. We need to take her to a safe space while I work on trying to gain access to Ether again."

"Of course, I'll help you, Sandra. I'd do anything for you both."

Alina arrived home from school to find Bob and Sandra gathered around the couch.

She darted her eyes between the two of them. "Hi Uncle Bob, I didn't know you'd be here today."

Sandra looked at Alina with sad, red eyes. "Honey, sit down. We need to talk."

"Okay, it was me who stuffed the clean laundry back in the dirty basket. I've just been so tired from school, and there's this guy in class who reeks of strong body spray, and it gives me a headache. So, I didn't want to do the laundry to—" Sandra cut her off.

"No, honey, you aren't in trouble," Sandra said as she stroked Alina's hair. "It's your father. He's planning something terrible. We need to leave. Now. I'll explain later," she said.

"What? Dad? He wouldn't hurt a fly. He literally wouldn't let me kill a fly that got in the house yesterday." Alina said.

"I know, but he's not acting like the man we knew. Trust me, Alina, I'll fix this and make it right," Sandra said, and Bob nodded in agreement.

Alina looked around the room and noticed six suitcases at the front door. She hadn't seen them when she walked in.

"Mom, just tell me now. What's happening?" she asked.

"There's no time, honey. You'll go with Uncle Bob, and I'll be right behind you. We're going to Bob's vacation home in Monterey, where you'll be safe," Sandra reassured.

Alina had tears in her eyes and was shaking. Bob grabbed the bags, and Sandra helped load everything into the car. Alina followed them outside.

"Mom, I'm scared." Alina's lip quivered.

Sandra wrapped her arms around Alina and whispered to her, "Everything is going to be okay, baby. I love you, my Alina Ballerina. Do you remember when I taught you how to ride a bike? You were so scared, but I was right there with you. Do you remember what I told you? Be strong. Be brave, and do not let go."

"I remember. I love you, Mom," Alina said, tears now flowing down her face as she got into the back seat of Bob's car.

"I'll see you soon, baby." Sandra closed the door on the passenger side.

She walked over to Bob, who was starting the ignition. "Bob, if anything happens to me, please watch over her. Keep her safe. Promise me."

Bob placed his hand on Sandra's wrist. "I promise. We'll see you soon." He backed out of the driveway and sped out of the court.

Sandra waited until she could no longer see the car and then ran inside. She was packing up the last of her belongings when she heard the keys jingle in the doorway. She froze when John swung the front door open and stepped inside.

"Did you really think I wouldn't find out your plan? I told you, MultiU knows everything. It sees what I want it to see, and it knows what I want it to know." He inched closer to Sandra.

Sandra took three steps backward and was cornered against the kitchen counter. She felt for a knife behind her and tucked it into her jacket sleeve.

"You had a chance to rule alongside Alina and me, not as this pitiful version of my family, the perfect version. You had a choice, Sandra." His eyes looked crazed, like a wild beast ready to pounce on its prey.

"And now I'm choosing for you." John lunged at her and tackled her to the floor.

She thrashed and kicked but to no avail. He dragged her by her ankles to the front door. She kicked him in the groin, and he recoiled, hunched over like the small man that he was.

She swung open the door and ran out to the side yard. There was no point running out onto the street; he'd catch her too quickly. She hid behind an apple tree next to their fence; she traced the initials that she and Alina had sketched into long ago.

"Where are you? You couldn't have gone far," John taunted as he stepped outside.

Sandra slipped the knife from her sleeve and etched into the fence:

Alina, Mom is here.

Sandra felt a hand on her hair as John dragged her from the tree. An unmarked white van pulled up to the driveway, and he dragged her down to the back of the truck. Sandra clenched her knife and slashed wildly in every direction.

"Ahhh!" John screamed but didn't let go. "You fucking bitch!" Blood poured from his cheek as he pushed Sandra into the van, locking the door behind her.

The plump guard switched to the passenger seat, and John entered the front. Sandra kicked against the door and tried to open the handle, but it was useless. The doors were sealed from the inside like a prison cell.

She heard a man approach the van.

Sandra screamed, "Help!" but he couldn't hear her.

John rolled down the window, and Mr. Jacob said, "Everything alright here? What are you doing with your wife?" He retrieved his phone from his pocket and began dialing 9-1-1.

"Daniel, if you know what's best for you and your daughter, you'll put your phone away and go inside right now. The police won't be able to help you," John said.

Mr. Jacob turned to look at his daughter, peeking through the window from inside the house. "I…I didn't see anything." He turned towards his house and retreated inside.

Sandra felt the jolt of the van speed off. "No! Help me! Come back. Help!" But it was no use.

She thought about her daughter during the drive as she kicked the van to no avail. She knew she had to help Alina, but how?

The van came to an abrupt stop beside Building C. The guard opened the door and dragged her to the entrance, where John stood, holding the door open. She spotted a teenage boy across the road, watching everything unfold.

"Help!" she screamed to the boy. "Go get help!" she yelled again.

The boy crossed the road and walked through the freshly laid grass. As the boy got closer, she recognized him.

"Alister, thank god. Get help, and get out of here," Sandra said.

Alister took off running.

"It will be too late by the time he gets help," John said.

The guard pulled her inside, and the metal door shut behind them.

"I can walk myself!" She swatted the guard's hands away as they led her to the unmarked room at the end of the hallway.

They entered the room where she saw *her creation* come to life.

"You bastard. This was my project. This was my design. And it was my biggest mistake. It shouldn't have been built," she said.

"I should really thank you, Sandra. Your kind heart has allowed this to come to fruition. What will you get for your effort? Infinite lifetimes of solitude. I hope you spend it wisely." He switched on the machine, and it whirred and beeped in excitement. Lights shot out from the holes covering it, and the computer system lit up with green code.

"The coding in your notes is genius. How you thought to make this track each universe in real-time is beyond me. All I had to do was build it." He ran his hand down the machine.

"What will you do with Alina? Please don't hurt her. She's my baby," Sandra pleaded.

"She's my baby too," he glared. "I would never hurt her. She will stand by me and rule the universes. And thanks to our other project, I will erase her memory of you and me in this universe, and the algorithm will give her everything she wants in the next universe. Power, fame, money, she will have it all. She will never know her original self will suffer a lifetime of unhappiness so she can have it all. This version of her does not matter. We will reign supreme in the next universe," he said.

John dragged Sandra to the illuminated mirror. He grabbed her head and forced her to stare at her reflection.

"She won't come looking for you. She won't know you; she won't know me. Not this version of me, anyway. Her poor mom left one day to go to work and never returned; abandoned her. Her father works far away at an oil rig to support her. She'll live out her days alone until she dies, just like you will. Only you will remember the pain. You will remember who created this suffering for her," he smiled.

"You underestimate her, John. She's a fighter, and she will find out the truth about you. I'll make sure of it." She stared at John's unblinking eyes.

"Sure, she will." John grabbed Sandra's shoulders by each side and, with all his strength, pushed her into the mirror.

The mirror shattered, and lights popped as sparks flew around the room.

CHAPTER FOURTEEN

UNIVERSE A-JOHN-PAST

John smirked as Sandra disappeared through the mirror, unphased by the shards of glass that spilled onto his face and scattered around his feet.

"You're another universe's problem now," he said to the mirror as it regenerated its glass like a chameleon that had lost its leg.

He walked over to the metal sphere; its lights faded as it recovered from swallowing Sandra. He observed the computer attached to the top of the sphere.

It read: *Successful transition to Universe X. Sandra lies on the grass; her eyes are shut.*

John typed in code.

"Hope you enjoy this gift," he said as he pressed enter.

He exited out of Sandra's new world and searched through the database. He found Sandra's file and entered the instructions.

Notify any person's access to Alina in Universe A, B, and C.

"Just in case you escape, my dear wife, I won't let you communicate with her without me knowing about it." Blood dripped from his cheek, falling onto his front teeth.

He wiped his face as he clicked the search bar, leaving the keyboard stained with blood and tiny shards of glass. *Find Alina, Universe A.*

The computer pulled up a blue map, pinpointing her location and marking it with a red arrow. She was in Monterey, located at 38945 Lygon Street. He pressed the button marked *Details*, and the computer screen produced line after line of real-time actions of Alina and Bob.

Alina and Bob enter Bob's vacation home.

Alina unpacks bags in the far left bedroom on the *upper floor.*

Bob reaches for his phone and calls Sandra.

Sandra's phone lit up in the corner of the room.

"Oh, Bob, you idiot. You're going to love what I have in store for you," John said to the phone, which, by now, had stopped ringing.

He made his way back to the van, where his guard was waiting for him.

"They're in Monterey on Lygon Street. Get them. And call the janitor to clean up that room," John said.

"Sure thing, Mr. Ether." The guard radioed through on his earpiece to the janitor and sped out of the parking lot.

John wasted no time and went back to the computer. He typed in more instructions for Alina and Bob's fates.

The janitor walked in with a broom and a mop and began picking up the shattered remnants of Sandra's memory. John sniffed in disgust.

"What is that foul-smelling cologne you're wearing?" John turned around to see a mottled brown- and grey-haired young man, who couldn't be older than eighteen, in an ill-fitted grey uniform. The young man's eyes stayed steady on the tiles as he swept the floor.

"My god, son, has no one told you that you reek?" John stared at Logan, who was placing the glass into a trash can.

"Sorry, Sir. I'm around trash all day," Logan said meekly.

"Trash would be a better smell," John covered his nose.

John observed the boy as he began mopping. "Make sure you scrub the floor over here." He pointed to where his blood had trailed through the room.

"Yes, Sir," Logan said.

He's obedient, John thought.

John's face lit up as if he had discovered the meaning of life. "Hey, how would you like a change in jobs?" John asked.

"I would like that very much, Sir." Logan was pushing the mop now with vigor and grinning a dopey grin from ear to ear.

"You'll be a manager in Building D. Just make sure you do everything I ask of you, and you'll be just fine. You start tomorrow." John stood up and extended his hand.

"Thank you so much, Mr. Ether! I won't let you down." Logan extended his hand, too, but John retracted his.

"You missed a spot." John's hand pointed down to the blood on his shoes that had been dripping from his face.

He turned back to the computer and pulled up Logan's file.

He entered: *Wipe Logan's memory in Universe A. He will report to me on Alina's behavior. The time of wipe will be at 0600.*

John's phone vibrated in his pocket.

"Yes?" he answered, annoyed. "Good. Bring them in."

"Get out of here, and we'll see you at work bright and early tomorrow morning," John said to Logan.

Logan hurried out of the room. Moments later, muffled screaming echoed from the hallway. The door opened, and the guard pushed a tied-up and gagged Alina and Bob inside. The guard exited and shut the door. He waited on the other side like a dutiful guard dog.

More muffled screaming.

"Oh, calm down, guys!" John said as he removed the gags from their mouths and tossed them to the side.

"I'm not going to kill you. Alina, you're my daughter. Do you really think that little of me?"

"I do now, you psychotic asshole!" Alina spat. "Where is my mom? What did you do with her?" Tears welled up from deep inside her.

"She's safe, Alina. She made a choice, and I put her where she can't cause more damage." John seemed to believe what he was saying was not unhinged.

"You asshole!" Alina fought against the rope tied between her hands and ankles.

"Yes, you said that already. Soon, you will see that I am doing this all for you. I am building a world where you will not suffer; you will live a perfect life. Well, not this you, of course, but the person you were destined to be will gain life due to me. You really should be thanking me," John said.

Bob sat hunched over in the corner. "What are you going to do, John?" he asked, raising his head to meet John's gaze.

"Well, I'm so glad you asked. Alina is going to get her mind wiped of recent events. She will think her mother went to work one day and just never returned. Her last memory of her will be one of my choosing. She will have fond memories of me, her supporting father who works so hard and lives far away at an oil rig. I'll alter her memory of my appearance so she has no idea who she works for. Oh, yes, and she'll be working for me in Building D." He looked to Alina. "What's that cute name you gave to the people who work in Building D, Alina? Dead-Weights? Yes, you'll be a Dead-Weight while I create the perfect version of you in Universe B." John looked around for an applause that was never coming.

"Universe B?" Alina asked, her face recoiling.

"Oh, your mother never told you? She created the blueprint for controlling another universe, well, not just one, but all universes. She didn't have the courage to make it come to fruition, but I did." He made a grand gesture with his arms to show off MultiU.

"How will you make her forget her mother and you? No one has mind control capabilities." Bob rolled his eyes.

"No one *had* mind control capabilities until now. I have connections in high places. Do you ever really know who your neighbors are? Your friends? Your family? You never know what someone is capable of until it's too late. That's some solid life advice for you, my daughter," he said.

Alina scowled. "You're the last person I would take life advice from. Tell me where my mom is!"

"Okay, no need to give me that attitude. Here is your mom." He brought up Universe X on the screen. "See, she's alive and well. She's resting in a replica of her parent's home." He stroked the computer screen.

"Send me there right now. I want to be with Mom!" Alina rushed to the computer. John grabbed her hands and pushed her to the floor.

"Stay there. I'm not finished showing you my creation. You really should be taking more interest, seeing as the better version of you will be part owner with me," he said.

"Now, where was I? Ah, yes. MultiU can control everything in every universe; watch." He excitedly entered code into the system, and an apple appeared in the middle of the room.

"Once you have mastered transporting matter from one universe to another, anything is possible." John walked to the apple and handed to it Alina. "Try it; it's real," he said.

"I'm not hungry." Alina turned her face away.

John scrunched his face, offended. "Suit yourself." He tossed the apple through the mirror, and it vanished.

"Enough games, John. What will you do to Alina and me?" Bob asked.

John walked over to Bob. "Well, I could kill you, and I still might. For now, you'll live out your life as a homeless man, forever walking the streets begging for pennies. You'll have no memory of how you got there or who you are. Alina will be safe under my watchful eye."

"That's not possible." Bob was alert.

Alina wailed beside Bob while she laid her head on his chest.

"It's very possible. Do I need to demonstrate more?" John asked.

They stayed silent.

"When will this happen?" Alina asked.

John looked at his watch: *8:57 PM.*

"You have three minutes. Say your goodbyes and get out." John retrieved the knife from the floor that Sandra had left behind and cut off their ropes. He held Alina's hand for just a beat too long and looked into her eyes.

"Bye, my Alina. I'll see you in another life," John said.

Alina took a brief last look at her dad and then grabbed Bob's hand as they hurried out of the building.

They ran to the most populated part of town and stopped next to *The Drinkery*, a dirty dive bar filled with patrons. Teenagers entered the building, passing as adults, and adults exited, passing as functioning adults.

Alina checked her watch, 8:59 PM, and hugged Bob. "I'm so scared. We need to find my mom. What do we do?"

Bob hugged Alina tightly and told her, "I don't know, but I promised your mom I would look after you. I intend to keep that promise. I won't leave you. We'll find her," he reassured her as they released their embrace.

She took a deep breath, and when she exhaled, she saw a man looking at her with tears in his eyes.

"Hey, Sir, are you okay?" she asked the man standing in front of her.

"Never better, sweetheart. Got any change?" Bob said.

Alina reached into her pocket but came up empty. "Sorry, I must have left my purse at home. I'll spot you next time."

Bob strolled away, muttering to himself. Alina took out her phone and scrolled down to recent calls. She clicked on the name *Dad*.

"Hi, honey, how's it going?" John said.

"Hey, Dad, I'm in the middle of the city and left my purse. Can you transfer me some money so I can get a ride home?"

"Of course, my dear," John said.

"When are you coming back from your work trip?" Alina asked.

"Oh, I think it will be a while," John replied.

Alina frowned.

"It's just that I miss you; I can't remember the last time I saw you," she said.

"I know; I'll be home before you know it," he lied.

"Dad? Do you think Mom will ever come home?" Alina asked as she picked at her wrists, which were bruised.

"I sure hope so, Alina. I've got to get back to work now. I'll send you money whenever you need it, but it will be a while until we talk again." John put on his most empathetic voice.

"Okay, I love you," Alina said. She heard a click, and the call ended.

An all-black cab with tinted windows pulled to the side of the curb.

She sat in the back behind the passenger seat.

A plump man sat in the driver's seat, glancing in the rearview mirror.

"Are you going home?" the plump man asked.

"Something like that," Alina muttered and sunk down in her seat. She stared out the window and watched the homeless man as he trailed along the sidewalk with his head down.

CHAPTER FIFTEEN

UNIVERSE X-SANDRA-PAST

A flash of light and a powerful force pulled Sandra through the mirror into darkness. She lay on the ground, motionless, while every inch of her body felt like tiny needles had pierced her skin. Birds chirped from above, but there was no light. She felt the sun radiating her face, but she couldn't see it in front of her. Her back felt twisted as she sat up. Her hands grazed the ground beneath her. She felt warm, soft tickles brush against her fingertips. The darkness in front of her turned to a light grey, and then pixelated images surrounded her. Color illuminated as far as she could see—green, vibrant grass beneath her and a bright blue sky with no clouds.

Sandra used what little strength she had to stand up. She looked around and wondered why John had sent her there. Was anyone else there? She observed the edge of the grass. Around her were fresh red apples growing on an army of trees laid out in an enclosed square.

Sandra looked back up at the sky, examining it further. It was too perfect of a day. The sky looked too blue; the sun shone down too brightly. Despite the sounds of animals chittering, the air felt hollow, no sounds of cars or tractors. It was quiet, and the world felt too still.

Sandra stood and walked toward a quaint white cottage. A white swing hung from the wooden posts, and square windows sat on either side of the front wall.

"It's beautiful. Just like my parent's house I grew up in," Sandra's face lit up.

"Am I dead? Will my family be here to greet me?" she said aloud.

She felt a sense of relief wash over her. If this was death, then maybe the worst of it was over.

She walked slowly to the porch and pushed open the door. Inside was a floral brown couch to the left with a fireplace filled with wood. The kitchen, to her right, had a brown countertop, a white sink, brown cupboards, and an oven. A lime green refrigerator stood at attention to her left. The wooden floors squeaked with every step she made. She opened the fridge to find a single-layer chocolate cake with a note on top. There was a large canister of cheap-looking coffee on a shelf. There were no other food items, not even condiments. *The cake must be from my mother, here to welcome me to the afterlife,* Sandra thought. She carefully placed the cake on the counter and picked up the note. It read:

"*Sandra, I hope you find your new life acceptable. I know you must think I'm evil and a terrible person.*

I am a man searching to create a better world. My world. I have loved you since the day I met you at the physics convention in our small town in California. I loved you when we struggled to afford to feed Alina while we created our dream together.

I loved you even when you surpassed my own competency in building Ether.

I loved you enough to let you go so that the new world you once envisioned could grow into existence. Alina will become the best version of herself because of you.

I only wish you loved me enough to thank me for the demanding work I put in to create the perfect world and worlds to come. You could have had it all, Sandra.

You will live out your days alone.

You will eat alone.

You will sleep alone. You will die alone.

Your time is up in all universes but this one.

Here, you will have eternity to reflect on the love you did not show me back.

Here, you will die by the slow hands of your own creation.

You will receive your favorite chocolate cake in the refrigerator each day. The one your mother used to make for you for your birthday every year before she passed, the one your daughter and I would make for you to continue the tradition.

This is my final act of love for you. May each bite be a reminder of my mercy.

Enjoy eternity alone, and don't worry, Alina will not suffer. She will not remember these events. She will only remember the void in her heart, and that is a weight you will have to bear for her.

All my love,

John

Sandra tore the note up in a fit of rage. This was worse than being dead. John had sentenced her to a living death. She picked up the cake and, with all her strength, smashed it against the window in the kitchen. She watched it slide into the sink in a heaping pile. Adrenaline rushed through her veins as she frantically searched the house. She was not dead, which meant she had a chance to save Alina. Was Alina here? Was she injured? Sandra thought, and she needed to find out quickly.

"Hello?" she screamed. "Alina! Are you here? Mom is here, baby. Hello?"

She saw three bedrooms with their doors closed. She opened the first to find her old childhood bedroom which was decorated with pink walls and had stuffed animals perfectly placed on her pink bedsheets. An old woven toy box sat in the corner, filled to the brim with toys. Next to it, a white vanity with colorful pallets of makeup lined the top. This room looked like a mixture of all the years it had been used, compressed into one.

Behind her was another door; she opened it to see her brother's room; blue walls, and baseball cards perfectly stacked on a desk. A model train ran the length of the floor. The walls were littered with pin-up models in bathing suits. The bed was neatly tucked in, something her brother never did. Her mother would sneak in and make it for him before their father woke up. He'd praise him for making his bed and give him his daily allowance while her mother winked at him. Sandra always made her own bed, but she continued that tradition with Alina and would secretly make her bed, too. She thought of Alina and wondered if she would start making her own bed now that she was alone.

She faced her parents' bedroom. "Mom? Dad? Are you here?" she yelled again as she started towards their room.

Her parents had died when Alina was a baby. She didn't know why she was calling for them, but she felt that maybe they might be there.

When she opened the main bedroom door, she saw no one. Her parents' wooden bed frame stood tall. It had a green and white floral comforter with too many pillows neatly stacked on top. The walls were pale grey, and a family photo was hanging above the bed.

Sandra ran outside, desperate to find someone, anyone. She didn't stop running until she reached the far left of the apple trees at the edge of the lawn. She pushed past the branches that poked and prodded her as she weaved between them. On the other side, she found more greenery. In the distance, beyond the grass, she spotted a brown and red horse stable. Signs of life were almost in her grasp. She ran to it, a smile almost formed on her dry lips. A faint gaggle of neighing and simultaneous moos increased with every step she took.

She slowly approached the back wall of the stable, careful with her steps so as not to spook anyone or anything on the other side. She found three horses; her old childhood horse, Winnie, was a soft golden brown with a chestnut brown mane. Next to Winnie was her mom's horse, Jessie, in an all-white coat with a blonde mane. The third horse, sitting down in the corner of the stall, was her brother's horse, Maybel, all black, and a gentle soul who just needed some warming up before you approached her. Winnie bucked up in excitement as Sandra came to her.

"Hey girl, you remember me, don't you?" Winnie placed her head against Sandra to receive some soft strokes.

"I'll take care of you all, I promise." Maybel looked up at her but stayed put.

Cows mooed from the other side of the stable, and Sandra left to investigate. Her neighbors, the Vonoghans, owned that part of the land, but they allowed her family to use their milk whenever needed. She walked down a long gravel path behind the stable. Maybe her neighbors were there, or perhaps someone else was in the house. She would happily welcome anyone at that point; anyone but John. She saw the surrounding apple trees that blocked the view of the house. She was close.

She quickened her pace and shouted, "Hello! Mr. Vonoghan, are you there?" Branches brushed her face as she weaved through the trees. "Mrs. Vonoghan? Hello? Anyone?"

The house appeared from behind the trees. She saw green grass and a white cottage with a white swing attached to the porch. The door was wide open. She sprinted up the porch and stumbled inside. John's cake was smeared against the window in the kitchen.

"No! No, no, no!" Sandra sank to the floor, realizing the truth behind John's note.

Sandra was utterly alone, trapped in his sick fantasy life for her. No one was there, and no one was coming to save her.

She heaved and wailed as she mourned her daughter. What had she done? She should have listened to John or tried harder to escape. She should never have created the blueprint for MultiU. Her daughter was in danger, and Sandra caused it. There had to be a way to save Alina.

"I'll find you, Alina; I promise." She wiped the tears from her eyes and pushed herself up. The refrigerator buzzed, and she walked to the drawer next to it and plucked a notepad and pen that her parents used to keep for taking phone messages.

She wrote *Day One* on the notepad. Her head throbbed, and her eyes felt heavy. She found a blanket tucked neatly on the floral couch and laid down as she spread it over her tired, sore body and went to sleep, thinking about Alina.

CHAPTER SIXTEEN

UNIVERSE X-SANDRA-PAST

Sandra hunched over the kitchen counter, staring down at the chocolate cake. That damn chocolate cake she swore never to eat. It seemed to stare back at her, mocking her. She drooled as she imagined the moist and decadent chocolate sponge hitting her taste buds. The creamy chocolate ganache would strike a perfect balance of sweetness and intensity. Her stomach rumbled at the idea of eating something other than apples, milk, and coffee.

She imagined Alina standing next to her, begging for the first bite, as she had done many times.

"You want to have some? Of course, baby," she said to an empty spot beside her.

Her hand lunged forward, as if it had a mind of its own, and dug her fork into the cake. She shoveled bite after bite into her mouth as crumbs and frosting flew down onto the who-knows-how-many-years-old clothing she had retrieved from her mother's chest of drawers. Leaving half the cake intact, she pushed the reminder of her failure into the trash can below the counter. Her legs gave way as she sank down next to it on the wooden floor.

The realization that John had won overcame her. She closed her eyes and sobbed as she thought of her daughter. She was missing so much of her life. She would never see her Alina Ballerina again. She sat there for hours, listening to the birds chirp and her horses neigh. She couldn't give up hope; they needed her to survive, and so did Alina. She decided at that moment that she would live. It was not the end for her; it was just the beginning.

The sun shone a spotlight of comfort through the kitchen window as she stared at the array of sticky notes that covered entirely the shelves and walls of the kitchen. She ran out of paper to write on long ago. The sun, shining its impressive rays onto her skin, gave her the strength to stand back up. She retrieved a knife from the kitchen drawer beside her, wiped the cake residue from her face with her sleeve, and carved into the counter *Year 5, day 100.*

Sandra had gone one year without eating any more of John's taunting gift to her. She spent her days picking apples for her and the horses and milking the cows. She imagined Alina was beside her, and she spoke to her as if she was there. She would visit the cows for other company but refused to slaughter them for sustenance.

One morning, she was so hungry that she took a knife out and marched over to them. She was going to kill a calf. She needed the protein; her bones showed through her ratted grey t-shirt, and her body was weak. She inched towards the calf grazing the field, blissfully unaware of the dangers approaching. She raised her knife to its throat when the mother cow mooed and started towards her. She dropped the knife and petted the calf while she cried.

"I'm sorry. I won't hurt you. You deserve to live," she said.

She imagined Alina's voice responding, "I know you'd never hurt me. It's okay."

The mother cow was approaching quickly, and Sandra jumped the fence. She threw the knife, which disappeared into the trees, and ran back home; if you could call it home.

Thoughts of Alina haunted her mind constantly. *Is she okay? Is she hurt? Does she remember me?* It played on repeat in her mind like a bad yet comforting song.

Sandra was not going to let herself die there. She made a promise to herself that she would see her daughter again, even if that meant eating sickeningly sweet chocolate cake every day to survive.

She spent hours searching the parameters of her universe, hoping to find a way out or find someone who could help her—but every exit led back to the entrance, an infinite loop of isolation.

She walked to the library, connected by the wall to the kitchen, where she spent her evenings reading. She searched the contents yet again even though she had read all of them twice. There were cookbooks, which seemed like a subtle taunt from John since there was no food to cook with. She read self-help books that were too old-school to fathom the type of help she needed.

She scanned the bottom shelf with her hands—old family albums consisting primarily of pictures of her and her brother as children. There was only one she came in there for. Sandra retrieved a red album labeled *Alina*. She had gifted her mother that album when Alina was one year old. Up until that moment, she had refused to look through it. The pain was too much to face alone, but as she envisioned her daughter sitting next to her, she felt stronger.

"Open it, Mama," a three-year-old version of Alina told her.

"Okay, my dear, I'll open it for you." She kissed the air beside her and before she could open it, she heard a loud, mechanical sound coming from the shelf.

Beep.Beep Beep.

Sandra jumped backward, startled by the sound of technology. Her prison world didn't even have a phone.

The bookshelf clicked and beeped as its floor-to-ceiling smooth wooden structure cracked down the middle and pulled itself apart. The floor shook beneath her feet, and she held imaginary Alina's hand. The bookcase opened to reveal a white wall with a rectangular fingerprint scanner the size of a small flat-screen computer.

"Oh my god!" She inched towards the wall and raised her finger to it.

It lit up green, and the wall broke away in a loud crackle like the bookcase. She stood there, frozen, in disbelief. A giant cylinder metal ball with holes surrounding it had caught her attention.

"MultiU," she said.

Sandra wasn't sure if she was happy or furious to see it again. She eyed the computer screen, wiped the dust off it with her cake-stained sleeve, and turned it on. It clicked and lit up with enthusiasm and the aluminum coil extending down the back rushed air through to the ceiling-high mirror that connected it. "This is my chance to go back home and save Alina. All this time, this machine has been here, waiting for me to find it," she said.

Sandra squealed, "My baby! I'm going to find you, Alina! Thank you, thank you." She cried and hugged the cold machine.

John may have built MultiU, but he didn't create it. His coding skills were much too weak to cover all the bases, and he must have overlooked the fact that if MultiU existed in one universe, then it must exist in all.

She located the instructions tab and, with energy that she hadn't had in years, she started her mission. She typed *Find Alina* and pressed enter.

The computer system popped up with:

There are infinite Alina Ethers. Please specify the Universe by letter first and then the number for subsequent universes.

Find Alina Ether Universe A. She tried again.

The computer instantly popped up with rows and rows of swiftly traveling green code. Sandra locked eyes on one line of code.

"It's tracking you in real-time." Sandra sat on the steel chair and observed.

Alina walks into Building D of Ether. She sits down at her desk and pulls up YouTube on the computer system.

A mix of emotions washed over Sandra. Her daughter was alive! She sighed a breath of relief and touched her hand to her chest. Joy spilled out through her pores.

"My baby, Mom is here. I miss you so much." She reached to the computer as more code appeared on the screen.

Alina rolls her eyes at her boss, Logan, as he walks to his office.

"Logan…Why does that name sound so familiar? Why does John have you doing busy work, Alina? I'm glad you're alive, sweetheart, but this is not you," she said.

She thought about when Alina came to the grand opening of the small building of Ether. Alina had been so excited, running around the office and imagining herself one day working there.

"Mama, I want to be a physicist like you one day." Alina had said as she ran into her arms.

"If that's what you wish, my darling, you will be." Sandra kissed her head.

John was punishing her. Or maybe he was punishing Sandra through her. Sandra slapped the keyboard, and a new window opened:

Universe B Alina Ether, the screen read.

She scrolled through the real-time actions.

Alina discusses with John the grand release of MultiU.

Alina hugs John.

Alina arrives in building A with Alister.

"Alister? Why does his name sound familiar too?" Sandra raised a brow.

Sandra sunk into the chair beside her. She mourned for her daughter, who must have had no idea what her father had done or the implications of what she was doing.

"I have to help her right now." She sat up straight and narrowed her eyes, focusing on the task at hand.

She clicked on the command bar and entered:

Contact Alina Ether Universe A.

A red flashing box spread over the screen with a blaring, loud tone.

Access denied. Cannot complete function. Access denied.

She growled. "Damn it!" She walked around the room and paced back and forth in the tiny seven by ten square foot room.

"Come on, think, Sandra, think." Suddenly, she stopped pacing; her face lit up the dim room.

She rushed back to the chair and input the instructions:

Place pole on Main Street. Put a flyer on the pole with the words 'Alina, Mom is here. Go to Building C.'

The system lit up green.

"I may not be able to talk directly to you, Alina, but this will have to do."

She set the computer's sound to the highest volume, ticked the box in the corner of the screen to *notify me*, and exited the room.

She entered the bathroom, stripped off her clothes, pushed the shower curtain back, and turned on the water.

Sandra felt hope that she would see her daughter again.

She spent every waking moment of her day reading Alina's life play out like a story in front of her. She felt closer to her, if not a little stalkerish.

She watched Alina in Universe A as she spent her weekends with Teddy. Sandra quickly realized that this was her best friend.

They watched movies together and ate Thai food every Friday night. Every Saturday night was taco night, and every Sunday was an everything night where they would use up whatever ingredients they had left in their apartment and make a mystery meal. Sandra started that tradition when her family struggled to make ends meet before they had built the Ether company. Alina would smile and laugh with Teddy, and she'd sing and dance like nobody was watching. But somebody was watching, and Sandra's heart would break repeatedly when, every night after Teddy went to sleep, Alina would lay in her bed and sob. She'd sob for her mother, who was no longer there. She'd weep for a life she could not remember. Sandra would sob with her; the pain of Alina feeling alone was too much to bear. She would occasionally watch over Alina in Universe B, too. She was still her daughter, even if she was an altered version of her.

She'd watch as Alina in Universe B would wake up in her mansion. She'd observe her being waited on hand and foot by staff as she got ready for the day. She'd be driven to work with Alister, and they would greet John. Alina spent long hours in the new empire John created. As Sandra stared at the code, she realized something: Alina B. never expressed any emotion beyond basic joy or determination. She used to be so full of life, so sarcastic, and averagely happy. It's as if John erased her personality. But sometimes, late at night, she would read the code that Alina B would get out of bed, stand at her bedroom windowpane that stretched from floor to ceiling, and climb out the window while Alister slept beside her. She'd sit on the roof and look up at the stars. Alister would wake up and ask her what she was doing, and she would look at him dazed and respond that she didn't know, but Sandra knew. Sandra knew that, although Alina B was a different Alina with different experiences, her soul was all the same in every universe. Sandra knew you can never truly erase someone's memory of their soul's experience.

That memory is stored somewhere deeper than the brain, and your body remembers what your mind forgets. Her daughter was still in there somewhere, and she would save her, too.

Sandra sent out many hints over the coming months to Alina A, but Alina didn't notice them. She coded MultiU to place a white teddy bear, the replica of the one that now resided in Teddy's room, into Logan's office. She put bright lights at the bank, trying to light up the pole from across the sidewalk. Yet, Alina always failed to notice. Alina would walk past it every day for work, and every day, Sandra would hold her breath, hoping that day was the day she'd see it. She wanted so badly just to let Alina know she was safe and that her mom was watching over her.

*****

After waking and stretching her arms, she stepped onto the dirty carpet, walked in a slow-motion haze to the kitchen, and pulled out a knife. She etched *Year Five, day 203*, into the countertop.

With a loud sigh, Sandra slumped down in her chair, where she'd spend the day, like she did every day, watching Alina. She pulled up Universe A and Universe B and surveyed the scene of Alina's life unfolding. In Universe B, Alina was walking with Alister along Main Street. They were both holding a cup from Coffee Couture. Alina walked to the left of Alister as they passed by a bank. Suddenly, from behind her, a woman walking four dogs lost hold of a Rottweiler, charging at Alina B. Alina looked back at the dog as she ran forward, attempting to escape imminent attack.

Sandra gripped the chair handles as she read in horror the following line MultiU spat out:

Alina hits her head on the pole, falls to the ground, and screams as the dog viciously bites her face.

"No! Alina! No, oh my god. Wake up, baby," Sandra screamed at the computer.

Alister tackles the dog, and it runs away, with Betty following.

Alister calls an ambulance.

Alina is taken to Hospital Ether urgent care.

Sandra quickly clicked on Universe A Alina and scrolled up to see the recent events. It read:

Alina walks furiously through Main Street.

Alina hits a pole and falls to the ground as coffee spills into her hair.

Alister runs from the bank to assist her.

Alina stands up.

Sandra placed her head in her hands. "Thank god," she whispered, muffled through her fingers.

She was thankful Alina was okay in that universe, but she worried for Alina B.

The ground shook beneath Sandra's chair. She dropped to the floor and covered her ears as the computer screen went black. It let out a loud, disorienting siren.

Woop. Woop. Woop. Malfunction. Fix immediately. Woop. Woop. Woop. Malfunction. Fix immediately.

This time, it didn't stop after two rounds. It continued its assault on her eardrums. She acted quickly as she went to the computer and pressed every button she could think of to stop the siren, but it was useless.

Woop. Woop. Woop. Energy overload Woop. Woop. Woop. Fix immediately. Woop. Woop. Woop.

A sudden rush of energy flowed through the connector tube between the mirror and the sphere, causing the sphere to illuminate a blinding light through each hole. It's as if the sun were right in that room—beams of pulsing rays shot through the holes, protruding in every direction.

Woop. Woop. Woop. Blending Universe A and B. Energy overload. Fix immediately. Woop. Woop. Woop.

Woop. Woop. Woop. Blending Universe A and B. Malfunction complete. Woop. Woop. Woop.

The ground slowed to a still, and the siren fell silent. Sandra peered at the computer while it switched back to its usual settings. She massaged her ears, which were still ringing from the sound. She focused her eyes on the screen and watched the code while Alina A continued to work, seemingly unharmed.

"Everything seems normal." She sat back in her chair, confused about what had happened.

Sandra eyed the light coming from the machine in her peripherals. It was too bright to stare directly at it.

"Okay, what do I know about light? Light is energy. Energy is in everything. Everything is energy."

Her eyes widened as she cupped her cheeks.

"My god. Both Alina's falling at the same time must have created enough energy to make the system malfunction. My version of MultiU in this universe created the pole, so it all leads back to this world. We're connected now."

Sandra's eyes lit up almost as bright as the lights. She typed *Universe X* into the system and brought up her coding. She typed:

Use light to guide Alina Universe A home.

Mom is home.

The ground shook again; this time, it spared her ears with no sound. The light within the sphere bled out like smoke from a fire and began swirling in a tornado-like fashion. It twisted and turned in the air and the ground slowed to a still when the light turned into a small spherical shape. The ball of light vibrated in the air as if had it sucked the vibrations up from the ground.

Behind it, the mirror lit up with swirling blue and green lights flowing in a patterned circle. The light floated towards it as if it were being pulled by a vacuum and disappeared into the mirror.

Sandra jumped from her seat to investigate. She could only hope this plan would work. If she wanted to get back to Alina, she had to outsmart John, which wouldn't be too hard, but she also needed to outsmart MultiU. Sandra approached the swirling colors in the mirror. She shouted at the top of her lungs with all her strength. Five years' worth of pain exploded from her from the inside out. "Agh!" she screamed.

She placed her hand against the mirror's mesmerizing lights, and a force pulled her in.

***

Sandra startled as a man shook her shoulder. A security guard in navy blue suspenders stood over her.

"Hey lady, are you alright? You can't sleep here," the man said.

She opened her eyes and took in her surroundings. She was in front of Ether Building C. Only there were no cars parked in the parking lot—in fact, there was no parking lot at all—just paved dirt.

"Sorry, yes, I'm leaving now," she said.

Despite the throbbing ache pulsating through her muscles, she maintained a rigid posture and a forced smile as she stood before the officer.

She looked to her right to see that Building B's doors and windows were patched with wood. Sandra furrowed her brows. *Hmm, that's odd.*

She walked over to where Building A should have been and found a large patch of dirt and builders with tractors moving the soil into a large bin. She walked down to the central part of the city, stumbling past mothers and fathers walking hand in hand with their young children. They laughed as they crossed the road and walked behind the dirt patch that led to a park. Sandra remembered that park vividly. Alina used to go there after school, and they spent many late afternoons picnicking there.

She approached the old Ether building, a small building on the corner of the street that had since been replaced with a makeup store. She touched the window longingly until a woman, who was applying red lipstick from the other side, glared at her. Sandra continued down the sidewalk and entered the building Bob worked in, hoping to get his help contacting Alina.

Bob owned his own business, Antique Me, which sold antique furniture. She spotted a worker there who she did not recognize.

"Excuse me, Sir, do you know where Bob is?" she asked.

"You're going to have to be more specific, darlin'." The man rolled his eyes as he finished with a customer.

"Bob, the owner, is he here?" Sandra remained calm despite her impatience.

"There is no owner named Bob here, sorry," he said as he moved on to another customer.

Sandra backed away. Where was her brother? This was his store. She turned and pushed the door open and walked faster, examining the city. Everything looked mostly the same but slightly different. The coffee shop that should have been Caffeine City was now a Little Cakes bakery. Everyone around her was using one of those old smartphones, not the Uchat technology she was familiar with.

A woman passed by talking to her friend about the latest TimeBook posts, but TimeBook had been obsolete for a few years before John had sent her to her living hell. She stopped walking and spotted a teenage girl dressed in black jeans and a blue T-shirt with a black backpack slung around her shoulder.

"Alina," she whispered. But how could this be? Alina was not a school-aged child anymore. Sandra had been gone for over five years. Sandra rushed to the nearest corner store, found a newspaper, and realized the date matched when Alina was eighteen years old.

"I'm somehow in the past, but who's past?" she gasped.

An older woman carrying a beer bottle stopped beside her.

"Ain't that the truth?" the older woman said.

Sandra sped out of the store to find Alina giggling with a blonde girl next to her. She desperately wanted to run to Alina, but she worried that John was tracking her. She had to be smart about who she interacted with there; in whatever world it was.

She followed far behind the girls as they approached a crosswalk.

"No, are my eyes playing tricks on me?" Sandra whispered.

Alina had turned around just enough that Sandra could see her protruding belly.

"You're pregnant? Oh my god!" Sandra blurted loudly.

Alina spun around, startled. Sandra stood frozen as she stared her daughter in the eyes from across the road, her mouth stuck in an open position. Sandra's mind screamed at her to say something, telling her to run to Alina and hug her, but her body wouldn't allow it. Instead, she ran behind the closest building and was out of sight. The thumping of her chest battled the noise of her finding out her eighteen-year-old daughter was pregnant. The girl wasn't *her* Alina, but it felt like it was.

Sandra waited until she could no longer hear the girls speaking before peering behind the wall. She could barely make out their silhouettes as they walked towards their house. This was once a version of Sandra's house, too, so she followed the trail behind them; this time making sure to keep a safer distance. The girls turned the corner into the court where Alina lived. She watched behind a tree as Alina entered the house, and Cecelia turned to walk toward hers.

This was her chance, the moment she had been hoping for. She waited for Cecelia to exit the courtyard. Cecelia was listening to music on her phone and overlooked Sandra until she bumped into her.

"You're Alina's friend, right?" Sandra said.

Cecelia screamed.

"Shhh, Shhh! Please don't be scared." Sandra stepped forward.

"You're that lady who was staring at us. Stay back!" Cecelia shouted.

Cecelia turned to run, but Sandra caught her arm and gripped it tighter than she had meant.

"I need your help," Sandra said.

CHAPTER SEVENTEEN

UNIVERSE C-CECELIA-PAST

Cecelia picked at the wood on her desk as Ms. Greenwald's health class seemed to stop time in its tracks. She showed the class how babies were born using a graphic video on the projector while she narrated every detail. Every. Detail. *Doesn't she know we're too old to learn this now? Or maybe we're too young,* Cecelia thought. *We're 18 and about to graduate, so I'd rather watch the paint dry than think about the birth of the placenta.*

She pulled her curly blonde hair into a loose ponytail and reached for a pack of gum in her backpack. Just as she was opening her gum, the woman on the projector screamed and a gooey baby was given life. *Oh, no thank you. That is not something I needed to see today.*

Cecelia focused her attention on the class around her to find they were also making faces and shielding their eyes. She caught a glimpse of the girl who sat behind her. A thin, quiet girl with chocolate brown hair who always had her head down in her notebook. Cecelia observed her as she seemed to tune out the birth schpeal, too, choosing to spend her time doodling and daydreaming.

"Pssst. Want some gum to wash out the taste of puke from listening to Ms. Greenwald talk about childbirth?" Cecelia winked.

Cecelia had a certain charm. She was sarcastic but kind, and she saw those traits in the quiet girl, too.

Alina looked up from her drawing and smiled. "Sure, thank you," she said as she unwrapped the gum.

Cecelia's eyes examined Alina's drawing of a mother and child on a green pasture.

"Why does the mother look so sad?" she asked.

"Probably because she was being bored to death by Ms. Greenwald," Alina smirked.

Alina's smile quickly faded as she stared at her drawing.

"She's not sad; she's just lost," she said.

Cecelia paused for a moment, and then her eyes lit up.

"Hey, do you want to have lunch with me today after class? We can get pizza and talk trash about Ms. Greenwald."

Alina paused to think about it momentarily and then said, "Hard yes on the pizza and trash-talking, I'm in. Can my boyfriend, Alister, come too?"

"Of course. Is that who, you know…" Cecelia's eyes gestured to her protruding stomach.

Alina placed a hand on her stomach and moved a stray hair behind her ear with the other hand.

"Yeah, he's the father," she smiled.

"You'll have an Alister junior running around pretty soon!" Cecelia whispered as Ms. Greenwald cleared her throat to get the girls' attention.

The girls faced forward in compliance.

Alina leaned into Cecelia's ear and whispered, "Actually, I think I'm going to name him Teddy."

Alina reached into her backpack and produced a small, white teddy bear with a blue bow tie around his neck.

"My mom gave this to me when she came with me to the gender reveal test." Alina stroked the bear's head.

"Teddy. What a beautiful name," Cecelia said.

From that moment on, the girls were inseparable.

The bell rang, signaling the end of the day, and they walked home together.

"I'm surprised we haven't met before this class. We live so close to each other," Alina said.

"I know, right?" Cecelia replied.

"It's funny what your eyes miss around you when you're not looking for it." Alina picked up a small, shiny rock off the gravel trail and threw it to the other side.

"So, how did you and Alister meet?" Cecelia asked.

She was nosey but not in a mean way. She was a girl who genuinely cared to know everything about everyone.

"We had physics class together and were paired up as partners. We had to discuss the Doppler effect to the class," Alina said.

Cecelia rolled her eyes. "Sounds…romantic," she giggled.

"Romance is for fairytales. I want a love that transcends time and space." Alina stared ahead; her eyes lost in thought.

The bell rang, and Alina and Cecelia left class. They walked along the trail that led to their neighborhoods.

They neared a crosswalk guiding their way to their respective homes.

A woman from across the street gasped and said, "Oh my god!"

Cecelia swiveled her head and caught a glimpse of a

woman with honey-brown curly hair staring at them. She was wearing a brown floral dress that looked like it belonged at Mighty Thrifty, a store that was one block over. She had a surprised expression on her face, which seemed to stay put as if she was made of stone. Cecelia shifted her weight while she observed the woman; she watched everyone, and the way this woman looked at her was not of this world.

Cecelia leaned into Alina and whispered, "Don't be too obvious but there is a woman staring at us to our left. It's giving me the creeps." Cecelia shuddered.

Alina stiffened and glanced to her left. She spun around when she spotted her mom. She was dressed odd, and her hair seemed a mess, but it was definitely her mom.

"Mom, what are you doing here?" She waved her over.

The woman bolted behind a stone wall.

"Alina, I doubt that was your mom. Come on, let's go." She grabbed Alina's hand and pulled her across the sidewalk.

When they arrived at Alina's house, they saw through the window that her mom had been sitting on their black leather couch, reading a book.

"I guess it wasn't my mom," Alina laughed.

"That woman probably thought you were crazy!" Cecelia said as she gave Alina a hug and continued, "I'll see you in class tomorrow. I'm so glad we're friends."

Alina started towards her front door and Cecelia turned her music on as she skipped down the road and made a sharp right, where she came to an abrupt halt.

Cecelia screamed, knocking her headphones out of her ears and onto the pavement. In front of her was the older woman.

"Shhh, shhh, it's okay. Please don't be scared," the woman said as she scanned her surroundings.

Cecelia froze, seemingly paralyzed.

"You're Alina's friend, right?" the woman asked.

Cecelia nodded as she planned her escape route.

"I need your help." Sandra grabbed Cecelia's arm harder than she had intended. Noticing Cecelia's fear, Sandra released her. "I'm not going to hurt you; my name is Sandra Ether. I'm Alina's mother, and I need you to help me," she said.

"No, no, you're not; we just saw Alina's mom in her house." Cecelia swiped her headphones from the ground and took quick steps backward, keeping her eyes steady on the crazed woman.

"I am from another universe, and I think I've also traveled back in time. Alina needs your help, too. Please believe me." Sandra choked back tears.

"Ah, of course! That's not crazy at all." Cecelia rolled her eyes, but she felt compelled to humor the poor woman. "Why can't you just talk to Alina yourself?" she quizzed.

"Because her father is a powerful man where I'm from, and probably here too. He is watching her and will know if I contact her. He wouldn't suspect you though," Sandra said.

"If you won't do it for me or for Alina, do it for her unborn child. Please, I am begging you." Sandra tried one last time to get through to Cecelia.

"His name is Teddy. You gave Alina the white bear that inspired his name. Do you remember that?" Cecelia quizzed again. She was not going to trust her that easily.

"No…but I am not from this universe. This Alina is my daughter, but she's not the daughter I know." Sandra rubbed her temples when she realized how insane she sounded.

Sandra's eyes darted up at Cecelia as her mind found clarity. "Wait a minute." She cocked her head to the side and stroked her chin. "Are you talking about a small white teddy bear with a blue ribbon?"

"Yes, that's the one," Cecelia said as she crossed her arms.

"My mother, Alina's grandmother, gave that to me before Alina was born. We all thought she would be a boy, but she came out with the most beautifully long, straight hair, and I was overjoyed to have a baby girl." Sandra brushed her cheek, remembering the first time she held Alina in her arms and nuzzled her daughter's tiny face to hers.

"My baby girl is having a baby boy." Sandra beamed with pride. "If you won't do it for me or Alina, do it for Alina's little boy."

"I know you're trying to pull at my heartstrings lady, but it won't work. Alina is my best friend, but would I risk my life for her? I don't know," Cecelia said.

"You make a good point. I don't know you, but I was sent to this universe for a reason. I don't know how or why, but I think you're the key to saving us all."

Cecelia eyed Sandra up and down before bursting out in a fit of laughter.

"Can I have what you're smoking?" she said while catching her breath.

Sandra hung her head down; she understood. Why would this girl help a crazy-looking woman claiming to be from another universe? Sandra would probably laugh, too, if she weren't living that reality.

"Sorry for bothering you. It won't happen again."

Sandra turned towards the main road and walked away. She would find another way to save Alina.

Cecelia observed the woman. She didn't believe her and was glad to watch her walk away, yet a nagging itch seeped under Cecelia's skin.

"Wait!" Cecelia ran to catch up with her.

"Okay, I'll help you," Cecelia said.

Sandra cocked an eyebrow. "Really? Why the sudden change of heart?"

"I need some adventure in my life anyway, and if what you're saying is true, I want to know why you were sent here to me...and I want to help," Cecelia mumbled those last words.

Sandra leaped in to hug Cecelia. It had been so long since she had felt the embrace of another human, and she imagined it was Alina she hugged. Only, Alina's hugs were much less stiff.

"Thank you so much. My daughter is lucky to have you as a friend. Come with me; I want to show you something." She clasped Cecelia's hand and walked her toward what should have been the Ether buildings.

"Don't you want to know my name? Or did your magical time machine tell you already?" Cecelia said as she tried to keep up with Sandra's pace. "My name is Cecelia. Thanks for asking." She rolled her eyes.

Sandra powered on weaving through people strolling through the sidewalk.

"Why did I agree to this?" Cecelia groaned as they entered through the door of the building, coughing through the dusty hallway to the unmarked door in Building C.

The floors creaked with each step. The lights above flickered—the remains of the demolished rooms on either side scattered across every surface.

Chills rushed down Cecelia's spine. *I'm going to be murdered here, I'm sure of it.*

Sandra opened the unmarked door and switched on the lights, stretching an arm out, to make a grand gesture.

"This is how you're going to help. Cecelia, meet MultiU. It is the smartest technology to have ever been created, and it should not have been created, but that's for another time," Sandra said as she switched the power button on. The machine surged awake, and lights shone through the holes.

"It just looks like a giant mirror with extra steps," Cecelia said as she approached it. She plucked her peach lip gloss from her jeans pocket and applied it to her lips. "Although, my skin looks like it's glowing. Wow, what is this made of?" She reached a hand out to touch the glass but stopped short as Sandra yanked her backward, pulling Cecelia away from the mirror.

"Don't touch that! Not yet. Without the proper setting, who knows where you'll end up," Sandra said.

"Jeez, okay, my bad. What are all those glowing lights in the sphere next to it?" Cecelia asked.

"It's pure energy. MultiU is malfunctioning. It shouldn't have those lights, and it shouldn't have this much power. I think it wants to help, and perhaps it sent me here for a reason. I believe that reason is you. I didn't know it could send me back in time, but I suppose it's smarter than I ever imagined it would be." Sandra said while Cecelia stood, mouth agape at the overloading influx of information.

"Okay, Lady, hold on. Let me think for a second."

"Call me Sandra, please."

"Sandra, sorry." She paused and took in the mirror, the long chord connecting to the sphere and the supercomputer sitting atop it as if overseeing the rest. "So, this is a time machine, and we're going back in time to help Alina and Teddy?"

"No, this is a man-made multi-dimensional portal that sent me to another universe, your universe, which is taking place in the past," Sandra said.

Cecelia's blank stare urged Sandra to try her explanation again.

"In my original universe, some of the events that have not happened here yet, have already happened for me and my Alina. My universe is on another timeline than yours, but they are happening simultaneously. Your timeline is further back than mine, so technically, we're in the past while also being in the present. The events and experiences here are not the exact same events and experiences in other universes. Think of it like baking a cake. All the ingredients are here, but each universe has a different baker, so no cake will be exactly alike," Sandra said.

"That still sounds like a time machine," Cecelia stated.

Sandra sighed. "Okay, let's move past that part for now and focus on the main reason MultiU exists."

"I still don't understand. This creates other universes?" she asked, mesmerized by the lights.

"It can, but it does so much more than that. It can control the already existing ones," Sandra replied.

"I'm not helping you control anyone." Cecelia crossed her arms and backed away.

"That's just it. I don't want control either. I want to save my daughter and her son, and then I want to destroy this machine. Alina's father is deranged; he wants the control. I won't rest until he and this abomination is destroyed."

"So, what am I here for? You said it brought you to me for a reason," Cecelia asked.

"Yes, I think you're the key to everything. I'm not sure how or why yet, but for now, I have a plan for you to get *my* Alina back before John finds out that I've escaped his prison world."

Cecelia paused for a moment and then perked up. "You're pretty badass Sandra. Okay, you've almost convinced me. What do you need me to do?"

"Not here." Sandra motioned to the mirror which had lit up its blue and purple swirls. She then typed code into the system.

"This will take us where it needs us to go," Sandra said as she held out her hand.

Cecelia took a deep breath in and grabbed Sandra's hand.

"Is this going to hurt?" Cecelia squinted her face tightly shut.

"Yes." Sandra pulled them through the mirror.

They were back in the small room connected to the library, and Cecelia groaned as she lay on the floor in agony.

"It gets easier every time you go through." Sandra extended her hand as she helped Cecelia up off the floor and allowed her to rest on the chair facing the computer. "I'm going to throw up." Cecelia clenched her stomach, hunched over. She caught her reflection in the mirror and touched her face in horror. She suddenly felt both less sick and sicker than before.

"Oh my god! Why am I old?" she screamed as she examined her face.

"I would hardly call twenty-three old, Cecelia. MultiU had me travel back in time to get you. I guess it wants us to be in this timeline now. And here you are, twenty-three, which is the same age as Alina in this timeline."

"You said this wasn't a time machine!" Cecelia stomped her foot. Although her body looked like a young adult woman, her mind was certainly still that of a teenager.

"It's time-machine-adjacent, okay? We have bigger things to worry about; like saving my daughter and grandson." Sandra did not hide the annoyance in her tone this time.

Cecelia examined her body and scrunched her nose while Sandra got to work, typing into MultiU's computer system.

"Come here and look at this. I have pulled up Universes A and B, and right here in this corner is Universe C. This is *your* universe." Sandra pointed to the right of the screen.

"My Alina is in Universe A, and your Alina is in Universe C."

"Then who is in universe B? And what Universe are we in now?" she asked.

"We are in Universe X. John Ether has hidden that universe on the system so that no one could find me, not that anyone would think to find me anyway. John made sure of that." Sandra's mind flooded with thoughts of Alina on the last day she saw her. Those memories were too painful, so she shook them away to focus on the task at hand.

"As for Universe B," Sandra continued, "that is home to the worst versions of my family you could possibly imagine, and it's where John has chosen his main universe to reside in. Your job is to travel to Universe A and lead Alina to Building C. You will then cross over to this universe. I will put my universe back on the map, but I will keep it from being visible."

"Why can't you be the one to go get her? This seems insane," Cecelia said.

"Because, like in your universe, Alina's father, John Ether, has blocked me from contacting Alina. He seems to have eyes on her interactions in Universes A and B. I guess he never thought I'd make it out of this world he put me in, so he didn't bother with the other universes. You're right, though, this is insane. John is insane, and we need to stop him," she said.

"Then why didn't you just contact Alina in my universe yourself?" Cecelia asked.

Sandra sighed. She didn't blame Cecelia for her never ending questions, but she did not have the energy for it. "Because I didn't want to risk being wrong and losing her forever. Besides, she has no idea what is happening. Her version of me in your universe is still there and hasn't disappeared yet. She likely wouldn't trust me. Just as you don't trust me."

"Well, that's true. I don't trust you," Cecelia exclaimed.

"That's okay. You just need to trust in yourself." Sandra rested her hand on Cecelia's shoulder.

"Are there more universes than these three?" Cecelia leaned forward.

"There are infinite universes. I am not sure how many universes John has manipulated. Infinite universes have always existed, but because of MultiU, John now has the power to manipulate each one of them if he so chooses. If we destroy the origin of MultiU, we destroy every version of it in every universe which, in turn, should destroy any alterations John has made."

"How can you be sure this will work?" Cecelia's questions were warranted, although frustrating.

Sandra stared through Cecelia's eyes as she searched for a response.

"Listen, we don't have a lot of time here," Sandra said then continued, "You can make a difference in this world and all worlds. Now, are you in or out?" Sandra had lost patience long ago.

Cecelia stared right back at Sandra, contemplating her next move. She could say no; she wanted to say no, but that nagging feeling kept her from turning to run.

"Okay, let's do this. I always wanted to be a hero. What do you need me to do?" Her eyes sharpened and a surge of energy jolted through her veins.

"Alina in both universes had a fall that resulted in the blending of Universes A and B. This universe we're in now, Universe X, created the malfunction. We are all connected. We are going to use this to our advantage. I will program MultiU to send you to a time before the collision occurs. You will find Teddy first and give him a note that I'll seal in an envelope."

"Wait, hold on. Teddy? As in her unborn child?" Cecelia's brain felt as fried as her bleached, blonde hair.

Sandra paused, contemplating how to explain the concept to her.

"Okay, in your universe, Teddy is Alina's child, and you are her best friend. In Universe A, Teddy is her best friend," Sandra said.

"Okay, so, I'm not her friend in the universe you're from?" Cecelia asked.

"From what I know, no, but perhaps your friendship was meant to start at a later time in Universe A. You see, in Alina's and my universe, she didn't meet Alister in school like she has in your universe. She meets Alister shortly after the collision, which means they haven't had a child yet in our universe." Sandra said.

"This makes no sense. How can there be multiples of anyone? How can there be multiples of me? I'm right here." Cecelia grabbed her temples.

"Okay, let's try this another way." Sandra typed in the computer system, and a whiteboard with markers appeared against the side wall to their left.

"Woah." Cecelia's eyes darted back and forth between Sandra and the whiteboard.

Sandra began drawing diagrams and squares of multiple colors, creating a vertical web.

"Your body is just a vessel. Picture a magnet block—the kind that children play with." She pointed to the colored squares. "If your soul is a magnet, and your body is the colored casing, you can place a magnet inside any plastic case you want—red, green, blue, purple, etc." She paused to observe Cecelia, who was nodding along with a blank stare, before continuing.

"Now, let's say you choose the casing colors green and blue to place your magnets in. These two magnets will be drawn together. Now let's say you take the blue and red casing and place the magnets inside. They will still be drawn together just the same. You see, it does not matter which color casing you choose, they will still find a way to connect to each other. Now let's take this one step further. You place the magnets in every available color casing and then stack each one on top of each other. Your magnets exist in the stack, although they can never reach each other outside of the casing. MultiU is the tool that allows you to reach any magnet in any casing that already exists. There were always multiple versions of you existing in infinite different realities. Your soul is like the magnet; it's in every one of those casing versions of you. MultiU is the mirror letting you see what you shouldn't be seeing." Sandra watched as Cecelia swallowed, hard. She didn't blame her; Sandra was packing many years worth of research into a single conversation. Still, she continued.

"Now replace my analogies with your body and your soul. Your body may differ, but your souls are drawn to each other. Your souls will always find a way back to the other souls they were drawn to. In this case, those examples would be Alina and Alister; and you and Alina. Your body exists in every plane of existence, right on top of one another. You just can't reach the other universes; until now." Sandra swiped away the whiteboard with her hand and it poofed out of existence.

Cecelia sat mouth opened, stunned into silence. After a long while, too long for Sandras's liking, she blinked twice and said, "Okay, I believe you now that you created this machine." She clapped her hands together.

Sandra smiled. "Good, now let's get on with it. Here is the plan. I will type instructions for what you must do when you reach Universe A. MultiU will be our communication source. Just read the code from Universe X, and I will talk to you through there. I will be here tracking your every move. Your job is to bring Alina back to Building C and get her to go through the mirror. You cannot directly tell her, or you will trigger the flag that John Ether has placed into the system. You must raise suspicion in Alina and get her to follow you on her own accord."

"I could dress preppy to make her dislike me. She doesn't strike me as the kind of girl who would appreciate that." Cecelia's eyes lit up with excitement.

"Uhm, yeah, sure. I'll type in code, and MultiU will provide you with everything you need on the other side," Sandra said as she typed. "Make sure to leave behind clues for her so she gets suspicious. I will send you an official letter for Alina to find, which should do the trick."

Sandra hurried Cecelia toward the mirror.

"Thank you so much, Cecelia. Find my baby and bring her back. One last thing, find Teddy and bring him back too. MultiU will give you everything you need, and I'll be right here in Universe X when you get back."

They embraced in a tight hug, and as they let go, Sandra grabbed hold of Cecelia's hand. She gently pushed Cecelia backward, and Cecelia disappeared through shattered glass.

CHAPTER EIGHTEEN

UNIVERSE A-TEDDY-PAST

Teddy handed his money to a barista with two different colored pigtails, square glasses, and a bright orange shirt. She cheerfully gave him his change.

"Have a caffeinated day!" she said.

Teddy gave her a bland smile and waited at the pickup station for his drink. He watched as a man in a grey suit with curly hair and a scruffy beard walked away from the ordering counter. Teddy noticed a fifty-dollar bill slip from out of the man's pocket. Teddy rushed over to pick it up for him.

"Sir, you dropped this." He waved the money around to the man.

"Thank you so much! I'm late for work today, and my mind is all over the place," the man said.

"No worries, man, it happens to the best of us. Where do you work?" Teddy asked.

"I work for Ether corporation. The top floor of Building A, but I sometimes help at the bank around the corner here," the man said.

"Wow, why would you need to work for a bank if you work for Ether?"

"I like the view from my desk." The man winked.

"My best friend works there too. You may know her—Alina. She works in Building D." Teddy perked up.

The man scratched his beard as he searched his brain.

"Hmm, no, it doesn't ring a bell. But you seem like a bright young man; come by the building sometime, and I'll see if I can get you a job there if you're interested?" he offered.

Teddy's eyes lit up. He would love to work alongside Alina, but he'd heard the horror stories of her boss, Logan.

"Thanks, man, I'll think about it!" Teddy gave him a fist bump.

A barista with black hair and buck teeth placed two drinks on the counter. "I've got a hot chocolate and a praline cappuccino for Teddy," he shouted.

Teddy thanked the barista and walked toward the door.

"See you around, Teddy," the man called out.

On his way out, a woman, still in her pajamas, opened the door for Teddy. He heard the barista call, "I've got a cappuccino for Alister."

The doors shut behind him, and he turned left toward the apartment he shared with his best friend, Alina.

A woman's heels clickity-clacked behind him. He walked slowly, careful not to spill the drinks. He stepped to his left, against the wall of an abandoned building, to let her pass since she sounded like she was in a hurry. To his surprise, she stopped right in front of him.

Her appearance did not surprise him but somewhat confused him. She wore pink leather pants with a pink crop top and a tiny pink handbag. He looked up at the clouds that were darkening with every passing second. He glanced back at the woman in front of him. *No jacket in sight*, he thought. He wondered if she was freezing in that outfit.

She held two envelopes in her hand: one red and one white. "Teddy?" the blonde woman said.

"Uhm, yes?" Teddy raised an eyebrow.

"My name is Cecelia Abernathy. We need to talk." She grabbed the hot chocolate from his hand and sipped. "Mmm, I needed this. Thanks!"

Teddy stared blankly at Cecelia; too stunned to object.

"A peppermint hot chocolate? Man, your world is cool. We don't have these where I'm from," she said as she wiped her mouth.

"Come with me." She grabbed his now free hand and pulled him in the opposite direction of his apartment.

"Uh, look, I'm not interested in whatever you're selling." He pulled his hand free.

"Gross! Never say that again." She glanced back at him.

"What do you want, really? Do you need money?" Teddy asked.

Cecelia turned around to face him. "No, I don't want your money. I want you to follow me."

"How did you know my name?" Teddy asked.

"Well, if you'd just follow me, then you would find out. I won't bite you," Cecelia replied.

"You're crazy. I'm not following you anywhere. Please leave me alone." Teddy said as he turned away from Cecelia.

"Do you ever feel like you don't belong in this world? Does it feel like there's a tiny hole with vicious spikes gnawing at you from the inside?" Cecelia asked him.

Teddy turned to face Cecelia but said nothing.

"You do feel that don't you? I know why. Come with me and you'll find out," Cecelia said.

Teddy glanced around the street, making sure there were witnesses before he agreed to follow her. "Okay, where are we going?" he asked.

Cecelia held onto his hand and led him to the Ether corporation.

"Keep watch; tell me if anyone is coming," Cecelia ordered.

They approached Building C, and Cecelia typed a code into the scanner.

She then led him down the hallway to the unmarked door.

"Are you going to kill me? Because I'm starting to regret my decision. Just so you know, I'm letting you drag me here." Teddy said as sweat formed on his brow.

"No, you cute little child. I'm here to save you," she said.

"Child? We look the same age." Teddy muttered.

She closed the door behind them and pointed to MultiU.

"Okay, little buddy, we have about ten minutes until you need to return to your apartment, so I will make this quick. This right here…" she made a circle with her finger at MultiU, "… will send you to another universe. You will meet your grandma there who will take care of you. You are Alina's son."

Teddy opened his mouth to speak, but Cecelia cut him off. "Yes, I know I don't have time to explain how weird that is, but believe me, it's true. Your father is a man named Alister. I'm here to get all of you out of this universe before we destroy it."

"We?" Teddy asked.

"Me, you, your grandma Sandra, your mom Alina, and father Alister. Keep up, Teddy Bear. We have two minutes left." She glanced at her gold watch.

Teddy's mind swirled with questions. Mostly, he was just wondering why this prostitute was making up some grand story for him.

Cecelia handed Teddy a red envelope. "This is for Alina. You'll give this to her and tell her you're moving out today and that you'll be gone before she gets home from work. When Alina leaves, I'll drop by your apartment and help you escape." She checked the time on her phone. "One minute left. Any questions?"

"Why do I need to leave?" he asked. Maybe she was telling the truth, or maybe she was lying, but he figured he better find out what he could.

"Alina is in danger here. She's in danger everywhere, and so are you. John Ether, her father, is a deranged man. He has been manipulating and controlling Alina for years and she doesn't remember. Her mom, Sandra, is stuck in another universe. You need to leave so Alina can find you, leading her to reunite with her mother."

"Alina's mom disappeared. You're telling me you know where she is?" Teddy asked.

"I know exactly where she is, and MultiU is going to take you both there," Cecelia said.

"Look, this was entertaining for a minute, but now it's creepy. Unless you can show me proof, I'm leaving," Teddy said.

"Oh my god, fine, but if you make us late, I'm going to have to go back in time and start this all over again. Sit at the computer system, and I'll show you," she said.

"Wait, this is a time machine?" Teddy asked.

"No, well, sort of. It's time machine adjacent, okay?" she replied.

Cecelia rolled her eyes as she typed into MultiU's system. "Okay, there's your proof."

Teddy glanced at the computer and back to Cecelia. "It's just a bunch of green code," he said.

"Yes, now read it," Cecelia said.

Teddy sighed. "Okay, the first window of code says Sandra is sitting in a library waving her hand." Teddy raised an eyebrow. "You're telling me that Sandra, Alina's mom, is watching us?"

"Not exactly, she's reading our code, too. She's in another universe, waiting for you. Now read the other window of code," Cecelia said.

"Okay. It says John Ether is in the surveillance room, watching Alina sleep." He looked up at Cecelia and continued. "Wait, is this in real time, too? She's being watched right now?"

"Yes. John doesn't have eyes on me yet, and that's why Sandra sent me here, to find you. You're both being watched and you're both in danger." Cecelia said as she grabbed his shoulder. "Okay, times up. You need to break the news to Alina and get out soon before John Ether realizes you're gone."

"But…" he said as Cecelia cut him off again. "Oh my god, child, go!" She shoved him out the door.

Teddy ran as fast as he could, mainly to get away from Cecelia. For some crazy reason, he almost believed her. He wanted to tell her to go away and yet, there was a glimmer of familiarity in her eyes he couldn't shake. *Just follow her instructions and see what happens,* he thought. He hoped the warmth of the coffee he bought would soothe the cold blow to Alina's he was about to cause. But as he peered down at the single cup of coffee that had long gone cold and its foam flat, he knew it wouldn't help.

Teddy knew that leaving Alina was going to cause her to spiral, but if what Cecelia had said was true, and Alina really was somehow his mother, then he had to protect her life over her feelings. If Cecelia was just some crazy woman making up stories, he could just come back and tell her it was all a terrible joke. Alina would be mad at him for a while, and he would have to clean the apartment and apologize repeatedly, but she would come around eventually. Alina was his best friend, and he knew she would forgive him. Teddy decided at once that it was worth the risk.

He rounded the corner of the apartment complex and saw Bob, the homeless man, who slept outside their building. He pulled out all his money from his wallet and gave it to him. *I guess I won't be needing this money anymore,* he thought.

Bob smiled and took the money from Teddy. "You're a good boy. May God be with you, may God be with us all," Bob said.

"It's been nice knowing you, Bob. Maybe we'll meet again in another life," Teddy muttered.

"Ain't no life left for me, Son. Be good." Bob leaned back on his crate and closed his eyes.

Teddy opened the main complex door, walked up the three flights of stairs, and down the sticky hallway floor. He took a deep breath and went into his apartment. He was not surprised, although relieved, to find Alina still sleeping; she was always late to work. He set down the coffee on the kitchen counter and took out the envelope. He peered down at the letter between his fingers, contemplating if he should open it before Alina saw it. He moved his fingers to the opening, and just as he was about to tear it, Alina cascaded out of her bedroom door. He quickly shoved the letter in his back pocket.

"Teddy! Good morning. Why are you so sweaty? Why aren't you dressed for work?"

Teddy's heart began to race as he followed the instructions from a crazy woman, hoping she was right while praying she was wrong.

***

Alina slammed the door shut, and Teddy felt the weight of the world crushing his chest. He imagined Alina was feeling much worse. She never truly recovered after her mom's disappearance, and this was Teddy's chance to help reunite them. He was doing this to save her; at least, he had to believe that, to keep his knees from buckling to the ground.

"What have I done? Why did I do that to her? Teddy, you screwed up so bad! What have I done?" He paced the living room in circles.

Tears streamed down his face, and he was about to chase after her, tell Alina it was all a sick joke, and beg for her forgiveness when there was a knock on the door. A knocking would be putting it lightly; it was thunderous pounding. *She's very impatient*, he thought.

He let Cecelia in, his shoulders slumped over, and he refused to look her in the eye.

"What have I done?" he said again to the floor.

Cecelia gave him a hug that wasn't reciprocated.

"You did the right thing. You will be reunited with her soon," she comforted Teddy. "I'm sorry to rush you, but we have to go. We have to get to Building C to bring you where you need to be." Cecelia walked towards the door.

"Okay, I just need to get something from my room." He walked to his bedroom closet and brought back a white teddy bear with a blue bow.

Cecelia's eyes widened.

"Where did you get that?" She asked.

"Alina gave this to me when we moved in together. She found it in her mom's closet while cleaning their old house. She thought it would be cute because my name is Teddy and well… you get it," he said.

"Yeah, I do get it." She smiled warmly. "Grab your keys, too; we're taking your car," Cecelia stated.

They drove on the main city road.

"Oh, there's Alina!" Cecelia shouted.

They watched as Alina approached the bank and ran straight into a pole.

"Oh my god, we need to help her!" Teddy gasped.

Cecelia continued to drive.

"She's okay. This is how she meets Alister, so it needs to happen."

Teddy watched as the man he saw at Caffeine City that morning ran out of the bank and attended to Alina.

"Alister. My father." The realization hit Teddy almost as hard as Alina hit that pole.

"What's that orb of light?" Teddy asked.

"It's energy. Alina caused a break in the energy flow of the universes. She doesn't know it yet, but she just saved us all." Cecelia said.

***

Cecelia started up MultiU, and it roared, its powers in defiance. It didn't seem to like being used, either.

"So, this machine will take me to another universe?" Teddy swiped his hand along the sphere.

"Yes, the mirror is the portal. Don't ask me how it works, and don't ask your grandmother, either; unless you want her to go on an hour-long rant." Cecelia shook her head.

"What does it look like on the other side?" Teddy asked.

"They're all different, and some are more similar than others. The place you are going to will be vastly different, but you'll be safe there," she reassured, taking note of Teddy's fidgeting.

"Okay, is there a magic phrase I say to get it to work?" he asked.

Cecelia snorted. "No, Teddy Bear. Walk up to the glass and look at your reflection."

Teddy did as he was told.

"Okay, now you need to look at yourself. Don't just glance; really look. Then touch the glass and go through the mirror. Sandra will be there on the other side," she said.

Teddy would do anything for Alina; he had to see this through. If she was somehow really his mother, then he needed to protect her, and if Sandra was his grandmother, then he believed she would protect him.

He clutched his teddy bear and observed his curly hair as he brushed his hand through it. His eyes looked tired, and his face seemed to look smoother than he remembered. He traced his skin as the blemishes on his face disappeared. Teddy's reflection slowly transformed into a teenager, and then, all at once, his figure morphed into a young boy, looking no older than five years old. The boy in the mirror hummed as his shoulders swayed back and forth. Teddy matched the boy's movements as the hum lulled him into a trance. He wanted to call for Cecelia, but his voice would not cooperate. His hand raised involuntarily, matching his younger image, then pressed it into the mirror to meet the boy's hand and was pulled in with a swirling force.

***

UNIVERSE X-Teddy and Sandra -past

"Teddy!" a woman's voice called to him from a distance. "Oh, thank God! It worked! I'm here, baby. It's okay." Sandra dug her knees into the grass and stroked his hair.

Teddy gradually opened his eyes, noticing a sudden change in his body. He felt different, smaller than before.

A four-year-old Teddy lay on the grass, pressing his teddy bear into his chest. Sandra scooped him up and carried him to the couch.

Teddy sobbed, "Mama! Where's my Mama?"

Sandra embraced him until he calmed. "Mama is coming."

Sandra wrapped a blanket around Teddy and rocked him to sleep. She sang the same lullaby she used to sing for Alina as a small child and that Sandra's mother used to sing to her and Bob when they were young.

"Hey, little bug, when your eyes feel heavy and your heart feels warm, sing this song to escape the storm. Down the trap, down the trap, close your eyes. Down the trap, down the trap to find your surprise. Hey, little bug, close your eyes."

Sandra kissed Teddy on the forehead as he drifted off to sleep.

***

The cows mooed in the field beyond the trees, as Sandra stretched her arms and stepped off from her bed. It had been three days since Teddy arrived. They spent their time picking apples that Sandra would later use to cook up a version of apple pie. Without any other ingredients, it was just baked apples, but Teddy enjoyed it without complaint.

The chocolate cake remained in the fridge, untouched and unacknowledged.

Every morning, they brought apples to the horses, and Sandra would tell many stories of his mother's childhood.

"Tell me another!" Teddy would say as he clapped his hands, and Sandra would happily oblige.

In the evenings, Sandra brought Teddy to the computer system that tracked Alina and read aloud her movements like a book.

"Mama went to her childhood home today," she said.

Teddy's eyes lit up.

"And then what happened?" he asked.

"She had a big meal, and your daddy came and picked her up, and then she went home," Sandra summarized.

"And then what happened, Grandma?" He'd lean forward in anticipation.

"Mama thought of you. She remembered how much she misses you and can't wait to see you soon." Sandra held back tears as she read.

"I miss her too." Teddy's big round eyes looked glossy as he yawned.

"That's enough reading for tonight; let's get you to sleep."

"Okay, Grandma." Teddy trotted to his room and hopped into bed.

Sandra kissed him goodnight, and he drifted off, clutching his teddy bear.

***

The cows mooed in the field, and Sandra opened her eyes. The days felt less mundane now that she had Teddy with her, but they still felt too repetitive for her liking. Her heart felt fuller now, but she knew that until Alina returned to her, she would never get rid of the nagging wound in her that ached with every breath.

She stepped onto the carpet and out of her mother's bedroom, peered through the door of her brother's old room, and checked on Teddy, who was sound asleep.

She walked to the kitchen, poured a glass of milk, and waited for him to wake up.

A flash of light illuminated the dawning sky.

Sandra stilled as she observed a body emerge from thin air and land on their back in the field in front of her house. Sandra couldn't contain her joy as she let out an excited scream, knocking over the glass of milk.

"She's here!" Sandra felt as bright as the light shining through on her skin. She ignored the spilled milk as she swung open the door and ran outside. "My baby, I'm here!" She ran down the steps and came to an abrupt halt.

"Ow, my back. Where am I?" A man with curly brown hair and a scruffy beard lay on the grass before her.

"Are you… Alister?" she exclaimed.

"Where am I? What happened?" He stood up slowly as he gained his bearings.

"It's okay. Please take it easy. You're safe. Where is Alina?" Sandra said.

Alister looked at the strange woman before him. "I don't know. She disappeared into a mirror, and I chased after her, ending up here." He gestured his hand outward.

Another light flashed, and Alister and Sandra shielded their eyes. Cecelia landed gracefully on her feet. Sandra's face paled.

"Don't be so shocked, Sandra; I told you I'd pull it off. Oh, and the key to landing without it hurting is to run and not stop kicking your feet until you arrive at the next universe." She dusted off her black ripped jeans and black hoodie, feeling relieved to wear comfortable clothes again.

Cecelia glanced at Alister, who had a perplexed expression.

"Oh hey, Alister," she winked.

She noticed Sandra's displeased expression and her smile faded. "What's wrong?"

"Where's Alina?" Sandra's worry was growing by the second.

"She's not here? I went in the mirror after the two of them went in," Cecelia said.

They shared a moment of silence and simultaneously ran to the library room, through to MultiU, leaving Alister outside.

They brought up Universe A, B, and C in the system.

"No sign of Alina in Universe A," Sandra said as she clicked on Universe B. "Oh no!" She backed away from the computer. "The system must have glitched, sending her to universe B. No, no, no! We must get her out, now, or her father will kill her. Her own self might kill her if she gets out of the hospital and finds Alina there, in her place," Sandra said.

Alister leaned by the bookshelf and cleared his throat. "Would you ladies mind telling me what the hell is happening?" He looked at Cecelia and scrunched his nose. "Aren't you meant to be the devil reincarnated? Who are you?"

"Ah, I see why Alina finds you so charming." Cecelia rolled her eyes.

Sandra, realizing the delicate situation, ignored her panic momentarily to tend to Alister.

"Cecelia, stay here and keep track of Alina, and report back to me on what you find." Sandra focused her attention on Alister. "Come with me, Alister; we have much to catch up on." Sandra guided Alister to the living room.

Cecelia joined the two, who were sitting on the couch, enjoying a cup of coffee—one of the few luxuries John had bestowed on Sandra.

Cecelia spotted Teddy sitting on Alister's lap, and she thanked the stars she didn't have to be there for that sappy reunion.

"Glad you're up to speed, Alister. Now, let's talk about how to get Alina back here before John—" She made gun sounds and gestured with her fingers.

"Cecelia, that's enough!" Sandra snapped.

"Sorry, sorry. I was just trying to lighten the mood. I actually have a plan. I'll go to Universe B and lead the way back to the mirror. She's still suspicious of me, so it shouldn't be too hard," Cecelia said.

Alister straightened himself in his seat. "I think I should go. She trusts me," he said.

"You work for Ether in that universe, Alister. MultiU will flag you and notify John if you go there and interact with Alina. Cecelia's plan is best, and she will go and bring her back," Sandra stated.

"Daddy works for Ether, too." Teddy perked up while talking to Sandra.

"This daddy doesn't, sweetheart," Sandra said.

"Yes, he does. He told me when I was big." Teddy nodded.

"Alister? What is Teddy talking about? Is this true?" Sandra asked.

Cecelia shifted in her seat.

"Well, sort of. I work in IT over there some days to make an extra buck. Teddy saw me at the coffee shop, although, I didn't know who he was then." Alister tensed in his seat.

"Well, that's good. Now we have another person from the inside who can help us take John down," Sandra said.

Cecelia eyed Alister up and down. "Right, okay, back to my plan. According to MultiU's tracking of Universe B, they're at the grand reveal of MultiU, for the elites right now. They think Alina A is their version of Alina. I'll go there and get her to follow me back."

"What if you get lost like Mama?" Teddy chimed in.

"I won't, buddy, but if I do, I trust you'll find me." Cecelia's soft spot for Teddy grew, reminding her of what was at stake.

Cecelia held Teddy in a tight embrace and Teddy hugged her back. Sandra's hand rubbed Cecelia's shoulder when she let go of Teddy.

"Thank you, Cecelia. You don't know how much this means to me," Sandra said.

"I won't let her get lost again, I promise," Cecelia said to Sandra.

"I know you won't." Sandra's lips curled upward.

Cecelia turned her attention to Alister, who had gotten up from his seat and joined the group.

"Alister, take care of them." She extended her hand and Alister shook it. His handshake was firm, like a businessman proving his worth.

"Of course I will," Alister said.

Cecelia pulled her hand away, fluffed her curly locks, and rounded the corner of the kitchen. "I'll see you all soon," she shouted as she walked into the library's hidden room.

Sandra, Teddy, and Alister listened to the rumble of energy flowing and watched the shadows of lights flashing until the rumbling stopped. The sound of glass pierced their ears as it fell to the floor, followed by clinks and snaps as the glass rebuilt itself into the mirror's rim. Silence permeated the walls.

The three of them stared at each other for what felt like hours but only lasted minutes.

"What do we do now?" Alister asked.

"We wait," Sandra said.

There was a long pause before Sandra spoke again. "I wanted to thank you," she said.

Alister cocked his head.

"For what?" he asked.

"I was watching MultiU as Alina ran into the pole. I saw that you ran out to help her," she stated.

"There is nothing I wouldn't do for her. I love her; I always have."

Sandra cocked her head up. "Always? Did you know her before that incident?" she questioned.

"Sort of; we went to the same school, but she didn't remember me. You don't seem to remember me, either." Alister's eyes diverted to the floor.

"Your name did sound familiar when I first read about you on MultiU, but I couldn't place where I knew you from," she admitted, embarrassed by her memory lapse.

"You were my mentor, but I don't blame you for not remembering me. I've changed a lot since childhood. I'm just grateful to be here to help Alina and her family. Well, our family." Alister smiled a warm smile while he rustled Teddy's hair.

"I'm grateful Alina has met such a lovely young man. I saw how you supported her. She needed someone to see her, and you did; you saw her. So, thank you." Sandra pressed her hand to her heart.

Alister looked around the room, noticing the worn-down wooden interior.

"So, John's kept you trapped here this whole time? That must have been hard," Alister said.

Sandra stiffened as she tried to block the memories of her time in her prison world. "Yes. Come, I'll show you around the place. Some fresh air will do us good."

Teddy latched onto Sandra's hand as they walked outside, with Alister following closely behind.

"This is how you spent your days?" Alister asked as he approached Maybel, who neighed and backed away from him. Sandra soothed Maybel with gentle strokes.

"Sorry, she's not used to new people yet. Yes, this is where I spent many days alone until I found the hidden room. Then, most of my time was spent there with Alina." Sandra paused. "Watching Alina." Sandra stared off into the distance as the trauma of being alone crept in again.

Teddy squeezed her hand, snapping her out of her trance.

"But then Teddy came along, and the world didn't feel quite as lonely anymore." She leaned over Teddy and kissed the top of his head.

"I'm so sorry you had to go through that," Alister empathized.

"Thank you, Alister. Here, let's go inside; I want to show you something else."

Sandra led them back into the house and around the corner to the library. She scanned the bottom of the bookshelf and retrieved the red photo album. "This is what saved me. I had plucked it off the shelf to look at photos of Alina when she was a baby, and the shelves opened up, revealing the hidden room and MultiU."

Alister looked at the album, and Teddy volunteered to turn the pages for them. Sandra smiled as she slipped a photo out from the clear slot.

"Ah, this picture is one of my fondest memories. Alina had just learned to walk, and just as she was about to take a step for the camera, she twirled around and landed on her back end, and she laughed; the kind of silly laugh only babies have mastered. That's when I nicknamed her Alina Ballerina." Sandra looked up at Alister, who had a warm smile stretched across his face.

"That's a great story." He rested his hand on her shoulder.

Teddy turned the pages until the very end. "Grandma, when is Mama coming back?" Teddy asked.

"Soon, baby. Come, let's make you a snack. Sliced apples, okay?" She scooped Teddy up in her arms and walked to the kitchen.

Alister studied the photo, still in his hands, and smiled. He slipped the photo of Alina into the inside pocket of his jacket and zipped it up. He carefully closed the photo album and gently placed it back on the shelf.

"Save some apples for me!" he called out to Sandra and Teddy.

Suddenly, Sandra screamed from the other room, and a knife clinked as it slammed on the wooden floor. A flash of light barrelled through the front yard.

"She's here! This is it!" Sandra could hardly contain her excitement.

Alister raced to the front door to be the first to greet Alina but was abruptly stopped by Sandra.

"Wait. Remember, she doesn't understand what is happening right now. We don't want to overwhelm her. Take Teddy and stay in the bedroom, and I'll call you to come out when I think she's ready for you both," Sandra said.

Alister looked to Alina, who was lying on the grass, seemingly unconscious, then met Teddy's eyes and held his hand.

"Come on, Son. We'll see your mom soon." Alister walked to the master bedroom, holding Teddy's hand in one of his and clutching the photo of Alina in his chest pocket with the other.

Sandra inhaled and exhaled with force as she stood at the doorway, blinking her eyes, to be sure it wasn't her imagination. This was it; she was really reuniting with her daughter. She held tears back when Alina's eyes opened.

Sandra ran to her.

"Alina Ballerina!" she exclaimed.

CHAPTER NINETEEN

UNIVERSE X-ALINA-PRESENT

"…and that's how you arrived here," my mom gestured to the room. Cecelia was grinning ear to ear and Alister's face looked pleased, yet hard to fully read.

My throat prickled at the back as I swallowed what little saliva was left.

"Where is the Teddy from my universe?" I asked.

"He's here. He's the same Teddy you knew in Universe A. When he crossed through the mirror, MultiU chose the path for him from there, the path he was always meant to be on. Teddy, like everyone else, exists in every universe, unless tampered with. My theory is that he was never meant to exist in Universe A as your best friend, and MultiU balanced out the universes when he crossed it," Sandra said.

"Are you saying someone tampered with Teddy's life, too?" I asked.

"I don't know, It's just a theory," Sandra replied.

"Are there other versions of Teddy out there or is he the only one?" I asked.

"There are other Teddys, who are not directly your child, who exist in other universes. His soul is all the same, though. In the same way that your soul is the same in Universes B, C, and the rest of them. Every version of you, me, and everyone has had quite different experiences that helped shape your current personality and life. Yet, just like Teddy, our souls are the same. You are my daughter in every universe, even if the other versions of you don't know this. You are the daughter I raised, though, and that makes you my family, my true family," Sandra smiled.

"Okay, I'm starting to understand, but can you explain—"

Cecelia cut me off, "It's like magnets; they stick together or something, I don't know; Sandra explained it better." Cecelia slumped back in her seat, embarrassed.

"It will all make sense in time. For now, you need to rest because we have a lot to do," Sandra said as she took the coffee cups to the sink to wash them.

Cecelia's eyes darted from Alister to me and back to Alister. "I'll go help." She stood from her chair and went to assist Sandra in the kitchen.

Teddy walked over to me and smiled his big grin. The same grin I remember from my universe, only he was missing a few front teeth.

"Hi, Mama." He curled into my arms, and I felt a warm, unfamiliar sensation for the first time. I felt warmth grow inside my heart as its thumps synced with his.

This is my son, I thought. *This is my Teddy. He needed to leave so I could find him.* I stroked his curly hair and rocked him.

"Hi, Teddy." I smiled down at him as he nuzzled his face into my chest.

Alister sat up from the rocking chair situated beside the fireplace and sat down next to me.

"This is pretty weird, isn't it?" I asked.

"Yes, but it feels right. You have always felt right to me, Alina." Alister rubbed his thumb on my hand as he held it, and we sat in silence, watching the warm flames flicker in the fireplace.

For the first time, the stillness of the world around me did not make me anxious; I felt peace.

"Dinner is ready. Sorry, it's not much." My mom placed three trays of baked apples and a pitcher of milk on the table.

"Nutritious." I looked down at my plate, trying to hide my disgust.

I ate until my stomach felt just full enough not to have to eat any more apples.

I collected all the dishes as my family chatted amongst themselves.

My family. What a beautiful phrase. I never thought I'd say those words again and feel their meaning.

Cecelia approached me and picked up a grey dish towel hanging from the oven.

"Can I help?" she offered.

I flinched because I still felt uneasy around her. Just hours prior, she had been the one causing all my pain and suffering, and there she was, trying to be my best friend, apparently.

"Sure," I muttered.

She dried the plates, and I moved to the forks.

"You know…I did all this for you and Teddy. In my world, you were so happy to have Teddy, and I couldn't let you both suffer," she said.

"I know; it's just going to take some time for me to comprehend that." I stayed silent for a moment and then glanced at her. She was placing the plates in the cupboard; she seemed calmer than in my world but still held her head high with natural confidence.

"The black clothes really suit you," I offered a crumb of kindness.

She faced me and tucked a blonde curl behind her ear.

"Thanks, the pink was a bit—" She twirled while making a vomiting gesture with her pointer finger.

I laughed. I guess she was kind of funny, in a class-clown kind of way.

"Thank you for helping me and my family." I smiled.

Maybe one day we would be good friends.

Mom gathered us around the library as we sat criss-cross in a circle while Teddy rolled around between us.

"Now that we are all together and caught up to speed, it's time to execute the final plan. It won't be long before John and the other versions of Alina and Alister notice something is awry," my mom said, and she avoided eye contact with me.

"Can the other versions of us help? There are infinite versions of us out there, right? They can't all be evil. We could create an army, and they wouldn't stand a chance," I suggested and eyed the group for their approval.

Alister said, "That would be too risky, wouldn't it? John would be keeping track. He probably already knows already we're here."

"Yes, you're probably right." Mom glanced at the mirror, looking increasingly uncomfortable.

"Besides, if there are infinite good versions of ourselves, then there must be infinite bad versions of ourselves, too," Cecelia added.

"That's right, and we can't take that risk," Mom said. She eyed the mirror again.

We all took a simultaneous deep breath in, except for Teddy, who went around the circle, bopping each person's nose.

"It looks like we're going to have to take down the Ether corporation and MultiU ourselves," I said, with unwarranted confidence.

"Can I help, Too?" Teddy asked me innocently.

"Of course, Teddy." He jumped into my arms, and I hugged him.

We all stared at MultiU as it seemingly stared right back at us. The holes in its sphere reminded me of hundreds of tiny eyes watching us like a spider waiting to catch its next meal. Or maybe it reminded me of a monarch butterfly. Perhaps its eyes would bring beauty and peace as it watched over us. I hadn't decided whose side this machine was on—ours or John's.

"Okay, since no one is going to get up, I guess I'll be the first to start." Cecelia rolled her eyes and walked to the machine.

She pulled up Universe B on the computer screen and read aloud.

"John and Alina are in Building C walking their investors through the process."

"Alina types in code as MultiU's mirror lights up. Mr. Leon, the investor, steps into the mirror and disappears."

Mom cut Cecelia off while the rest of us circled around the computer. "They have begun the widespread launch. That version of Alina is back from the hospital, which means they probably know our Alina was impersonating her. Let's start erasing universes while they're distracted," Mom said.

"Good idea. Sandra, tell me what to type, and I'll do it," Alister chimed in. His taking charge made my heart beat faster. He was even more handsome than his other selves. He was more attractive than the husband version of him in Universe B. Power does not look good on him. But here, it was inspiring to watch him take the lead and protect the family he didn't know he had until recently. I shook my head, knocking the daydreaming out of my mind, and turned my attention back to the task at hand.

"Let's start with worlds we don't know anything about yet. Who knows what they could be up to," I suggested, and the group nodded in agreement.

Mom instructed Alister to enter a code I didn't understand. I did catch the last part Alister typed; it read:
<-UD-Z-1-all>

I watched as Alister clicked a button, but it didn't look like it was the enter key.

Beep. Beep. Beep.

MultiU blared so loudly that everyone fell to their knees, cupping their hands over their ears, except Teddy, who was screaming. I ran to him, covered his ears with my hands, and guided him out of the room to bring him outside. Horses neighed from their stable, and the cows mooed angrily. The noise was still loud outside, but not ear-piercingly loud.

"It's okay, Teddy. I'm here. It's going to be okay." I cradled him for a long while until the air was finally still.

"Everything's okay now. You can come back in," Alister called from the front porch.

I picked Teddy up and returned to them as he clung to me.

"What happened, Mom?" I asked.

"Your father put a tracker on every universe, and it seems that MultiU just exposed us," she said.

"We've successfully destroyed those universes, but we have to act quickly," Alister said as he clicked on Universe B.

Mom peered over his shoulder. She was silent momentarily while she read the words on the screen, then looked up, but not directly at me.

"Guys, we have a problem. They've gone through the mirror." She pushed Alister out of his seat and furiously started typing and entering code:

<-D>UB-UA-UC>

She faced the group who were hovering over her anxiously.

"Why haven't you pressed enter?" Cecelia asked as she bit her fingernails.

"Listen, guys, when I delete this, they will come here, and we'll have to destroy the machine to truly destroy them. I am going to stay here and fight them off. All of you need to run right now. Run as far as this prison will allow you to and hide," she commanded.

"No, Mom, we aren't leaving you!" I protested.

Mom stood up and wrapped her arms around me and Teddy, who was nuzzled into my neck.

"Alina, I am going to keep you guys safe no matter what it takes. If they take me hostage or worse—just stay hidden until they're gone," she said.

"What if they take you? What do I do?" I asked.

"You found me once; you can do it again. Do you remember what I told you when I was teaching you to ride your bike when you were five?" She pulled away and placed her hand on my cheek.

"Yes," I said through tears.

"Good." She looked at Alister. "Take care of my family."

Alister nodded.

Mom rubbed Teddy's back and leaned down to hand him his teddy bear, which was lying on the floor.

Cecelia hugged my mom, and mom whispered, "Thank you" to her.

"You need to leave now." Mom's eyes held back tears.

The rest of us ran out of the cottage together. We ran to the horses and stayed with them. That was as far as we could go before the sirens started wailing from the house, which was loud, but bearable from that distance. We held our ears until the alarm stopped.

Everything was still. The cows stopped mooing. The horses stood at attention. I wanted to run to my mom, but as I held onto Teddy's hand, I knew I couldn't make any risky decisions. Alister stood up; he slowly crept to the apple trees and peered through. We followed but kept a safe distance behind him.

"Guys, something is happening in the grass, just there. Do you see it?" He pointed to the grass a few feet away from the front porch.

A swarm of light radiated from the ground and ascended into the air, forming a circle, pulsing in rhythm to a beat I couldn't hear.

"It's the light! I think it wants us to follow it," I said then continued, "It's going to save us!"

CHAPTER TWENTY

UNIVERSE X-ALINA-PRESENT

We moved quickly as we hurried toward the light, crossing the barrier of trees, and I reached out to touch it.

"Alina, no!" Mom sprinted down the porch and leaped across to push Teddy and me out of the way.

Teddy and I rolled to the side, and my back thumped against a tree stump. Teddy was next to me, hugging his bear.

The light turned a deep red as Mom pushed herself up from the ground and yelled, "Run, Alina!"

Sparks of red light flew out in every direction like fireworks, singeing everything they landed on. One fell on my leg, burning a hole through my dark blue jeans.

Alister picked Teddy up and dragged him behind the trees. Cecelia followed Teddy. I knew I needed to run but couldn't look away from the flares. The vibrational humming called to me like a siren.

"Alina!" I heard my name, but I didn't look away.

"Alina!" the voice was louder.

Suddenly, the voice was clear. My mom was dragging me by both arms and pulling me behind the tree to join the others. Holes peppered my clothes, and my cheek felt hot and tingly.

"Stay right here. Do not come out, and do not make a sound," Mom was direct, but her voice was shaky.

The shards of light dissipated, and the air felt thick with an unseen smoke. The haunting sound of an immense earthquake roared through the ground, followed by the softer thuds of bodies hitting the grass accompanied by loud groans.

"Agh!" a man moaned.

"My head," another man whined.

"Where are we?" I recognized this woman's voice.

"Dad, where are we?" I heard my own voice talking and clenched my hands to my mouth to stay quiet.

"Hello, John. Welcome to your prison." Mom was acting tough, but I knew she was scared.

"Where's the girl?" I heard my father say.

"That girl is your daughter, and she's not here," Mom said.

"She's no daughter of mine. My daughter, the perfect Alina, is right here."

"In the flesh." I imagined Alina 2.0 smiled a dumb grin.

God, is that what I sound like? I cringed.

"Alina, do you know who I am?" Mom said.

"No. But Dad told me not to trust you," she said.

"I'm your mother. Your father has been lying to you this whole time. He sent me to this universe to stop me from seeing you."

"Wow, really? That's so sad, for you." Alina 2.0 laughed.

My heart ached for my mom. That was not another version of me; she was a shell of me; her brain manipulated by John.

I looked at Alister and used my eyes to ask what we should do.

Alister shrugged and mouthed, "We wait."

Cecelia held her legs to her chest as she bit her nails down to nubs. I looked at Teddy, who was reaching his arms out for me, and I mouthed that it would be okay. I then pressed my finger to my lips to signal him not to make a sound.

"I know she's here, Sandra. Did you think the machine that *I built* wasn't going to tell me that?" John scoffed.

"Well, I deleted the other universes, so I don't know where she is or if she's still alive," Mom said.

"You tried to delete them, but of course, you failed; just like you failed to create the blueprint for MultiU," John taunted.

"I chose not to build it so that I wouldn't become a monster like you," Mom spat.

"Sandra, just tell us where they are. We don't want to hurt them. We just want to put them back where they came from," Alister 2.0 chimed in.

I looked at my Alister and smiled. Alister shook his head and mouthed, "No, don't believe him."

My smile faded.

"They aren't here. I told you. You can just kill me now, go create another universe, and leave," she said.

I wanted to scream, but I held back for Teddy's sake.

"Actually, Mom, that's a great idea," Alina 2.0 said.

I heard movement and struggling sounds but couldn't decipher what was happening. My body shook like I'd had seven coffees.

"Alina, this is Alina. I have a knife to your mom's throat. You have five seconds to come out before I jam it into her neck. 5…"

I looked to Cecelia and Alister for what to do. They were both shaking their head no. I looked at Teddy, who was unaware of the gravity of the unfolding events.

"4…3…" Alina 2.0 shouted.

"Come on, princess, you don't want to see her bleed out now, do you?" John said. The sound of his voice made me want to vomit.

"2…" Alina 2.0 sounded impatient.

I thought about what my mom said; she didn't want us to move. I decided to listen to her.

"1," Alina's voice sounded angry. I clenched my eyes shut and held my breath as tears flooded my face.

I whispered, "I'm sorry," as I awaited my mom's fate.

"Alright, you called my bluff. I told you we aren't going to kill any of you. We just need you to live in a shitty universe so MultiU can let us live in a perfect one," Alina 2.0 said.

She seemed to believe she was doing nothing wrong, and I hated her. I hated John for what he did to her, to my mom, and to Alister. I sure as hell wasn't going to let them hurt my son.

I retrieved a stick from near my ankle, careful not to make a sound, and slowly sharpened it against a rock.

"Guys, they aren't going to show themselves. Let's just have a look around," Alister 2.0 suggested.

I heard Alina tell John she'd check the stables. John said he'd check inside the house, and Alister would stay put to watch my mom. As their footsteps faded, I heard my mom speak again.

"Alister, don't let them control you like this. You're a good man."

Mom tried her luck to win over the new Alister.

"Am I a good man? You don't even know me." His voice was cold.

"I know you love my daughter. And I trust she's chosen a good man," she said.

"Alina hasn't chosen anything for herself in her entire life. Isn't that right, Alister?" Alister 2.0 shouted at the trees.

What does he mean by that? Does he know we're hiding behind the trees? I thought but stayed silent.

"But you're right. I am good," Alister 2.0 continued. "Good enough to notice that shoe popping out from behind the tree over there."

I heard Alister 2.0's footsteps approaching the tree to my left.

"Alina, run!" Mom yelled, just loud enough for me to hear, but insufficient to alert John and Alina 2.0.

There wasn't enough time to run.

"Boo." Alister 2.0 crouched beside me so close I could smell the tuna sandwich he had for lunch.

I raised the stick and jammed it in his chest, but it barely made a dent against his shirt. He grabbed me by my hair as I waved my hand frantically along the soil, searching for another stick. I grasped something sharp that cut my hand and I glanced down to find a knife clutched in my fist. As Alister 2.0 dragged me off the ground, I swung my arm into his face, driving the knife into his eyeball. Alister released me from his grasp, and fell to the ground, screaming.

I bolted up and grabbed Teddy from Alister's arms while gesturing for my Alister and Cecelia to get up.

Tuna Breath Alister was on the ground crying in agony as his eye poured blood into his hands.

We had to take our chances with John to get to MultiU and attempt an escape. I immediately regretted that decision when we were face-to-face with John, who was in the chair waiting for us, with an unnerving grin.

"Hello, my family, and random girl, who I do not care for," John said.

He glanced at each of us individually, but his stare seemed to linger when he looked at me and then at my mom. *Why is he smiling like that?* His smile faded as he met Alister's eyes and cleared his throat.

"Idiots, all of you," John said. This time, his lingering stare was aimed at Alister.

"You're a monster." I looked at John with hate in my eyes.

"You'll see that's not true, in time," he said.

Alister stepped forward and clenched his fist, but I held him back.

"Big tough guy, are you Alister? Why don't you show your family just how tough you are?" John taunted him.

Alister stepped towards John, again.

"Don't," I whispered to Alister, grabbed his hand, and pulled him back.

I glanced at Alister, who then straightened his posture, and cleared his throat as he rubbed his chest.

John took a step towards me while Teddy held on so tight to my neck that it was leaving marks.

Cecelia and Mom jumped in front of us and blocked him from getting closer.

"You touch that boy, or my daughter, and I swear, John, you will regret it," Mom said, clenching her jaw.

"Don't get so worked up, Sandra. I just wanted to properly meet my grandson," he said.

John looked sad. His face didn't match all that he had done to us. I studied him like I would a car crash. I wanted to look away, but I couldn't. He glanced at Alister again and continued.

"Okay, I'm bored of this conversation. Here's what's going to happen. I will send you to your own personal universe where you will live out your lives alone. Sound good? Good." John turned to MultiU and typed in some code.

Alister lunged toward him, tackling him to the ground.

"What are you doing?" I heard Alister say to John as they struggled on the floor.

"Dad!" a familiar voice shouted from behind me. I turned around to see Alina 2.0 charging at Teddy and me.

Cecelia grabbed Teddy from my arms seconds before Alina 2.0 threw me to the ground. We tumbled and turned on the floor. I pulled her hair, and she punched me in the stomach.

My body didn't feel the pain as the adrenaline surged through my veins. In the flurry of fighting, I saw Alister 2.0 run into the room.

Mom ran to him and punched his good eye, and the rest was a blur as I fought off the evil bitch version of me. I clawed at her perfectly hollow face as she tried to rip me limb from limb. My body was tired, and I struggled to gain my bearings after the third blow to my face. I saw Teddy standing in the corner, screaming, "Mama!" as tears streamed down his face. I needed to get to him; I needed to help him, but I was pinned down.

Where is Cecelia? Why is she not protecting my boy? I can't fight any longer. My brain was foggy, and my eyes were blurry from the blood dripping down my brow.

"Mama!" he shouted again.

"Mama!" His voice was all I heard.

The blows to my face stopped. Alina 2.0 looked up at the crying boy, seemingly frozen for a moment in time.

"Teddy?" Her voice was shaky as she crouched over me, unmoving, looking at him. *I guess somewhere deep down, she has a soft spot for Teddy, too.* I used this opportunity to push her off me. Mustering all the strength I had left, I crawled to Teddy.

I held him as tightly as I could when Alina 2.0 slowly emerged from her trance, stood up, and inched toward us.

"I wasn't going to kill you. But I've changed my mind," she said.

She looked deranged as if she'd start frothing at the mouth at any moment.

I looked to my mom for help, but she was still on the floor, fighting John. Alister was winning his fight with Tuna Breath but didn't notice Teddy and me in the corner. He didn't hear my shouts, and I couldn't risk Mom looking away for a second.

I covered Teddy as much as I could and braced for what was to come.

Out of the corner of my eye, I saw Cecelia rushing in, holding an axe. She hit Alina 2.0 with the end of it, and the bitch fell to the floor, unconscious. Cecelia kicked John's head over and over until he fell unconscious, too. Alister didn't need any assistance because he had just delivered a blow that knocked Tuna Breath out cold.

"Cecelia Abernathy gets shit done. Brace yourselves, it's about to get weird," Cecelia said as she raised the axe above her head and, with all her strength, smashed the axe into MultiU. The machine crackled and popped as glass shattered to the floor.

The ground beneath us rumbled, and piece by piece, the room began to erase like a puzzle being picked apart. I tried to hold Teddy tightly, but he broke away, too, until my hands were empty.

The room swirled and warped in a patterned fashion. The world around us dissolved into shadow, swallowing all colors, and plunged everything into an abyss of darkness.

CHAPTER TWENTY-ONE

UNIVERSE ZERO-ALINA-PRESENT

Darkness clung to every curve and crevice like a secret waiting to be revealed. The air around me whispered with an eerie stillness.

"Teddy!" My voice echoed, but everything else was silence.

"Mom!" I shouted. I thought I heard a faint voice in the distance but couldn't decipher it from my echoes.

"Alister! Cecelia! Can anyone hear me?" The ground beneath me was cold.

I stretched my arms out in front of me to feel for something to hold onto. My hands landed on a cold, rough surface, which stretched upwards. They felt like jagged rocks or crystals, but I couldn't know for sure.

"Mom!" I yelled again.

From far away, my ears focused in on barely audible voices. I held my hands against what I believed was a wall and let it guide me forward—or backward. I didn't know which way I was going or if I was even hearing anyone. *It must be in a tunnel*, I thought. I blinked my eyes; trying to see something, anything, but this tunnel was an impenetrable cloak of pitch black.

I walked through what seemed like a never-ending course. My hands had gone numb from the cold rocks grazing my palms. Droplets ran down my arms, soaking my sleeves. *Is it water or my own blood? Is it someone else's blood?* I shook my evil thoughts away.

"Teddy!" I called out again.

"Please be okay, Teddy," I whispered.

My feet had gone numb now, too. Somehow, I lost my shoes in the fight, but I'm lucky that's all I lost. Each step on the ground sent a piercing jolt of cold through my bare soles. I willed myself to take another step as each stride became a negotiation with agony.

"Mom! Teddy! Alister! Can anyone hear me?" I shouted again, but my voice felt weak.

"I'm here, Alina!" someone said.

"We're over here!" came another voice.

Two people shouted back at me. I couldn't determine who was talking, but I knew I was getting closer. A jolt of energy burst through me, and I walked faster.

"Mom! Where are you?" I shouted, stronger this time. I took longer strides and ignored the shards of rocky ice beneath my feet.

The voices were close now, and I could hear clearly.

"Alina, I'm here," my mom said.

I took one hand off the wall and stretched my hand out to feel for her. It met her hand, and she pulled me in for an embrace.

"Oh, thank God, Alina. I was so worried. Are you okay?" She held me close as I let out a wailing sob.

"I'm okay, but where is Teddy?" I asked through heaving breaths.

I felt a hand on my back.

"We don't know. Alister and Teddy aren't with us." I recognized Cecelia's voice.

"We'll find them," my mom reassured.

"Are you both okay? Is anyone hurt?" I asked, suddenly realizing my own body's pain again.

"We're okay, but we need to get out of here before hypothermia sets in. It's too cold in here," Mom said.

"We need to keep walking to find the boys. Let's hold hands so no one gets lost," I said, taking my mom's hand and then feeling around for Cecelia's.

I was relieved to feel their slightly warmer hands against mine.

We walked in a line, our steps synced together, creating an eerie hollowness the tunnel seemed to swallow.

We took turns shouting Teddy and Alister's names, which proved useless.

Time seemed to stretch; with no visual references, we could have been walking for five minutes or five hours. We walked silently, holding in our suffering, as we searched for hope in an endless void.

I stopped abruptly, and Mom and Cecelia stopped with me.

"Did you see that?" I whispered.

"All I see is my death sentence," Cecelia said.

"No, honey. What are you seeing?" Mom asked.

"It's there," I said, realizing that I couldn't point, nor could they see where I suggested. "Look really hard. Do you see it?"

A light from far away, or maybe close by, was now visible. Its beaming rays vibrated as if welcoming us to approach it.

"I see it now!" Mom exclaimed and clenched my hand tighter.

"I see it, too. Let's go!" Cecelia yanked on my hand, pulling me forward and dragging my mom to follow suit.

The light seemed to get further away as we walked to it.

"Maybe it's a mirage," I said, questioning if we were all losing our minds, as we neared death.

"Maybe, but we have no other choice. The boys may be there," Mom said. My chest felt heavy as I thought about Teddy. *I can't lose him again.* I shook off the thought and focused on the light that finally appeared to be getting bigger.

"We must be close," Cecelia said, as we could see our silhouettes. The air surrounding us felt warmer, as if someone had turned on the heat, and I was grateful.

A vibrating orb buzzed and glistened, illuminating the surrounding area. It floated between two large mirrors connected to two metal spheres.

"The light led us to MultiU," I said, a smile formed on my near-frozen lips.

The light was bright enough to brighten where we were.

We let go of each other's hands and looked at each other and then at the tunnel. My mom's lips were a shade of purple and chapped, but she seemed otherwise unharmed. Cecelia had bruises on her arms and cheek, yet her hair was still in perfectly curled ribbons.

I observed myself in the mirror, and I looked sickly. My hair was akin to a rat's nest, and my face was pale with a tinge of purple. My hands had lost most of their color, and my palms were smeared with blood. I didn't dare look down at my feet.

I looked to the punishing walls and saw jagged rocks from the ground up to the top, stretching over the ceiling to the other side.

Without a moment to lose, Mom switched on the left mirror and gestured for me to turn on the other.

They clicked and whirred on with force, further illuminating the room. We shielded our eyes from the sudden burst of light until our retinas acclimated.

The mirror no longer showed my reflection. Instead, it swirled its mesmerizing blue and purple lights, dancing as if inviting us in.

"Which one do we go through?" I asked.

"I don't know, but I think we should choose quickly," Cecelia said.

We held each other's hands again and started toward the mirrors.

Before we could choose, a voice powered through the tunnel. John's voice spoke to us, but we couldn't see him.

"You thought you could destroy what I created? You have no idea what I am capable of. Sandra, I warned you many years ago that if you tried to interfere, you would regret it, and that promise remains true. Before you are two mirrors. You have one choice to make; choose wisely." John seemed to enjoy playing with his mice, which were trapped in a never-ending maze.

We looked on with horror as Alister appeared in the left mirror and Teddy appeared on the right.

Alister's hands were tied up with rope as he pleaded, "Alina! Don't trust them."

I looked to the right mirror, and Teddy clutched his bear as he cried, "Mama! Help me."

Their images snapped out of existence, and the mirrors continued their alluring swirls. We stood still for a moment before simultaneously realizing we needed to act. I looked to both my mom and Cecelia, who were now standing in front of me.

"You guys need to save Alister. I'm going to save my son," I commanded.

"We will get him out and save him. Don't worry," Cecelia said.

Mom pulled me in an embrace. "Be safe, Alina. We will wait for you on the other side," her voice calmed my nerves.

I released her, looking her in the eyes.

"I'll find you again; I promise," I said.

Cecelia and my mom held hands and ran into the left mirror. I protected my face as glass shattered outward and fell to the ground.

"Mom will save you, Teddy. I'll find you, too," I said to myself before taking a deep breath in. I took a few steps backward and charged the swirling lights of the right mirror with all my strength.

***

I flung into the air, where I saw Teddy standing on a hill; I grasped him with both arms but couldn't slow my momentum. We toppled over and rolled down a hill. Screams from Teddy and me were muffled by mouthfuls of dirt and dandelions. We reached the bottom and abruptly stopped against a park bench. My body took the brunt of the impact, and Teddy recovered quickly.

"Mama! You saved me," he cheered innocently.

I grabbed his teddy bear, now soaked from a puddle under the wooden park bench, and handed it to him.

"We can't forget your bear." I ruffled his hair and held his hand as we explored our new world.

I still had all my injuries from the fight at the white cottage and my time in the dark void, but at that moment, I felt no pain. We were in a large park; the sky was cloudy, and the air crisp. It was not nearly as cold as the tunnel of death, though. I straightened Teddy's grey, long-sleeve shirt, which had turned a brown and green shade, covered in mud and grass. A soccer team of pre-teens played and cheered in the field ahead of us. Children swung on the swing sets, and mothers chased their toddlers around a water fountain that erupted periodically. Fathers played frisbee with their sons, and dogs chased each other's tails beside them.

I smiled at Teddy when he tugged on my arm.

"Can we play?" he asked.

"We sure can, buddy. But let's play tomorrow after we get cleaned up and get some much-needed rest," I said.

"Awe, okay, Mom," he replied, and we continued back up the hill.

I could never get tired of him calling me mom. Just the other day, he was my best friend, and now I'm *Mom* to him.

I think we'll still be best friends. The normalcy of whatever new world we were in, was refreshing. It was not perfect, but I thought it felt like home. We stood at the top of the hill and peered down the other side; a gravel pathway led to a parking lot packed to the brim with cars. We walked down the main road past the parking lot, and I recognized where we were, or rather, where we used to be. I turned back around to face the park again. My hand raised to my mouth as the realization flowed over me. This was the land where Ether was built. This world must have been a world without the Ether corporation.

"Mommy, are you okay?" Teddy peered up at me as tears filled my eyes.

"Yes, baby, everything is perfect. Let's go home." I smiled, and we crossed the road to Main Street.

I observed the people around me, and my shoulders relaxed to match theirs. They seemed happier and lighter as if their bodies moved in a wave. The kind of movement you can only get when you've not been traumatized. Their jaws remained unclenched and their arms open, inviting people in. In my old world, everyone looked tense. Everyone's jaw was one grind away from cracking a tooth. I waved as kids trotted past us, playing, and giggling to a game I'd never understand.

Couples enjoyed their coffee at the local Bean café. I opened my mouth to tell Teddy how our favorite coffee shop had changed but realized he probably didn't understand, or maybe, those memories were still there somewhere hidden in his brain. I wanted to joke with him that my eyes were not assaulted by intrusive lighting, nor were they saddened by all the chrome coatings. This world felt colorful without trying. As I peered down at Teddy, I remembered he was so much more than the Teddy I used to know. We had a lifetime of new memories to make, better memories.

We arrived at my apartment complex, and I was startled to see a familiar man standing before us.

"Alina! My niece, it's so good to see you. We have a lot to catch up on," Bob said.

Niece? What is he talking about? I thought.

Bob no longer looked scruffy; he was dressed in clean jeans and a black jacket.

"Bob! You're not dead! Oh my god, I thought they killed you when I heard gunshots in Universe B," I said.

Bob shook his head and said, "I managed to escape, and I've been waiting for you and the rest of our family to find out the truth, and you did! When Sandra arrived, I was overjoyed! And…"

"My mom is here?" I cut him off.

"Yes, sweetheart, your whole family is here. I told you we had a lot to catch up on," he chuckled.

I opened the complex's front door, and Teddy pranced up the stairs as Bob and I followed behind him.

"So, you're my uncle? I'm guessing Ether is behind your homelessness, but why didn't I know who you were? Why have I never met you as my uncle?" I asked as we started the second flight of stairs.

"You have—many times. You can thank John Ether for wiping your memory and punishing us, but let's get you and Teddy inside and get some clean clothes. There's plenty of time for catching up." He patted my back.

I had so many questions to ask him, but Bob was right, we had time. All I wanted at that moment was to see my mom again, so I put my questions on hold.

We walked on the floor of level three, which was neither sticky nor pristine. Bob opened the door, and the chatter in the room stopped as my mom, Alister, and Cecelia rushed over to greet us.

"Alina Ballerina! Thank heavens you're alright!" Mom hugged me and Alister swooped Teddy up.

Cecelia took turns hugging Teddy and me.

"It's so great to see you all. How did you guys get here? How did you save Alister? I have so many questions for all of you!" I was overjoyed yet, bewildered.

"When we arrived at the other end of the mirror, we ended up in this universe. Alister was not in danger at all. We found him with Bob, who was helping him out of the parking lot," Cecelia said.

"We did it, baby. We're home," my mom said as she brushed my cheek.

Alister cleared his throat behind me. I twirled around and wrapped my arms around him, and we kissed. It would have been more magical if my family weren't observing the performance.

"I'm so glad you're here, Alister. A life without Ether's control. Can you believe it?" I said in amazement at all we had accomplished.

"Of course, I can believe it. You're a badass," he winked.

"Alina, why don't you and Teddy get showered and cleaned up? I'll cook some food, and we can have a nice picnic dinner at the park." Mom started in the kitchen, pulling out pots and pans.

"Sounds perfect. Just no apples, please," I quipped.

Everyone shuddered in disgust and let out a belly laugh.

"Never again," Mom said.

I turned the hot water tap on in the shower, and Teddy and I stepped in. The water ran down like a blanket of heat as the soap washed the dirt away. Teddy splashed in the water and giggled while he splashed me. For the first time, I didn't daydream of a better life. I was right where I wanted to be.

I reached for two soft, brown towels and wrapped one

around Teddy. We walked to my bedroom. White bedsheets lay tightly fitted around my bed. I thought of the bedsheets Teddy had gifted me and wondered if I'd ever see them again. I opened the black wooden dresser drawers beside my bed and found rows and rows of little boy clothes for Teddy. I handed Teddy fresh clothes and searched the second drawer to select mine, which happened to be exactly my size.

We joined the others in the kitchen. Mom passed out food for each person to carry. We exited the building and strolled together as a family to the park. The sun beamed down on my face, and I beamed back at it. The sky looked almost perfect. I locked my eyes on a single cloud that was graying with every passing second.

Alister placed his arm around me with his free hand, the other hand balancing mom's famous pasta salad. Cecelia wiped her brow as she carried water bottles while Mom held a tray of chocolate muffins. Bob brought the cheese and cutlery. I was sure I had caught glimpses of him sneaking bites of the cheese on our walk.

We arrived at the park, picking a spot along the grass, next to three other families.

Teddy sat next to me, and we dug into the food.

"So, what's next for us?" Mom asked.

"Anything we like," I said, watching the sky as it showed off its yellow and red palate.

It was beautiful, but that single cloud kept catching my eye. It was so dark now that I felt a storm would erupt on us at any moment.

"Mama, let's go play on the swings." Teddy stood up and pulled my hand.

"Okay, but we'll have to be quick before it gets dark. I looked down at Teddy's hand and realized his bear was not with him.

"Hey, Teddy, where is your bear?" I asked.

"Grandma took it," he said.

"Why would she do that?" I asked.

Teddy shrugged. Come to think of it, I hadn't seen his bear since we went into my bedroom.

"Mom, have you seen Teddy's bear anywhere? Teddy said you took it?" I asked as my eyes scanned the grass surrounding us.

"What bear, honey?" my mom said.

I shot my head up at her, confused. "The bear he never lets out of his sight. Have you seen it?"

Mom shooed away my question with her hand.

"Oh, it's just a bear; I'm sure you'll find it." She turned her head to continue a conversation with Cecelia and Alister while they laughed amongst themselves. Mom knew how important her old teddy bear was to all of us. Irritated, I pressed her further.

"Teddy said you took it, and I believe him. Where is it?" I asked.

"You know how kids are. They have wild imaginations," Mom said.

I looked to Bob, who always had a kind thought to share, but he would not look at me. He was concerned with opening his water bottle after consuming half of the cheese plate.

"Cecelia, any thoughts on where the bear is?" I asked.

"Oh my god, Alina. It's not that serious," Cecelia said.

Alister chimed in. "She's right, sweetheart. Come sit next to me and relax."

I clenched my jaw. *Why are they acting like this?*

I looked back at Teddy, who was still holding my hand, gazing longingly at the swings. In the distance, beyond the hill and behind the trees, I spotted a pulsing light.

I slowly glanced back at my mom, observing her. I then shifted my focus to Alister, Cecelia, and Bob. They looked happy—too happy. Their smiles seemed as if they were stapled from either side. Their eyes looked dull and empty, not matching the smile plastered on their face. Their skin looked off like it didn't quite fit their bones. I squeezed Teddy's hand tighter as chills swept up my back and down my arms.

"Well, okay, we're just going to go on the swing for a bit. We'll be back." I pushed Teddy along until we took enough steps to where they were out of earshot.

"Oh, Teddy, here, let me tie your shoe," I announced dramatically.

I bent down and whispered, "Teddy, I need you to listen to me and keep looking at the swings." I didn't look up to check if he followed my directions and continued. "These people are not our family. I don't know who they are, or what universe they came from, but we need to leave now. There is a light just over the hill and down through the trees. On my count of three, you are going to hold my hand and run to it."

I looked up at him, brushed my hand along his cheek, and hugged him. Teddy nodded in agreement, seemingly understanding what was at stake. I stood up and placed my body between him and the others. I whispered to Teddy, "Be strong. Be brave. And do not let go. One …two…three, RUN."

CHAPTER TWENTY-TWO

UNIVERSE A-ALISTER-PAST

Alister watched the swarm of students pouring in through the door of classroom 201 for advanced physics. It was his favorite class to attend, and it was not because Mr. Brian was a great teacher, although he was. It was not because Alister was considered too intelligent for this class either, but he certainly was. It was because he got to spend the day with the love of his life, Alina Ether.

He sat on the furthest desk against a back wall littered with graffiti which Alister had drawn on throughout the semester. No one ever noticed the wall, and, sometimes, he couldn't tell which was more invisible, the wall or him. He twiddled his pen between his fingers, which would not stay put, while he waited for her every day. Every day at 2:02 PM, she would stroll into the classroom.

Alister tensed his shoulders and smoothed his curly hair as she, like clockwork, made it to class. Alina seemed to float as she walked in, clutching her physics book to her chest as her straight chocolate-brown hair billowed behind her. Alister gazed up at her as she walked toward the back row. Her smile radiated light into his soul. She placed her notebook on the desk in front of him.

"Hi, babe!" She wrapped her arms around Logan Needleman, who was sitting at the desk to her left.

She kissed him on the lips and Alister's jaw clenched at the sight.

"Mmm, you smell so good. Is that cinnamon?" she said to Logan.

"It is! I bought a new cologne over the weekend." He smiled and Alister recoiled. *Logan didn't deserve her*, Alister thought.

Logan was the typical bro guy who was at the top of the football team. Alister hated him because Logan was too popular and confident. He hated how he clearly must have tricked Alina into liking him by being nice to her and charming. Logan was handsome in a rugged way, while he was handsome in a shy way. Logan was loud and funny, and Alister was quiet and serious. Logan was a snake. The way he gazed into Alina's eyes; no one was that nice. Alister released the pen which had made an indent in his desk.

Mr. Brian entered the classroom and raised his hands in front of him.

"Okay, class. Settle, please. Today is a big day. We're going to be learning about the big bang theory. And, no, not the television show." Mr. Brian looked at the class, amused.

Alister slumped back into his seat. He already knew what Mr. Brian was going to say. Alister knew he could teach the class better than Mr. Brian. He daydreamed about walking to the front of the class and telling the teacher everything he knew. He would explain how the big bang created bubbles of space-time that expanded at different rates, creating infinite bubble universes with other laws of physics, and many similar to ours, thus creating infinite versions of ourselves, existing in infinite universes. In Alister's mind, the class cheered for him, and Alina stood from her seat and swooned over Alister in front of the class while Logan sulked in his seat.

In reality, Alina doodled on her notepad while Logan playfully poked her as she giggled.

Alister should have taken college courses instead of being stuck in the *dumb* class, but he stayed for *her*. He stayed for his Alina. If she would only notice him, he would have the perfect world.

The bell rang, and the class started packing up faster than cheetahs, who saw a gazelle resting nearby. Logan and Alina walked together through the hallway, and Alister trailed behind them. He took in Logan's muscular physique and scoffed when he thought about how easily he could win in a fight against him. He imagined Alina's legs wrapping around his waist as she thanked him for saving her from Logan. Alister walked down the stairs outside to the pick-up zone, put his hoodie over his curly hair when it started to drizzle, and watched Alina and Logan step inside the bus together. Alister waved to her through the window, but she didn't see him. He stayed behind, waiting for his community service case worker to pick him up.

Three months prior, Alister had fought with a boy named James at school. James had bumped into him in the hallway, and Alister punched him straight in the face. The cops were called and decided that instead of suspension, community service would suffice. They went lenient on him because they knew he came from a troubled home. He was in the foster system because his mom and dad were both alcoholics and lost custody. Alister played up this reasoning to the cops as he cried in the hallway. He wiped his tears and replaced his frown with a smirk as the cops walked away.

Jim, the community service case worker, picked Alister up in his silver Mitsubishi.

"Hey buddy, how's it going?" Jim tried too hard to be nice.

"Fine." Alister rolled his eyes and hopped in the front seat.

"How's the community service going at the Ether's research lab?" Jim pried.

"Good, only one session left," Alister responded dryly.

Alister leaned his head against the car window and allowed his mind to drift.

Relieved to be almost done with his community service, Alister exhaled. Having to pretend like he was too dumb to understand what Mr. and Mrs. Ether would teach him was excruciating. He had to play dumb so they wouldn't suspect what he was doing under their noses. Besides, he got to be close to Alina's parents. He imagined how he would be a good son-in-law, and they would thank him for one day marrying their daughter. John Ether was smart, but he wasn't as smart as Mrs. Ether. He used that advantage by buttering up John and pretending to learn much from him. John, in turn, would trust Alister alone in the lab room, allowing Alister to create his prototype. Sandra trusted him, too, but she'd never let him be alone unsupervised. It was John and Alister's little secret—one of many to come.

Alister wiped the smirk off his face as he turned to look at Jim, who was pulling up to a small office building at the end of Main Street. It was situated across from a park filled with happy kids and gleeful but burnt-out parents. He stared at that park every afternoon. *What a waste of space the park is.* If he had it his way, he'd tear it all down and build a palace for him and Alina to live in, a palace where she would have to notice him, and one she could not escape.

"Thanks for the ride," Alister muttered as he shut the car door behind him and opened the front door of Ether's research facility.

John and Sandra were waiting for Alister's arrival, holding balloons and a sign that said, *Congratulations!* Alisters eyes darted between the cheesy decorations and the too-bright colorful lights shining down on them, and he made a mental note that their terrible taste would come back to bite them one day.

"Alister! Good to see you. We're so proud of your progress with us. We got you a last-day congratulations present!" Sandra said and eagerly handed Alister a box of assorted chocolate.

John shook his hand. "It's been great working with you. You are a very bright and promising young man. If you can keep up with managing your anger, I would happily offer you a job at our company," John said.

"Maybe one day I'll even replace you in your position," Alister said.

"Now, don't get too ahead of yourself," Sandra chuckled.

"We thought we'd give you your last day off, seeing as you really put in the hard work these last few months. But first, can you tell us what you enjoyed the most from this experience? We need to add that to the notes for your case worker." Sandra raised a clipboard and positioned her pen.

What he enjoyed the most was his prized work. Mr. and Mr. Ether were too naive to understand his plan, so he figured candor would go past their small minds.

"I enjoyed creating ideas for the future, like mind control," Alister said.

"Ah yes. Your vision for mind control, to assist students affected by personal tragedies and thus help heal them, was a phenomenal contribution. After you graduate, we can work on making that blueprint of yours come true. What do you say, Alister?" John patted him on the back like a proud father.

"Sounds great, Mr. Ether." Alister shoved a chocolate in his mouth. "Hey, do you mind if I go to the bathroom before I leave?" he said while clearing the caramel from his teeth.

"Of course, dear. You know where it is." Sandra gestured behind her.

Alister's shit-eating grin returned as he walked through a long hallway and down the end where the bathrooms were. He glanced behind himself and then slowly opened the door to his left.

He entered the room where he'd been working on his ideas for the past three months. Creeping inside and carefully closing the door, Alister felt with his fingers underneath the round wooden table for the circular metal device taped to it.

John and Sandra underestimated his intelligence; everyone seemed to underestimate him.

They thought his mind control was some silly futuristic

idea, but while everyone was busy looking away, Alister was looking at them. Alister created what no one else could, and he was going to show the world that he was deserving of genuine praise and love. He would force them to look if he had to. The start of his plan was to make Alina love him, but he knew it wouldn't be that simple. You can't make someone love you. You must change the world around them and show them that they need you; that they need your strength. You must let them find you while you hang back in the shadows, pulling the strings.

He shoved the device into his backpack and exited the room as quietly as when he entered. Alister crept to the end of the hallway, straightened his posture, and continued regular strides while observing John's face for any sign he had been caught.

John spoke on the phone. "Okay, Alina, be safe; I love you," he said and clicked the end button. "Alina's going to the park with her boyfriend and will be home after," he said to Sandra.

Alister's body tensed up. He wiped his palms on his grey jeans and smoothed his hair. She was nearby, with Logan.

He grabbed the chocolates and started for the door "Well, thanks, Mr. and Mrs. Ether. It's been really… eye-opening for me." Alister walked out the door before they could get another word in.

CHAPTER TWENTY-THREE

UNIVERSE A-ALISTER-PAST

Alister wiped off the wet swing set with his sleeve and sat down. He gazed up at the cloudy sky. The swing creaked as it swung back and forth, and his curly hair peeked out of his grey sweatshirt hoody. His bony butt ached in his seat, and he smacked his chapped lips together, contemplating going to the drinking fountain across the park, but he didn't want to miss the chance to see his Alina. He held onto the metal handles with one hand while he unzipped his backpack and pulled out his mind control device. He fiddled with the buttons, admiring his work. His heart raced as he heard Alina's angelic voice sling daggers through his eardrums.

"Logan, oh my gosh, you're so funny!" Alina playfully tapped Logan's shoulder, as they strolled onto the freshly cut grass, two feet away from where Alister was swinging.

Alister looked up to see *her*. He watched the sway of her hips glide effortlessly through the field of grass, He laughed as

Logan unknowingly stepped in dog poop. He wondered what Logan was saying to her to make her eyes light up with a belly laugh. Alister knew he could make her laugh that way too, if only she would notice him. He imagined the conversation he would have with her if he were in Logan's place.

"Your smile radiates my soul," he said aloud as he kicked his feet off the ground beneath him. "Let's get married. Let's run away and build our perfect life together," he said to Alina, who was gazing deeply into Logan's eyes.

He watched them as they kissed, puckering his own lips into the air, and kissed what he imagined her soft lips would feel like. Saliva pooled in his mouth when he imagined the taste of her watermelon lip balm he'd seen her apply countless times in class.

Alister opened his eyes and sunk lower into the swing, as the realization slammed back into his mind that he wasn't kissing Alina; Logan was. Alister's hot breath filled the air surrounding him while he clenched the metal handles of the swing. He snarled at the two lovebirds. *Logan doesn't deserve this life with her.* The sight of them kissing made his stomach turn. His calloused hands released from the swing, and he fiddled with his device in his pocket. His frown turned and his left lip flipped upwards. Calm replaced the rage he felt, and a smile crept across his face.

"He does deserve *this*, though," Alister said as he jumped off the swing and stumbled to the ground.

He shot to his feet and swept the dirt off his pants while looking around, embarrassed. Alina didn't even notice his fall. *Am I that invisible to her?* He held the device tightly in his hand. Its edges dug into his skin like a cat's claw begging to be freed. He made slow movements towards the unsuspecting couple. "H-hi." He cleared his throat.

They didn't look at him. Alister straightened his shoulders and tried again. *Be bold, Alister,* he encouraged himself.

"Alina." He commanded her attention.

Startled, Alina jumped back and released Logan, who stepped forward, shielding her.

"What do you want, creep?" Logan said to Alister.

They had never spoken before, but Logan knew of the fights.

"Nothing; I just wanted to show you something I made for you." Alister raised his device, showcasing its metallic perfection.

"Wow, very cool, now go away." Logan rolled his eyes.

Alister looked to Alina, who was avoiding eye contact with him.

"You know what? I think I'll stay." He pressed down on the button marked C and pointed it to Logan.

Logan froze as if he had been pulled in every direction with invisible magnets.

"What are you doing to him?" Alina screamed but Alister ignored her.

"You are Logan Needleman, a dorky guy with no friends, no ambition, and no girlfriend. You wear ill-fitting clothes, and you smell terrible. You will spend your life trying to earn the approval of people better than you, but you will never succeed. Oh, and you'll never remember dating Alina Ether. You won't remember meeting her at all." Alister released the button and Logan's body returned to full function.

Logan looked to Alina and then to Alister. His gaze remained vacant as if lost in the depths of his own thoughts, unable to find clarity amidst the confusion.

"Logan! Are you okay? What did he do to you?" Alina's eyes were wide with fear; her hands trembled as she shook his shoulder.

Logan said nothing as he turned around and walked away. Alina ran to catch up to him but froze mid-run as Alister followed her with his hand pressed firmly on the control button.

"Alina, I'm sorry it had to be this way, but you will thank me one day. I've been here with you the entire time, but you couldn't see me; you could never just see me. That's all I wanted, was for you to look up and just fucking SEE me!" Alister raised his voice as she stood frozen under his control.

Alister straightened his posture, cleared his throat, and rubbed his chest. He self-soothed often, a technique he learned from Jim, his case manager.

"But you see me now," Alister continued. "You'll see me for the rest of your life. You won't remember dating Logan or interacting with him at all. I won't make you love me, Alina; that would be cruel, and I'm not a cruel man. You will learn you have always loved me, in time. Every time you see me, you will feel an inexplicable pull towards me, but you won't know why; that's for you to figure out on your own. Forget this conversation happened and go be with your family. I'll be seeing you soon, sweetheart." He blew her a kiss.

Alister released the button and Alina continued running, despite not knowing why.

He watched as Alina ran to her parents' research facility. Moments later, she was accompanied by John and Sandra as they walked to their car parked against the sidewalk. They seemed happy and clueless as they entered the vehicle, and Alister felt relieved.

He waited until they drove off before walking to the building's back entrance and slipping inside. Sandra's office was at the other end of the hallway. She was the true genius, and he knew if he was going to find something useful, he should start with her.

He rifled through her drawers but only found pens, papers, and plastic forks; nothing of use.

"Come on, Mrs. E. I know you've got something for me here," he said, opening every book on the shelf and rifling through every page in her notebooks. Alister let out a grunt in frustration.

"Come on think, Alister. What would you do if you were hiding something big?" he pondered.

"Oh, of course, I'd tape it to something. Geniuses think alike," he chuckled.

He slid his hand against the wooden underside of her desk and felt paper brush his fingertips. He carefully peeled the tape from the desk and lifted the papers from underneath.

"What is this Mama E?" His eyes rested on an image of a spherical metal device with a long tail connected to a mirror. The heading was labeled **Project MultiU,** and it had a red X crossed through the page.

He focused on the second paper that read, *"Blueprint for altering universes proven a success by my calculations."*

A smirk crept across Alister's face as he shoved the papers in his backpack. He cleaned up the mess he had made, covering all traces of his presence, and left the way he had come in.

He walked to the Cozy Nook coffee shop, which had just had its grand opening last week, and ordered a water and a coffee. He needed his energy for it was going to be a long night. He observed the coffee shop; the dull, lifeless baristas made half-assed attempts at getting people's names right as they called out each order. He wondered if the workers felt as invisible as he did.

"This place could use some color." he said to the girl as she typed in his order.

"Yeah, I guess." She mumbled without making eye contact.

"I'll make this place so bright people will have to notice it," he said. "What?" The barista looked up and frowned.

"It will be my gift to you. The ignored recognizes the ignored," he said. "Uhm, okay. Well, your total is $15.99, not including the mandatory tip," she said.

"For one coffee?" Alister raised an eyebrow.

"Yes." She stared at him blankly.

He handed her a twenty dollar note and walked to an empty table in the corner of the room, facing the window.

Alister sat unmoving for hours, admiring the paperwork sprawled out on the table, planning his next move.

"Excuse me, kid, we're closing now." A woman in her late 40s began sweeping under his table.

Alister retrieved his things and exited the café. Following the trail behind the central part of town, he made his way to

Alina's house. He had been there many times before, watching her. Not through the bushes or anything; he wasn't a stalker. He'd sit in his car parked at their neighbor's house and watch through the living room window. Sometimes, the man would come out and inquire what Alister was doing, and he would say he was a food delivery man waiting for his next customer request. The neighbor would leave him alone every time. *Some people are way too trusting of others.*

Alister waited until all the lights were out before retrieving the spare key from under a fake rock in the dirt beside their house. He'd seen Alina use this often when she got home from school.

He knew they had no cameras or security alarms from watching the family enter their house and walk in without stopping to enter a security code.

After leaving the door open for an easy escape route, he sharply turned to the stairs.

Surprised to see a wooden plaque hanging from a bedroom door with ALINA etched into it in pink letters, Alister traced his fingers through the letters. It was as if she were inviting him in, so he slowly turned the knob to find Alina sprawled out in her bed. His sleeping beauty was dressed in white pajamas, and he had hoped she was dreaming of him. He smiled while he observed her mouth, which was wide open, and her hair tousled around her pillow. He reached his hand out to stroke her hair but recoiled. *No, not yet, she needs to come to you. Love cannot be forced. Only manipulated,* he thought as he willed himself to leave and shut the door behind him.

His attention shifted to another bedroom across the hallway. He knew it was her parent's room because, on nights when he observed them through his car, he could see them. How easy it was to be watched when you think you're not worth watching. Alister entered their room as quietly as he did Alina's, ensuring to turn the knob as slowly as possible. He found them sleeping at either end of the bed, holding hands. John lightly snored while Sandra slept as silently as she was brilliant. He walked over to John, taking notice of his gold watch rimmed with tiny diamonds. After plucking it off the nightstand and slipping it into his pocket, he gently tapped John's shoulder to wake him.

John startled awake to find Alister standing over him.

"Alister, what the fu—"Alister cut John off with a finger to his lips and held up the MultiU blueprint with the other.

"Come with me, and no one gets hurt," Alister whispered, and Sandra stirred on the other side of the bed.

John jumped up and did what he was told with no hesitation.

"Where are you going, dear?" Sandra mumbled; her eyes still closed.

"Just to get a snack, darling. I'll be right back," he said stiffly as Alister led him down the stairs.

They reached the basement and closed the door.

"Are you out of your damn mind? What do you want? How did you get in here?" John asked.

"I want to show you what your wife has been doing behind your back." Alister threw the paper down on an old, leather couch and motioned for John to sit down.

John plucked a pair of glasses from a round table beside the couch and read through the papers.

"Okay, so she created something groundbreaking. My wife is brilliant and kind, so that's why she didn't follow through," John said.

"You're not mad that she's overshadowing you?" Alister asked.

"No, of course not. We're a team, and we've created a beautiful daughter and a successful business together. Now, please leave my home before I call the cops." John stood up and ushered Alister towards the basement door.

Alister remained firm on the carpet. "John, we have a chance to change the world. You have a chance to lead your family to greatness, and I'm going to help you. You said you would hire me one day, remember? Well, that day is now."

"Son, I was just being nice to you. You are obviously a troubled kid, and I would never allow you to actually work for me," John said.

Alister took a step back, and his wounded eyes drooped.

"But you liked my mind control idea." Alister found himself desperate for John's approval. He rubbed his chest while clearing his throat.

"Your mind control idea is childish. No one has that capability, and no one should have that capability. Alister, I was being kind, okay? Now, get out of my house, and do not come back." John grabbed Alister's arm and pulled him towards the door.

Alister shoved John to the ground, causing him to stumble over a cardboard box and land on the floor. John's head slammed against the wall, and he stared at Alister in a daze.

Alister approached John and crouched down so he was inches from his face.

"I expected you to be stronger, John," he sighed, "but I guess I have to do this the hard way." He pulled his backpack from his shoulder and revealed his device.

John watched the circular metal in Alister's hands, too dazed to speak.

"You know what this is, don't you? I can see it in your eyes. I didn't want to hurt you; I'm not going to. You will be safe, and your family will be safe. Let me show you my creation; MY creation, the one you called childish. I'll forgive you this time. Though, if you cross me again, you'll be sorry." Alister waved his device in front of John's face. "This, right here, is my gift to you. You'll see what I mean soon enough." Alister clicked the C button, and John raised his hands to his face before his body tensed up, frozen.

"You will build MultiU exactly as Sandra designed it. You will create a better universe for your family. I am part of your family, John. Alina and I will rule the new worlds beside you, and you will have all the glory, for now." Alister paused, enjoying the dramatics of his speech. His plan was coming together better than he had hoped, and the exhilaration left him wanting to draw out every word.

"You are furious at your wife for being more intelligent than you. You are angry at Alina for not being the perfect daughter. You will build out that hideous park next to your pathetic office building and create the Ether empire. Sandra will help you because she believes you're still in love with her, and when she is no longer needed, you will discard her. You're filled with rage, the only emotion you can feel. Oh, and yes, I will accept your offer to work for you when I finish school. I will be your business partner. I have much to do in this world for my Alina, so I'll be residing in this world. You will not remember this conversation happening. You will fall asleep and wake up a new man; a stronger man, someone with purpose. The time of reset will be 0400."

Alister took a deep breath in. His heart raced from exhilaration.

John closed his eyes against the wall.

"I'll see you in the next world, John," Alister muttered as he glanced at the clock that read: 3:59 AM. He walked up the stairs and through the front door. He closed the door behind him and placed the key from his pocket back under the mat.

***

The bell sounded as the cluster of students barged through the doors, laughing and screeching. Alister sat at his desk, hiding his amusement, as Logan slumped into the classroom, eyes looking down at the ground while he took his seat. Alister watched Alina zip up her white jacket as she approached her seat in front of him. Alina's nose scrunched up when she sniffed the air. She looked at Logan, who rested a hand on his head, and then at the empty seat at the end of the row. She gathered her book and bag and moved to the less offensive-smelling spot in the room. Logan did not look up from the floor when Mr. Brian entered the room.

"Okay, class, today we're learning about quantum consciousness," he said as he wrote the words on the whiteboard.

Today, Alister didn't mind Mr Brian's rambling. Usually, the sound of his too-enthusiastic voice would be enough to make him see red. But today, he saw green. He didn't mind Logan's new, foul-smelling cologne that brought most of the class to tears; it was a reminder of what was to come.

Alister focused on Alina, who doodled in her notebook. He admired her long fingers as she grasped her pen while shading a patch of grass.

He retrieved his own green pen, the exact brand Alina liked to use, and etched a message into the back wall.

You don't love me yet, but you will.

CHAPTER TWENTY-FOUR

UNIVERSE X-2-JOHN-PRESENT

"God dammit, Alister. You are a worthless piece of work, aren't you?" Alister snapped at his other self while he patched up the bloody eye.

"I'm sorry! She was too quick; I couldn't stop her." Alister 2.0 peered up at Alister with his one bruised, but good, eye.

"And you!" Alister sneered as he pointed to John. "You let them escape! The plan was to scare them into jumping into this new prison universe. How did you screw that up so badly?" Alister asked.

"I...I don't know." John looked down at the floor; he couldn't bring himself to look Alister in the eyes when he was angry.

"Half-brain-Alister, do we have eyes on them? Excuse me, eye." He mocked.

"They're in a tunnel, Universe 0, but…" Alister 2.0 trailed off.

"But what?" Alister's fist tightened into two balls.

"The boy isn't with them," Alister 2.0 said.

"Well, you're going to fix it. Think of a plan to get them back here; now," he said to John and stormed out of Building C.

John sat on the floor with his hands on his head. His plan almost worked, and he almost set his family free. When the two Alinas fell simultaneously, fusing three worlds, its energy force lifted the mind control Alister had placed him under. John had spent every waking moment since trying to communicate to Alina that he was there to help her, without being caught by Alister and his minions. John was there the day Alina stumbled into Building A. He saw her, disheveled and shoeless, running up those steps. He told the guards to let her in, and he knew he had to stop her from making a scene before Alister found out. His heart broke into pieces as she stared at him in Building A's lobby, not recognizing her own father standing in front of her. Alister had forced John to lead her to a miserable life for far too long. Now that he had his mind back, he needed to keep his daughter out of danger as much as possible, so he told her to leave, hoping she would back down while he handled Alister in the background.

When Alina 2.0 was in the hospital, all John could think about was his *real* Alina, the daughter he raised. He checked on her through MultiU every day, and even protected her throughout the night, watching her on the cameras Alister had put in place. He knew it was his original Alina when she arrived in Universe B; a father knows his daughter.

He wanted to tell her to go to Universe X to be with her mom, where she would be safe, but Alister would have found out. He called the only person who could help her. He brought Bob from Universe A through to Universe B. Bob was still under mind control, but some of his memory seemed to have returned. John helped him fill in the blanks and instructed him to help Alina at the auditorium. When the time came, Bob was less than subtle and made a scene at the grand opening, leaving John no choice but to play along and report him to protect Alina and not blow both of their covers. The guards were not on John's side, and Bob's fate was in the hands of Alister, who instructed the guards to shoot him. After the presentation in the auditorium had ended, John searched Building C for Alina and Bob. He found his daughter safe in Universe X with Sandra, after searching for her in MultiU's system. Bob's body was nowhere to be found, and John didn't have enough time to search for him in the system before he was questioned by Alister. He made up a lie, which steered Alister's suspicions elsewhere.

When Alister notified Alister 2.0 of their whereabouts in Sandra's prison world, John knew he had to think quickly. While the others were busy outside with his family in Universe X, John set MultiU to a randomized universe setting. He had hoped this would buy his family time to escape, but it wasn't enough. Alister noticed John's suspicious behavior in Universe X and tackled John to the ground.

John glanced at Alister 2.0, who had been under Alister's control, too, and maybe he still was. But this version of Alister looked softer than the son-in-law he was used to, although less bright. John remembered all those years ago when this deranged man was just a troubled boy. He really did want to help him, but he saw an unsettling darkness in Alister's eyes. John couldn't have known how truly evil he could be.

John observed Alister 2.0 and saw something in that version of Alister that gave him hope. He saw weakness in him, or was it his humanity?

John walked up to Alister 2.0, who was crying out of his one good eye.

"Hey, pull it together, we need to come up with a plan quickly before he gets back, or he's going to kill you." John rested a hand on his shoulder. "I have one. It's not a great plan, but we don't have enough time for another; they're in the tunnel right now. We will create a deepfake of Alister and Teddy asking for help. My wife and Cecelia, who think Alister is on their side, will come here to save him. I will be able to keep an eye on them here and keep them safe. Alina will choose to save Teddy, giving my daughter and grandson a chance to escape."

"You'll get yourself killed if he finds out you're helping them. Do what you want, but I didn't see anything if you get caught," Alister 2.0 said.

"I'm already a dead man walking. Look around, man, look what I've done; better me than them. Please, it's my family, my daughter. Save them, and I promise we will be free from Alister's control." John didn't know if he could keep his promise, but still, he held his breath for an answer.

"Okay. I'll look away and whatever you do is on you," he said.

With shaking hands, John typed code into MultiU and pressed enter.

John breathed out a sigh of relief, and before he could thank him, Alister entered the room, fists still clenched.

"Well? What have you come up with?" he demanded.

"They'll be here soon," John said.

"Good man, John. You know, I almost feel bad for destroying your family. Maybe in another world, we would be friends." Alister laughed as he pulled rope and duct tape from his satchel and slung them around his shoulder.

"When they arrive, tie them up. We don't want another incident on our hands." He clenched his jaw as he eyed Alister 2.0 up and down.

Moments later, the mirror began its colorful dance and Sandra and Cecelia ran from the other side, stopping just short of the wall. Alister stood tall with his arms folded like an angry teacher.

"Alister, are you okay? Did they hurt you?" Sandra said as John straddled her with the rope and tied her hands behind her back.

"Oh, I'm perfectly fine. We have a lot to catch up on. It's time you knew the truth," Alister said.

John yanked Sandra up by her tied hands while Alister 2.0 finished tying Cecelia's.

John leaned into her, taking in her sweet scent mixed with sweat. He wished he could tell her everything right then, how he missed her so much, how it wasn't his choice to do what he did. He yearned to hug her again. To her, it had been over five years. To him, it was as if she was never gone; even though, logically, he remembered everything that had happened, it didn't feel like it was him who did it.

"Don't trust them," John whispered into her ear.

Sandra's eyes widened and quickly darted to her husband's. His face looked less tense, his eyes, less narrow. There was a sparkle in him that she hadn't seen in a long time.

"Alister, what's going on?" Sandra asked as her eyes remained on John's face.

"Well, you see, dear mother-in-law, your husband here has been assisting me in creating a world where no one can step over me, or him. No one can look down on me because I already look down on them. I created worlds where your bitch-daughter finally loved me, respected me. She never gave me a chance to show her what a great man I am, so I created a world where she had to love me. I manipulated worlds where everyone would love me, or fear me, same thing. And it was all thanks to you and your blueprint of MultiU. I tweaked it a bit and improved it, but I'm not one for bragging." He winked and his eyes glittered with pride.

"You. It was you? You did this to us? Alina trusted you." Sandra switched her intense gaze to Alister. If her eyes were daggers, then he was the target.

"I know. That was by design. Can't you see, Sandra? Your daughter became the perfect person—well, not your daughter, but a version of her. You really should be thanking me," he said.

"That's disgusting," Cecelia said.

"Ah, the pot calling the kettle black. Wasn't it you who lied to Alina and lured her into Building C?" Alister asked Cecelia.

"She did that to help her," Sandra said.

"And I did what I had to for her. We're not that different," Alister replied.

"We're nothing like you," Sandra spat.

"What do you need original Alina for anyway, if you've already manipulated other versions of her? You got what you wanted," Cecelia said.

"They're still versions of my daughter, though. You're harming all of them," Sandra said.

"You think I want some random version of her to love me? I want MY Alina to see the truth on her own. The truth is that she has always loved me. The other versions of her are just helping me move that along."

"She will never love you," Sandra said.

"She already does. You should have seen the look in her eyes when I helped her navigate your little scheme. You made it easy for me. My backup plan was to have us connected in all worlds through our son, Teddy," he said.

"What did you do to Teddy?" Sandra balled her hand into a fist.

"When I saw how close she was to her best friend, Teddy, in Universe A, I recreated his DNA through MultiU, and with the help of my mind control device, I worked my little charm on her in other universes, and now we are bound together by the person she loves most. Since these versions of Teddy are not naturally occurring in all universes, like the rest of us are, if one Teddy dies, all of them do. Who will she turn to when I take away that love by removing Teddy from the equation? Oh, that's right. She turned to me when you removed him the first time. See, we are similar, we both caused her pain for our own selfish reasons," Alister said.

Anger surged through Sandra's veins as she hurled her

body towards Alister and wrapped her rope-tied hands around his throat.

"I'll kill you right now, you son of a bitch." She pulled the rope tighter, trapping Alister's head between her chest and the rope.

"Yeah, try us, asshole; we'll take out your other eye," Cecelia said to both Alister's.

"If you kill me, infinitely more Alisters will come to destroy you," he said with choked words.

John pulled Sandra off Alister while Alister 2.0 blocked Cecelia from intervening.

John looked at Sandra and mouthed the words, "Not now, trust me."

Cecelia noticed their interaction and backed down, too.

"Tie them together, and don't forget their feet this time," Alister said as he massaged the rope burn on his throat. "You can sleep here tonight and think about what kind of life you'd like to have: one where you never see the light of day in this room, or one where you are free to live your life in this prison world while Alina and I live in pure bliss together? The choice is yours, well, sort of."

"You're a psychopath," Cecelia spat at Alister as he, John, and Alister 2.0 gathered their belongings.

Alister opened the door and paused.

"No, Cecelia, a psychopath does things without purpose." He ushered the men out of the room, shutting the door behind him.

"What do we do?" Cecelia said.

"Maybe we can inch ourselves toward the mirror and get out," Sandra responded.

They moved across the carpeted floor in unison until they approached the mirror.

"Just a little bit further," Cecelia said.

The door swung open, and John entered the room. The girls' eyes widened as shivers rippled through their bodies. The color paled from their cheeks like water swirling down the drain.

"It's okay. Please don't be scared of me. Listen, the more you try to fight this right now, the angrier he will get. He will find you even if you run. Stay put, and we will fight him together," John said, noticing the fear in their eyes.

"Fat chance we're going to trust you," Cecelia growled.

"You're right. I don't deserve to be trusted. But I promise you I'm on your side," he said.

Sandra's eyes softened as she observed the twitch in John's lips. His lips always quivered when he felt emotional. "John? Is it really you?"

John leaned down, embraced Sandra, and kissed her cheek. "Yes, my love. I'm so sorry for what I've done; Alister used mind control on me. He made me believe I created all of this. He made me…" John composed himself and wiped the tears from his face. "I'll fix it, Sandra, I promise. Alina and Teddy are safe if he can't find them." He kissed her cheek and warned them, "Just stay put for now, and act clueless," then walked out of the room.

"Do you believe him?" Cecelia asked.

"We don't have much choice not to believe him right now." Sandra sighed.

"I say we break these restraints and get out of here," Cecelia said.

"And go where, Cecelia? Anywhere we go will put my family in danger." Sandra shook her head.

"And what about me?" Cecelia asked.

"Honey, you're my family too. You might be an Abernathy, but to me, you're an Ether," Sandra replied.

Cecelia couldn't help but smile, as she felt the warm air rise to her cheeks.

They sat in silence for who knows how long. There was no clock on the wall, and there were no windows to see the night sky or maybe the sunrise. Cecelia counted the paint spikes on the off-white walls, while Sandra observed the room for anything to set them free. The room was spotless; there were no knives or tools on the floor, no lamps or glass either, nothing they could use. The two were stuck there, helpless, for at least the night.

Their eyes opened to John switching on the light. He held a bag containing two muffins and a tray with two coffees in travel mugs. I guess they didn't have a Coffee City in this universe. He gently placed the tray on the floor and gestured with his eyes that he did not arrive alone.

"Rise and shine." Alister entered the room with a skip in his step.

"Any sign of my girlfriend and son?" He awaited a response, but everyone remained silent.

"I'll take the silence as a no." He rolled his eyes.

"Where is Alina 2.0?" Sandra asked.

"She's back in Universe B running the company while I attend to my men's failures." He glared at John and Alister 2.0, who averted their eyes.

Everyone but Alister jumped when the roar of MultiU's energy burst to life. The mirror lit up and swirled in an eerily slow pattern, and Alina and Teddy jumped through and over Sandra and Cecelia. They tumbled to the floor, still holding hands.

Sandra looked on with horror as her daughter, unknowingly, just sealed their fate.

CHAPTER TWENTY-FIVE

UNIVERSE X-2- ALINA-PRESENT

"Alina! It's so good to see you." Alister rushed to me, squeezing me in a tight hug. I felt so relieved to find him safe and feel his warm skin against mine.

"My boy." He looked at Teddy and ruffled his hair.

Mom yelled out from behind me, "Alina, get away from Alister. It's him," she warned.

"What do you mean it's him? Why are you tied up? Alister, what's going on?" I asked.

"He built MultiU; he did this to us. Get Teddy away from him, now," Cecelia said.

My mind swirled in every direction, my vision caving in on me.

"Wha—what do you mean? Alister?" I looked to Alister; my eyes begged for an explanation.

Alister's face warped as if he had smelt something terrible and heard something funny simultaneously. "Okay, yes, the jig is up. This isn't going to be some grand speech. I already did that with your family. Here's the gist, sweetheart: you didn't love me, so I made sure you would, eventually. You were an imperfect girl who needed direction in her life, so I created MultiU from a blueprint I stole from your mother, to make you perfect and to make a perfect world. Other versions of Alina love me. You took your time, but you eventually came around. It's too bad about Teddy, though."

I wanted to punch that smug look from his face but chose to take Teddy to a safer distance next to my mom and Cecelia. He said it so matter-of-fact, as if he'd been dangling a carrot in front of me the whole time, and I was too hungry to look up at the beast holding it.

"I thought you weren't going to give a speech? What about Teddy? What are you talking about?" I rolled my eyes in defiance. I was scared, but I wouldn't let him see that. *How could he do this to me? I trusted him. He made me trust him.* I wanted to hunch over in a ball and cry my eyes out, but I needed to be brave, for Teddy.

"You really missed a lot while you were away. I made multiples of Teddy and made it possible for him to be our child so you and I would be bound together forever, by Teddy. I know you love him the most, so I gave you that gift," Alister said and then continued. "But I'm not happy with the outcome, so I'm going to get rid of him. They're connected, so they'll all die."

"You're insane, Alister. I won't let you touch him. Besides, your logic doesn't make sense. What about the other Teddys that do exist in other universes; the ones you didn't create yourself? They can't all die."

"I'm not concerned about those ones, just the ones that connect you to me. They've served their purpose. I'll give you some time to spend with him before it happens, don't worry," Alister said.

I could not believe what I was hearing, and I would not believe it. I didn't know what to do, but I had to think of something to save my family.

The door swung open, and John entered the room.

I shoved Teddy behind my mom and myself, creating a barrier. Mom leaned in and whispered the faintest of words in my ear. "He's on our side, I think," she said.

I could just barely make out the words. *How is my father, John, on our side? Has the world gone mad?* Well, I suppose it had.

"Alina, let me re-introduce you to your father. This is John, my little puppet who does whatever I say. You should know that before I turned him, he loved you very much. But there is no room for his love when you have me. I can and have loved you far better than anyone ever could, and you will soon grow to love the real me." Alister's face looked hopeful but void of real emotion.

"And if she doesn't, you'll just erase her memory?" my mom said.

"Well, I'm going to do that anyway, but yeah, that's the plan. See, I knew you were the smart one, Mrs. E," Alister said.

I stood frozen, unable to form words. I didn't recognize this man, and I don't know how I could have ever believed he was charming and kind. He looked so tiny and pathetic; it made me want to vomit.

"Hey, Alister. There's something in my hand. Could you check it out?" Cecelia said as she wiggled her cuffed hands and let her middle finger free.

"Thank God I don't have to pretend to care about your little girl drama with Cecelia anymore; that was so annoying." Alister frowned at Cecelia, his face then stiffened.

"I will cut that finger off the next time you get smart with me." Alister reached into his back pocket to reveal a blade.

Cecelia put her finger back into a clenched fist.

I stepped in front of Cecelia and my mom, while Teddy hovered behind them.

"How did you know we knew about MultiU before I told you about it? Were you the one watching me and the city in that basement of Building A?" I asked, my mind moving a million miles a second.

"Ah, good question, Alina! I like to see those wheels turning. Of course it was me watching you. I've watched you since we were in high school, ever since I laid eyes on you. I then had your father place cameras everywhere you frequented. You're very cute when you sleep, you know. Yes, I knew everything well before you did. MultiU sees and hears everything I want it to. I played along and went on your little witch-hunt for Cecelia because I knew she would lead you all to the same place. I needed you all together so I could finally erase your universe. The original universe, Universe A, was filled with despair and disappointing people who never respected me. I planned to gather you into Sandra's prison world and keep you there until you were ready to love me—or kill your family; I hadn't decided yet. But now my plan is ruined because someone fucked that up." He glanced over to John, realizing Alister 2.0 wasn't there.

"Where's my dumber half?" Alister asked.

"He's getting the house ready for them, Sir," John replied.

Alister continued his speech as if he didn't ask a question.

"But your souls must live on somewhere, so I chose this universe for your family to die in. If you thought your original Universe was bad, just wait until you see this one." He finally ended his speech.

My god, does this man ever stop talking? How could I ever have been in love with him? How did I not see all his flaws? My mind raced to the memories of when we first met.

Alister had been the first, and only, person to help me when I fell. He just happened to be right around the corner when I needed help when I visited my old home. He was the only person not frozen in time after I fell. He didn't question my sanity when I told him about my suspicions of Cecelia.

Yet, I knew he was acting weird when we went into the Ether basement, and, apparently, he was the one watching me on those screens. He was the one showing proof of Cecelia being the one following me. He is the one who put it in my head that John Ether tortured his family with experiments. John Ether, my father, is a victim of Alister, just like the rest of my family. How did he get a hold of MultiU? I wondered but couldn't bear to hear his voice grind my eardrums further, so I saved the questions for another time. My heart shattered as I realized that I didn't know Alister at all, and I didn't want to.

"John, tie Alina and the boy up like the rest and take them to their home," Alister commanded.

"You're not touching my son!" I reached my hands back and held onto Teddy's shoulders.

"Excuse me, our son," Alister corrected.

"A version of you was his father, maybe, but it was never you, and it will never be you." My words flowed from my mouth like hot lava. I looked at Teddy, who was quivering and crying.

"None of that will matter soon enough. It's cute to watch you all try to fight this, but you can't win this one, Alina. The sooner you realize this, the sooner we can be together and live a happy life." Alister sighed and looked bored. "Okay, his hands can stay free. I'm not a monster." He gestured to John to tie my wrists and connect the rope to my mom's and Cecelia's.

John picked Teddy up and placed him on his side. With his other hand, he tightened the rope and forced us forward out of the unmarked door, through the desiccated hallway, and out of the building. We stumbled forward in utter disbelief, our eyes struggling to comprehend the desolation around us. The once bustling city streets now lay eerily silent, devoid of the familiar hum of activity. The towering silhouette of the Ether building loomed ominously against the horizon, its reflective surface starkly contrasting with the dusty landscape that stretched endlessly before us.

As John urged us forward, each step felt like we were marching to our end. The air hung heavy with a sense of emptiness, broken only by the faint whisper of the wind as it swept through the abandoned streets.

Turning a corner, our gaze fell on a familiar solitary structure—a white cottage perched atop the desolate earth like a beacon of solitude, a haunting reminder of the life Alister had taken from all of us.

Time itself seemed to stand still. The absence of vibrant greenery and the silence devoid of even the chirping of birds—all served as a chilling reminder of our isolation. We were prisoners in a desolate realm, and Alister and his army were the guards.

John led us up the steps into our prison home, and I glanced at my mom, her face etched with a haunting expression of dread. Years of solitude in this house had taken their toll on her, leaving her frail and weary. Yet her eyes still held a flicker of hope as they searched for mine. She had clung to her belief that I would find her, and now that I had, I couldn't let her down. Guilt gnawed at the edges of my mind, but I couldn't afford to dwell on my shortcomings, not now. I shook my body to wash away the guilt, saving it for a later date. I had to be strong for her and Teddy. I would not let Alister get away with this.

We walked inside to an exact replica of the cottage I found Mom in.

John set Teddy down, who then clung to my leg. John retrieved a knife from the brown kitchen drawer and sliced the ropes from our wrists and ankles.

We all stood awkwardly, eyeing each other, not knowing what to do next. John cleared his throat, breaking the silence.

"Alina, my beautiful girl, I am so sorry for what I've done. Alister was controlling me; you must believe me that I would never wish this on you." He paused and looked at Teddy, then Cecelia, and then met Sandra's gaze. "Any of you." John's lip quivered.

I wanted to believe him. I wanted to believe my dad wouldn't destroy our family willingly. I wanted to believe he wasn't some power-hungry maniac who tried to take over the world. I wanted to remember him as my dad, who would bandage my knee after I fell off my bike and scare away the monsters under my bed by singing the monster-repellent chant, but I couldn't yet. I couldn't trust him until I was sure he wasn't the monster under my bed in the first place. He needed to prove himself first.

"If that's true, then help us get out." I crossed my arms.

"I will, but it's not that easy because Alister doesn't know his mind control stopped working on me. I have to pretend that I'm still with him," John said.

"That's convenient," Cecelia scoffed.

John looked to my mom for reassurance, but she averted her gaze.

He slumped forward and walked toward the front door. Placing his hand on the knob, he turned around. "I'm sorry. I'll fix this," he said as he moved to the porch, closing the door behind him.

I waited until I saw John leave and turn the corner before running to the door to open it. "It's locked! He trapped us in here." Heat rushed to my cheeks as I yanked at the door.

Cecelia came to my aid, but it was no use. I turned to Mom, who was tending to Teddy, giving him a glass of water from the sink.

"Mom, what do we do?" I asked.

She looked at me with drooping eyes, and her shoulders slumped over. "I don't know," she said meekly.

"That's not good enough. I'm not going to let them do this to us!" I shouted, then ran to the library and proceeded to pull out every book and every photo album on the shelf, letting them scatter to the floor. The wall behind the bookshelf did not open. My fingers grazed every inch of the walls in a futile attempt to find some hidden passage, another secret door, which would lead to our freedom. But all I felt was the cold, unyielding surface beneath my touch.

The walls mocked me as I tore away their floral paper.

"They removed the secret wall this time," I shouted.

Mom and Cecelia didn't respond, and I heard them playing with Teddy, relieved they were tending to him.

I paced the room; my movements were frantic and agitated as if trying to outrun the suffocating walls closing us in.

I wiped sweat off my brow, unzipped my jacket, and threw it to the floor. I opened a wooden desk drawer to see an assortment of pens next to a small stack of notepads. I laid the notepad out across the table and uncapped the pen. At first, I scribbled as hard as I could, releasing all my frustration on the paper while I yelled until my voice cracked, and I sank to the floor, panting and coughing. I slowed as I listened to Teddy's laughter from the other room. I took deep breaths in and out. *I need to be strong for Teddy; I need to pull myself together.*

My breathing calmed, and I closed my eyes, searching from deep within to find a way out. I thought of the note Teddy's left me, which had felt like so long ago that I almost forgot. I guess it was my mom who actually wrote it, but it still felt like Teddy's voice. The words, *I had to leave so you could find me,* played repeatedly in my head. I had found him, but we were still in this mess, trapped in Alister's fantasy worlds.

What did I miss? I had to leave so you could find me. The phrase haunted me as I dissected each letter.

My eyes shot open; *I get it. I see it so clearly now.* He did have to leave, but it wasn't me who needed to find him. I jumped up with newfound energy and grasped the pen in my hand. I brought it to the paper and wrote the words that were swirling into my mind. I tore the paper off, neatly folded it into a small square, and palmed the note in my hand.

I walked over to Teddy, who was sitting beside my mom and Cecelia. I ruffled his hair, and he turned to me and hugged me tightly. I took in his embrace for a long time; his scent, which smelled of chocolate cake and sweat. I've never appreciated such a mixture before now. I felt his heartbeat sync with mine and stroked his hair, placing the paper in his back pocket with my other hand. I held him for as long as he held me. Though he didn't understand how much that hug meant, he would someday.

Our embrace was gently interrupted by Mom and Cecelia, who placed their hands on both of our backs. I could see the light dim in their eyes. They were giving up, but I wasn't going to let this be our ending. I couldn't tell them my plan because they would never allow it, but this was our only way to freedom.

"Let's get some rest, guys. It's been a long…how long has it been?" Mom said.

"Too long," Cecelia said.

Mom took short steps to her room as if she needed to be pushed from behind to make it to bed. Cecelia sang a quiet lullaby I had never heard of as she soothed herself and closed the door to my mom's childhood room. I crawled into Uncle Bob's old room and snuggled up to Teddy while we fell asleep in each other's arms.

I found myself in the middle of a busy road. Cars and trucks rushed past me and swerved in the opposite direction, narrowly avoiding collision. Horns blared from behind me as tires screeched. I zig-zagged between the cars, calling out for Teddy. I saw him standing twenty feet away from me as an oversized truck barrelled towards him at full speed.

"Teddy!" I shouted as I sprinted to him. My arms and legs moved faster than I could process.

"Teddy!" I screamed again as I made contact with him and pushed him out of the road. I turned to see a bright light, beautiful and elegant. I stared at it, as if in a trance, mesmerized by its rays shining out from every direction. A potent force collided with my body and the light slowly dimmed out of existence.

Warmth tingled through my cells, and I heard Teddy's voice calling my name from a place I couldn't see. A white silhouette walked towards me in the darkness until he was all I could see; Teddy, my old Teddy, the one I went to school with, and the Teddy I shared an apartment with. He kneeled as blood poured from my mangled body and whispered, "You found me."

My eyes shot open, and my heart pounded so fast I swear it would have leapt out of my chest. I ran my hands down my body and checked for any injuries; I was still alive. The night was silent but filled with an almost tangible energy as my thoughts raced through my mind. I peered down to my side to find Teddy still snuggled up next to me, and I watched his chest rise and fall, rise and fall.

I stepped out of bed and tiptoed to the window, where I pushed open the dark green curtains. I was up before sunrise, my body forcing me awake before the world was ready for me. Staring into the night sky, my brain was an overworked clutter of thoughts, as my mind cycled through my plan.

I had to believe this plan would work; it was our only chance at beating Alister in his twisted game. A tiny hand grasped mine, and I looked down to see my son.

"What are you doing, Mama?" Teddy said as he peered up at me with sleepy eyes.

I kneeled to his eye level and pointed to the sky. "Do you see those three stars in a vertical row up there?"

Teddy leaned into the window, leaving a foggy mark against the glass. "There?" he pointed to Orion's belt.

"Yes, baby. If you ever feel lost, find those stars, and you'll know Mama is keeping you safe; always follow the lights," I said.

Teddy yawned and held my hand again as he led me back to bed. I sat up, watching over him as he slept. He stirred when the sun rose from the sky instantly. I guessed in this universe, Alister controlled our sun, because the calm, starlit sky immediately turned bright and intruding like an impatient god flicking a light switch.

Alister really was trying to play God. And maybe John, too. I still didn't trust my father, but he needed to believe I did for my plan to work.

Three knocks sounded on the door, and I opened it. John was standing with a tray of breakfast items: oatmeal that looked like it had been sitting out for two hours, dried up and withered scrambled eggs, toast with no butter, and a single glass of orange juice for us to share.

"I'm sorry. It's the best I could do. Alister said to give you chocolate cake, but I snuck this from my refrigerator for you all." He looked genuine, like a puppy dog begging for approval, but I was going to proceed with caution.

"Thank you. John…dad?" I corrected myself.

"Yes, baby, what is it?" He set the tray down on the glass counter.

"Teddy lost his white bear. Do you think I could take him to Building C to see if he left it there?" I asked innocently.

"Well…I'd have to escort you both there, and Alister would have my head. But, yes, of course, my grandson needs his bear." He smiled.

The others sleepily approached the counter, barely acknowledging John. I guessed they didn't believe him either.

Cecelia ripped into the dry bread while shovelling spoonfuls of oatmeal in her mouth, taking large gulps of the glass of orange juice between bites.

"Okay then, let's go; we'll need to be quick before Alister sees us." John headed towards the door.

"Where are you going?" Mom asked through a bite of her bread.

"It's okay, Mom. We're just going to get Teddy's bear that he left in Building C. We'll be back." I widened my eyes toward Mom to let her know I was up to something.

She seemingly understood and nodded. "Okay, my Alina Ballerina, I'll see you soon. I love you." She didn't take her eyes off me as I swooped Teddy up in my arms and moved toward the door.

"I love you too," I said. I mouthed the words "It's okay," as we walked to the porch.

I heard Cecelia ask my mom, "Wait, where are they going?" as John shut the door.

He walked behind Teddy and I as he escorted us to Building C. I coughed and shielded Teddy's face as the dirt kicked up into the air and thickened around us.

John stepped before us to type the code in, *Eight-five-seven-five.*

The floors creaked below my recovering feet, and the lights above flickered. Teddy hugged me tighter and said, "I'm scared, Mama."

I held him close and told him, "Remember what I told you, Teddy, look to the light and the stars above. I am always with you."

John flicked on the lights and began searching the floor for Teddy's bear as I eyed the chair in front of MultiU. I set Teddy down on the floor and whispered to him, "Look away for a minute and hold your ears." Teddy complied.

"Hmm, it doesn't seem to be—" John said before he collapsed to the floor, unconscious. I had swung the chair and whipped him in the face.

I flipped the on-switch of MultiU, and it hummed and

clicked in all its glory. I moved to the computer system and typed in code.

"Follow me, baby. We don't have much time," I said to Teddy as I grabbed his hands from his ears and brought him to the front of the illuminated mirror.

I plucked the note from his back pocket and placed it in his hand.

"Teddy, Mom can't go with you right now, but you must go through this mirror and look for me there. Show this note to whoever finds you, they'll know what to do."

I pulled him in for a hug which felt like, perhaps, it was the last one.

"Be brave, Teddy; I will find you, I promise," I said.

Teddy didn't cry.

He held onto me and whispered, "I love you."

I clenched him tighter, as if letting go might mean I may lose him forever.

"I love you too, Teddy," I said as I gently pushed him into the mirror. Just as I was about to let go, his body transformed, stretching into his familiar six-foot form. His stubble returned, and he nodded to me before he poofed out of existence. I shielded my face from the broken glass flying out. Shards fell to the floor, coated in my tears.

I turned around to see John struggling to get up. He gained his strength with every movement. As he took slow, thumping strides toward me, I made steps backward until I was cornered into the mirror, ready to plunge into another unknown world.

Maybe I would make it out alive; perhaps I wouldn't. But they'll chase me before they go after Teddy, so I know Teddy will be safe. I took one last deep breath in of this prison world as John charged at me. I closed my eyes as I anticipated his push. To my surprise, he wrapped his arms around me in a tight embrace.

"I would have done the same thing. I told you, I'm not the one doing this to you," he whispered.

I opened my eyes, overwhelmed with the unexpected emotions flooding my body. He didn't attack me; instead, he held me. Suddenly the sound of his voice felt warm.

"Dad? Is it really you?" my voice cracked.

"Yes, Alina Ballerina. I'm so sorry for what I've done. I'm going to get you all out of here," he said.

"I forgive you. I missed you so much, Dad. I have a plan, and you aren't going to like it, but I need you to trust me. When it's all over, I need you to guide Mom and Cecelia to the mirror. It's programmed to where I sent Teddy," I said.

"What about you, though? I'm not going to leave you here, Alina." Dad said.

"Just trust me, like I'm trusting you," I said.

My dad nodded.

The door swung open and slammed into the wall. Startled, I jumped away from my dad's embrace, and he followed suit.

Alister was seething, steam practically flowed out of his nose, while he held a knife to Mom's throat. Cecelia was not with them. Mom's eyes were red from tears as she struggled against Alister's grasp.

"John, I will always be one step ahead of you. You, of all people, should know that MultiU notifies me of everything. It's Robotics 101," Alister said.

"Let my family go. Please, Alister. I'll do whatever you want." John stepped toward Alister and Mom.

"You already were doing whatever I wanted. I see what you're doing. You're trying to take my wife from me, my perfectly pathetic Alina. She's not yours to take, and just to make sure you understand that, I'm going to take your wife from you so you understand what it would have felt like for me." Alister's eyes darted in unnaturally sporadic movements.

Alister raised the knife, ready to plunge it into her heart. I screamed and lunged toward him, but just before he reached her skin, he pulled his hand back and released her.

"Oh, you thought I was going to stab her? No." He laughed as if he just remembered an old joke.

"I poisoned the bread John made for you. I hope it was extra tasty." He winked.

"Cecelia ate so much of it; she died first. It's a shame because I wanted her to see the reveal. I would have enjoyed watching that smug look melt from her face as much as I enjoyed the look on yours, John. You think I don't know you got your memory back?" Alister said.

My dad pulled both me and Mom behind him.

Mom whispered, "I'm sorry, baby; I failed you. I wish I could have protected you. I love you." She held my hand.

Her face was pale as a ghost, and her eyes drooped.

"I love you too, Mom. Don't be sorry. Everything is going to be okay." I squeezed her hand.

I didn't eat any of the bread, although I wish I had.

My mom collapsed to the floor, too weak to fight any longer.

"You son of a bitch. I'm going to kill you," John said, then punched Alister in the face. Alister stumbled backward but then steadied himself. I pushed in front of my dad and approached Alister.

"Alister, if you love me at all, please stop now before it's too late," I said and Alister's eyes softened.

I grabbed hold of his hands, which were clenching the knife, and gently cupped them.

"Please, Alister, we can be together. Don't kill my family, just give me the knife." I carefully pried it out of his hands, and he leaned his head into my forehead.

"Alina, I love you; I will never hurt you," he said.

"I know you won't," I replied.

The knife was entirely in my grasp, and I knew what I had to do. I gestured behind my back, pointing toward the mirror, signaling to my dad that he needed to go through it. I stroked Alister's hair as he breathed in my scent, and then I took the knife and slowly raised it. His eyes were closed; he didn't see me coming.

I whispered to him, "Goodbye, Alister."

I mustered up all my strength and jammed the knife in as hard as I could. Alister released me and stumbled backward when he realized what I had done.

I pulled the knife out from my stomach and slipped back while my blood shot out over him.

"No. No! Alina, what have you done? You can't die! I need you," Alister cried out as he moved toward me, but he stopped when my dad tackled him to the floor. My dad didn't listen to me; he didn't leave. John and Alister held each other back as they both fought for the knife.

I fell to the ground next to my mom, who was dry-heaving. Blood continued to spout from my stomach, and the room spun.

A familiar face ran into the room, holding an axe.

Cecelia?

Alister and my dad stopped fighting and gazed with their mouths open at the girl they thought had died.

"How are you still alive?" Alister asked.

My dad ran to the knife while Alister was distracted and cornered him.

"You didn't really think I was going to swallow that dry bread right? You should have removed the axe from this universe. I don't miss twice."

Cecelia charged at MultiU with all her strength and slammed the axe down into where I imagined its heart would have been if it had one. Sparks flew out in all directions as the machine made a loud roaring boom. She ran to me and crouched down as I bled out beside her. I wanted to thank her, but I couldn't speak.

"Oh Alina, I'm so sorry. I wish I could have saved you, too. Maybe in another life, I'll get the chance."

I used every ounce of energy to form the word, "Teddy."

Cecelia looked around the room, landing her eyes on the mirror, and then back to me. She nodded then said, "I understand." She cried as she hurried to the mirror and disappeared.

From the corner of my eye, I watched as Mom inched towards me, mustering all her strength to grab my hand.

We looked at each other through fading glimmers of hope; the sounds of my dad and Alister's battle dimmed in my ears.

She mouthed to me, "I love you," or maybe she said it; I couldn't hear her.

Her eyes glossed over, replaced by a vacant stare. She was gone. Still, I held her hand.

I turned my head to see a blurry silhouette of my dad pushing Alister to the floor with the knife no longer in his grasp. He ran over to Mom and I and stroked our hair. "I trust you," I think he said.

I watched his blurry form stand and enter the mirror, his body vanishing through it.

I squeezed Mom's hand, but she didn't squeeze back. She lay lifeless next to me, and I prepared to join her.

Alister hovered over me; his features were blurred. I felt rumbling beneath my increasingly numb body.

My eyes darted above me as MultiU roared its energy through the room. Its rays shot through every tiny hole and leaped out of its metal prison. It zipped around the room, pinging each corner.

Alister shielded his eyes from the brightness, but I found the light comforting. I observed as it formed a giant sphere; its heat warmed me as if welcoming me home. There were faint screams from Alister from a distance and the smell of burning flesh permeated my nose.

The light grew brighter until it was all I could see. Its humming siren sang to me until the light zipped through the mirror, disappearing into a better world. As my mind faded out, I thought of Teddy. I knew he was safe somewhere; I could feel him. My plan had worked; I had to die to break the obsession that original Alister had on me, and MultiU's energy took care of the rest. Teddy made it out alive, and maybe another version of Alister would try to find him, but I sent him to someone who could help. I allowed the darkness to overcome me, knowing I had won.

ERROR-TEDDY-UNIDENTIFIED

Teddy landed in the middle of a bustling city. Angry drivers slammed on their horns, veering around him as he stood frozen on the warm pavement. A semi-truck barrelled towards him at full speed.

"Hey man, watch out!" a woman yelled as she leaped from the sidewalk and into oncoming traffic, pushing him to the other side.

The man in the truck had jumped out and ran over to Teddy.

"Oh my god, are you okay?" The man rushed to Teddy's aid as the woman knelt over him.

"He's awake but in shock." The woman found a pulse and brushed Teddy's curly hair from his face.

Teddy's eyes were open, but he didn't respond.

"Can you hear me? What's your name?" she asked.

Teddy fluttered his eyes, as if coming out of a trance and gasped in air; he looked at the familiar woman above him and smiled. "Alina."

A puzzled expression clouded her features. The corners of her mouth drooped slightly as her eyebrows furrowed.

"Do you know him?" the man asked.

"No, but my name is Alina. What's yours?"

"My name is Logan. Let's get this guy somewhere safe."

Teddy's eyes lit up as he abruptly sat straight, staring behind them.

"She told me to look to the stars; she's here," he said, pointing behind Alina and Logan.

Alina turned around as three spheres of vibrating lights rose vertically from the ground, taking the form of Orion's Belt.

She turned to Teddy, who was holding his arm out to reveal the note his mother had sent with him.

"What's that you're holding?" Logan pointed to the note.

Teddy handed the note to Alina, and she gently unfolded it.

She read it aloud:

"Dear reader, if you are reading this note, then it was meant for you. Follow the light to find me."

End